"Bajema's prose combines the pre[   ]
with the surreal haziness of a fever[   ]
stories treat a range of topics, from[   ]
dom and infatuation with a local be[   ] to Eddie's encounters with his emotionally battered father, described as a 'dog of war' with a 'soul in pieces.' A raw and direct pathway into the mind of an independent youth 'trapped in the culture of Southern California.'" — *Publishers Weekly*

"From the moment you meet the thirteen-year-old Burnett in a San Diego suburb, to the moment many years later when he awakens with a bad hangover from a life that used to welcome him, you'll find yourself silently cheering his every small triumph over gravity. Bajema is an enviably powerful storyteller . . . a walking badass of a book." — *Rolling Stone*

"Bajema touches all the bases of American life: the pervasiveness of violence, the pain of loss, the strange calculus of race, the bittersweet agonies of family attachments and, always, the signals and skirmishes between men and women." — *San Francisco Chronicle*

"Eddie constantly seeks a nobler perspective, only to find an illusion, a trick of the mind. . . . As the distinction between right and wrong continues to erode, [Bajema] unveils a very dark answer in the quest to illuminate the human spirit." — *LA Reader*

"Bajema's prose is surly and mesmerizing, snakes down your throat like a pickup's exhaust. Fans of Sam Shepard will dig these desperate and beautiful tales." — Joshua Mohr, author of *Damascus*

"Don Bajema is one of my favorite writers. His stories are tough, honest and sometimes brutal yet they're also merciful, wise and transcendent. Reading Bajema's work is like hearing an ancient, mysterious folk song played by a great rock and roll band in a dark bar somewhere in the Mojave Desert on a hot night. Don Bajema's stories makes me want to go write songs and play guitar too loud." — Dave Alvin, Grammy Award-winning singer/songwriter

"Don is a great writer. His work is worth reading." — Henry Rollins, singer-songwriter, publisher, author of *Black Coffee Blues*

"Don gives an articulate voice to the outsider. He captures the fragility of adolescence and the awkwardness; how the random collection of our childhood experiences shape us into the person we are reacting against, coming to terms with and always becoming." — Dred Scott, jazz musician

"A smidgeon of Shepard, a bit of Boyle, a cry of Kerouac and maybe a taste of Morrison flavor these original stories of a California life." — Robert Englund, actor

"Discovering Don Bajema's literary genius before the rest of the world has caught on is akin to stepping into Gerde's Folk City in '61 and catching a young kid from Minnesota fixing his harmonica in place and launching into a song about 'Hard Rain' or finding yourself at London's Marquee Club in '63 when a group of scruffy hooligans are reverently and rebelliously inventing a groundbreaking, world splitting, stone rolling, blues rock 'n' roll. Bajema's writing ignites agonizing heartache, prophetic insight, immortal swagger, and a redemptive, triumphant love of life. You will beg him to keep on singing." — Pete Sinjin, musician

Winged Shoes
and a Shield

Winged Shoes and a Shield

COLLECTED STORIES

Don Bajema

City Lights Books • San Francisco

Cover design: emdash

These stories were previously published in two collections, both
published by 2.13.61 Press in 1996: *Reach* and *Boy in the Air.*

This book is also available as an e-edition: 978-0-87286-594-5

Library of Congress Cataloging-in-Publication Data
Bajema, Don.
  Winged shoes and a shield : collected stories / Don Bajema.
     p. cm.
  ISBN 978-0-87286-588-4
  I. Title.

  PS3552.A3944W56 2012
  813'.54—dc23

                                    2012025574

.

City Lights Books are published at the City Lights Bookstore
261 Columbus Avenue, San Francisco, CA 94133
www.citylights.com

For Ramona, Nick, Epifania and Luke

Also, John Fawks and Pete Sinjin, the best friends a boy and man could ever have, "There is a house . . ."

CONTENTS

ROCK-A-BILLIES

THEY WERE ROUGH, WILD-HUMORED TEXANS. Their house rang with laughter and singing, steamed with heartfelt conflict, occasionally spattered with their blood. That house rocked with a lust for the next expression of love, the next fight, the next joke to sum it all up. Five kids raving under the roof of two Rebels. They left their pit bulls in Waco, moved out to San Diego and put a beagle named Chino in the back yard. But the blood lust and heart of those pit bulls seemed as much a part of them as the black Indian eyes of their mother, and the sloping shoulders and wry squint of their old man.

They had audacious courage, stubborn determination, and a fierce brotherhood, because they kept their dead alive. In fact they were on a first-name basis with death. He was like a visiting uncle who carried a straight razor and told glorious stories as he bounced each of us on his knee. He appeared in cars late at night, across the border in brothels, in the bottle, staring at us with blood-red eyes. His were stories sung to the slow low keys of the piano at night, or told with laughter in the kitchen by day.

When our thirst raged hotter than water could quench, they'd take me to the ancient well that keeps the souls of our past beneath its surface. When I took their dare and peered over the edge down onto that black pool, one of them would slap my back and holler, "See, there it is" — I'd see my own reflection. We each took our turn pulling to the surface another song, pouring out another story. We'd fill ourselves with the desire to accept the next dare by gulping the cold elixir of our unique American heritage, part romantic, part psychopathic.

Until this very day when my heart drops into a dry hollow pit, or during those times it beats with the universe, or even when I'm just catching my breath, I hear a slow rhythm of inhalation and exhalation, a whisper of inspiration from those down in that well. When I fail to live as the man I was born to be, I hear a chorus of low moans as they recall their own regrets, before their time here expired.

We can't see our ghosts, but we can hear them. When their voices echo in our songs, in our blues, in our dreams, it's our own voice we're hearing. Because they were who we are, and what happened to them, happened to us.

Gettysburg. Still-Breathing Ghosts.

Promise them the love of God and country; then watch them become the sons of Satan, transformed by the alchemy of war, from boys crying for their mothers into their brothers' butchers. Long after you are sick of the sound of the victor and the vanquished, long after your heart is broken observing their astonishing efforts to prolong a life no longer worth living, you'll hear their last song. It'll sound just like a rebel yell.

I'm one of those still-breathing ghosts. The last few battles, I remember pinning my father's name under my gray jacket. I wanted to go home one way or the other. I did the same thing for a few boys new to the regiment who had not seen this kind of fighting before. Without ammunition, we'd have to run more boys at them than they could kill all at once, and get it down to hand-to-hand just as fast as possible.

These new boys' hands shook so badly I penned their names in for them. They said their fingers were too cold. I took it as a white lie. We'd get up in the morning and vomit, squat somewhere and empty our bowels, and do the things you might imagine a body has to do when it is expecting to die, beside itself with numbing fear.

The older boys start yelling curses across the pasture. The answer returns in the form of a collective jeer filling the black field. The sound of voices preparing for battle drifts disembodied across the low morning fog. The momentum for hysteria builds into a peak as the fingers of the sun clutch another morning. The quiet fear in the darkness comes to light and thousands of men and boys begin to take the first steps toward true wrathful bloody passion. You'll need it, believe me, when men are killing each other by the thousands in a ten-acre pasture on a single summer morning.

I remember I hated the sound of the clubbing and stabbing and crushing. That crunching wrong sound. The evidence of it in my hair, covering my clothes, on my face, under the nails of my hands. I hated the red pile of agony under my feet, clawing at my legs in blind animal panic. You have to teach them that a boot caving in their face is a lot worse than trying to die there quietly. I'm young, fourteen, and not the youngest by far. I've killed boys younger than me. I've pinned their arms to their sides as a couple of men with jack-off voices shouted insanely to "Stickemstickem . . . stick that little son of a bitch, . . ." watching as the boy's white face opened in a shriek for his mother.

I'm one of the last ones left. Since I'm small, they use me to kill the wounded and the dying enemy we leave behind our advancing ranks. It's an important job, because you never want trouble behind you. If a few wounded can somehow mount a move, you can get cut off, surrounded, which is the worst thing that can happen. Some of them were tricky, and you had to stay on your toes.

Struggling for each breath of air yourself, you stumble over a field of groaning, wild-eyed men. The man covered in blood, straining on his hands and knees, howling like a hound, shaking his gory beard — kill him. Move over to the boys encouraging each other in some desperate assurance that the fighting is over for them. Kill them. It is too early in the battle for prisoners. Out of the corner of your eye you see a blue uniform crawling fast and resting, then scrabbling again. The man crying for water, and thanking God when he sees your approach, mistaken that you have come to help him — kill him. The man you saw crawling senses your approach and drags his useless legs toward the trees lining the pasture. You hear his gasping breath falling into sequence with your own. Kill him. Stab a dead man just in case. End the sentences of a hundred whispered prayers. Kill, until everyone there is dead, even the ones still breathing.

BAD GIRL FROM TEXAS

IT'S ABOUT NOON, AND ALREADY over 100 degrees. The novelty of this kind of heat has the energy level climbing all over this Southern California town.

The bad girl from Texas must be making a ragged terry-cloth robe very happy as it clings tightly around her body. She is fifteen. She hasn't been to bed yet. One hand clasps the robe in a knot under her throat. The other hand holds a garden hose; its mouth is open, and a clear cylinder splash-splatters a torrent into the mud that surrounds some geraniums.

Eddie Burnett is tall, thin, and thirteen. Moments ago he woke up startled, kicked off his semen-stained sheets, pulled the oversize white T-shirt over his head, yanked on the Levi's that lay on his bedroom floor, and walked barefooted into the street.

Eddie is approaching her from a few houses up the street, watching her profile bent over at the waist, the robe contouring her hips. She knows he knows who she is and she's not in the slightest ashamed of it: his friends' bad sister, who had to be sent out of town because the boys up the canyon fought and screamed like cats all night long under her window.

Eddie likes the length of her black hair, which has grown

from a short bob to shoulder length in the months since he's seen her. Her voice becomes audible as he gets a few yards closer in a studied nonchalant stroll. She is singing under her breath in a whispering deep register. . . . "Saddest thing in the whole wide world, is to see your baby with another girl. . . ."

The sound of her voice draws a feeling from between his legs, not in his dick, but under his balls, inside. It comes as a jolt that nearly lifts him on his toes. His heart begins pounding as he realizes he cannot stop his stride and must pass within a few feet of her to enter his friends' house.

At times like this, Eddie usually looks to some sort of omen. He believes in magic. The moment he sees a smooth brown stone, about the size of his palm, lying near the gutter, he knows exactly what he will do with it. The girl does not see him picking it up. He looks four houses down the street where the cop, who doesn't like Eddie much, lives. The ex-Marine, Sgt. Johnson, loves his Chevy Bel Air. Although he is nowhere to be seen, he has set out his plastic pail, the Turtle Wax, the chamois. In direct line with the shining pride of Sgt. Johnson, and Eddie, is a wooden telephone pole. Eddie knows that if he can hit that pole with the hot stone in his hand, from this distance, then the gods of jasmine, heatwave nights and bad girls will smile on him. If he dents Sgt. Johnson's Chevy, he can expect no mercy.

Eddie calculated all of this the instant he saw the stone, felt its smooth hot curves fit perfectly against the heel of his hand and his forefinger. He focuses on the pole with the intensity of a cat under a mockingbird. His arm is already drawn back. In a flash his whole body whips outward, and the stone is launched in the final instant of the whirl. Eddie watches the stone climbing in a wide arc, promising all the velocity needed to reach the Chevy, or the telephone pole. As his heart stops in sheer terror, he sees Sgt. Johnson happily swinging open his screen door, heading toward the object of his affection. The stone begins to lose altitude, dropping with a line up on the pole that is deliciously close. Eddie is walking as though he had nothing on his mind. The girl has stood up to her full height and he notes she is a little taller than he is. Sgt. Johnson hears the stone thunk into the wooden pole. He sees that Burnett kid twisted in a moment of ecstasy, pumping his arm like a hometown umpire calling a strike to end a no-hitter.

Eddie regains his composure. The girl looks up toward the source of the sound of the impact. She locks eyes with Sgt. Johnson for an instant, noting the confused and suspicious stare on his face. She turns to see Eddie Burnett stepping onto her lawn. He passes without a nod. She shrugs and returns to the search for snails in the geraniums. Sgt. Johnson watches the brown stone bounce along the grass of his sweet-smelling, just-mowed lawn.

Eddie walks to the side of the flat-roofed stucco house, putting a hand on the top slat of the redwood fence as he disappears over it into the bad girl's back yard. She hears the exchange of greetings between Eddie and her little brothers. "Say, Grant, Robert." "Hey, Eddie." "Hot." "Yeah, hotter'n snot." "Play catch?" "Yeah." She walks into the house thinking that Eddie has grown since last summer.

Ten minutes later she's in bed, dreaming about canyons with fire running along their ridges, and boys from the demolition derby driving out of tunnels, cars' back seats in flames, trailing a plume of black smoke.

Late that afternoon she drags herself down the hall. Eddie had it timed by the sun reaching her bedroom window. He told her brothers he was going inside for a glass of water. Grant looked at Robert and shook his head. "Sure," he muttered in contempt. They knew he always drank from a hose outside. There was no reason to go inside unless it was to see their sister.

As he leaned over the sink, with the faucet turned on

and pouring water directly into his upturned mouth, he caught a glimpse of her walking to the refrigerator. She was beautiful with a sleep-swollen face, wearing a huge T-shirt. The smell of Noxzema filled the kitchen. She disappeared into the front room carrying a popsicle and a transistor radio, singing along and harmonizing pretty well with Ronnie Spector. The phone rang and she flew into a rocking chair. One leg crossed over her knee, her bare foot nodding in the air with the song's bass line, she sprawled there until her mother started calling her lazy names. Phone under her chin, she was in the process of making the night's selection. She laughed an intimate laugh and sighed with approval. She hung up the phone and stood on her toes, arms reaching for the ceiling, back arched, T-shirt climbing up her thighs.

Eddie backed out the kitchen door into the dark garage, and into the back yard. Five minutes later the patio screen door swung open and she walked into the full glare of the heat wave, black wrap-around sunglasses, hair hiding most of her face. She answered her mother's calls coming from inside the house.

"In a minute." "I will." "I did." "Oh, I forgot."

Eddie wanted to tell her he'd do anything for her. Steal, lie, leave home, take her anywhere. Instead he played catch with her brother. Without showing the least effort, he threw electric blue lines that smacked into her brother's glove the instant they left his fingers. He knew she could hear the ball hissing from where she slouched against the doorjamb. Eddie threw harder. Her brother showed his bravery, standing in front of an eighty-mile-an-hour fastball with a casual blank expression on his face, his eyes as big as saucers. Eddie spoke to her as Grant's return throw popped into his own glove. "Hey, Sis."

She let his words hang in the air, timing her response to the moment before he'd think she was ignoring him. "Eddie, don't throw so hard."

To show her who was king of this street, who ruled her brothers and the other boys around those canyons, Eddie jerked his chin over the back yard fence and he and the brothers vanished in silence for those canyons, and the shore breaks, and the ballparks, and the matinees, and the girls Eddie's age. Girls he lured out at night into the canyons and behind the bushes, or into unlocked cars. Girls who removed his hands from their breasts. Girls who pressed their knees together, or crossed their legs as Eddie felt their sweating faces, and heard their strange throaty whispers telling him, "No. No. No, Eddie." Girls he had been pretending were the bad girl from Texas, ever since she had left town.

BOY IN THE AIR

A STACK OF BOOKS CUTTING into my forearm, the wind blowing in my face, I'm a seventh grader walking home from school. I've made it a couple of blocks and am presently making my way past the high school athletic field, I'm noticing cars and kids converging with loud chatter and a certain kind of anticipation toward the wide-swung chain-link gate. There must be a couple of hundred kids flowing through that gate and taking their seats in the stands. I won't ask anyone what's going on, but it seems to be something pretty good, although I haven't heard about it. I'm standing in the way, getting jostled, and doing a slow spin trying to balance the stack of books and to "get the hell out of the way," as I am being advised. I manage to get to one side of the river of teenagers and pretend to be doing something other than trying to find out if it costs money to get in, because I don't have any and I don't need the embarrassment. Most of the time I feel invisible, and in fact I never attract much attention unless I'm in the way. So I stand there shirttail-out in my Converse All-Stars, my orange hair and freckles, getting tired in the hotter-than-usual April sun. I don't recognize any of these kids, except for one or two of the older brothers or sisters of my friends, who pass by me in silence. I know my place.

Sitting on my books waiting for the crush of kids to

lighten, I dig some wax out of my ear casually, burp loudly with a certain aplomb, spread my knees wide and pull my socks up so that my white legs don't show beneath my khaki pants. "Fuck you guys," I think. "I'll rule this place in a couple of years." One of those old Fords that have all the edges rounded out and have dusty, vomited-in-smelling upholstery screeches up and runs over the curb. The Ford is full of girls. Not three in front, and four in the back, but more like five in the front and ten in the back. All the windows are down and arms and an ankle stick out. The radio is loud. The girls are singing "Angel Baby," as loudly and sincerely as possible. I stand up, and put my hand in my pocket. Then I sit back down, resume my former position but twist my butt over so that I can get a better view of them. By now they are untangling and swearing at each other as shoes scrape down unlucky shins, and elbows balance awkwardly and painfully in sensitive, newly formed places. More laughs, and the doors bounce open. If I look up a skirt no one notices and I am poker-faced.

I've seen girls in packs before and I know that one does not want to be noticed by them under most circumstances. As they always do, they wait until their full number is standing in a close knot beside the door. Purses are found, hair is brushed, mirrors are flashing, and lipstick is borrowed. This takes twenty-five seconds. As though by genetic imprint, like a flock of birds, they make the final dress-press with hands, tilt their chins just right, and stroll slowly and silently toward the gate.

I see their calves. Their feet are as big or bigger than mine. They have veins showing in their feet, and the calves are shaved smooth and tanned brown. I breathe deep and notice it before I sigh. I close my mouth and the chestful of air stops at my closed mouth and passes silently out of my nose. My eyes are bugging so I turn toward the opposite direction and notice that the gate area is empty and there is no ticket booth. Okey dokey.

I turn and three of the flock are standing next to me. They are saying something to me. They are asking me an urgent question. They are expecting an answer. I am still sitting on my books. I stand up slowly, gathering my thoughts as though I were a rodeo star recovering from an eight-second ride on Oscar. I brush off my butt, why I don't know, and I say, "Huh?" I notice that my eyebrows are somewhere around my hairline and that my voice has squeaked. I clear my throat and compose my face. It doesn't work. The girls are looking at me with a great deal of impatience and they know I am a little jerk. One girl has already given up in disgust. Another one is saying "I said, is Rick Hanks jumping here today?" I don't have any idea. But I know that someone might see me talking to these high school girls with their women's bodies and I have to somehow prolong the occasion. I do not want to be lacking in anything, information about Rick Hanks, whoever that lucky boy must be, wit, or anything. I get too worked up, and the sentence I begin turns into a stammer. My mouth will not cooperate and it keeps stammering. The best-looking girl looks right over my shoulder and this makes me turn around. I hear her voice saying, "There's the bus." All the girls see the bus from Hoover High pulling into an adjacent parking lot. These are Hoover girls looking for a jumper named Rick Hanks.

My moment has passed. I imagine I hear a "never mind" as the girls disappear but I am probably being kind to myself. I see Junior Osuna looking at me out of the corner of my eye. I stoop to pick up my books and try to act like maybe I'm with these girls and I follow a pace and a half behind them toward the gate. I give that up pretty quick and feel foolish. I then acknowledge Junior with a "Did you see that?" leer behind the girls' backs. But Junior is walking across the street picking his nose. I'm still walking forward with my head turned. I am not looking where I am going, in other words, and manage to stumble in the dirt. This kicks up a fair amount of dust and sand, which coats the heel and instep of one of the girls walking in front of me. I bump into her as she empties out her shoe. I mumble an apology. She's so happy to be seeing Rick that she smiles and says, "That's OK." I melt. She leaves and I look for a place to sit in the stands, which are full.

Now I am in front of about a hundred kids and even a few adults. I am facing a sea of faces. I feel like a complete goon. I cannot stand to look for a seat for more than four seconds, I would rather sit on roofing nails. I wander off to the side of the stands and lean on a fence with the little brothers and sisters of the athletes on the field. Little kids. I move to the other side of the stands, walking behind the stands this time, and stand near some trees that obstruct most of the view. The place smells to high heaven from the piles of neighbors' dog shit. I am alone at least.

Hoover's track team wears maroon sweats. They are an integrated team of Negroes and whites. They are walking in the direction of the field in knots of five or six. The home team wears white sweats and is all white. I wonder which boy is Rick Hanks. I search the thirty or so maroon figures looking for someone who could pull a carload of bitchin' girls to see him jump. I can't tell.

A smallish white boy appears in the bus doorway. All his teammates are on the field. One boy with three coaches steps down the stairs. As soon as he is out of the bus, he smiles a huge smile. The girls in the stands are on their feet yelling "Rick" and waving at him. He is walking like this happens all the time. He breaks into a light trot toward the high-jump pit. This is enough to get the girls louder for a second. They sit down in silence, and then they start mumbling to each other. I can hear them. Most of the words are along the line of cute, so cute, or sooo cuuute. Well, cute I don't know, but certainly improbable. He's got a baby face, a Kingston Trio haircut, and with the three other guys he now walks with, he looks like a younger brother. Except for something.

What, I don't know. I look into the stands and I can tell that all the Hoover kids are feeling pretty good to be going to the same school as Rick Hanks.

The track is bright in the sunshine, the wind is dying down. There are red, blue, and white plastic triangles hanging in long lines all around the infield. The chalk is in even lines all around the huge track. The hurdles are sitting in stacks by the straightaway. The high-jump pit and the pole-vault pit are mountains of fragrant wood shavings and sawdust. The athletes are jogging, stretching, jumping up and down, passing batons, and every face looks like it means business. Men in red jackets are carrying pistols. Coaches are standing in conference with clipboards, pointing and directing the occasional athlete that approaches. A man sits at a table with two large loudspeakers, one facing the stands and the other facing the infield. The man at the table shuffles a stack of papers. The stands sound like a gigantic beehive. I am beside myself with energy.

The jumpers take turns warming up by jumping over the bar at a fairly low height. It looks about 5' or 5'6". Well, I should say that the home team jumpers are jumping. The Hoover guys are elsewhere. Finally they join the three white-uniformed jumpers. One Hoover guy jumps a couple of times clearing the bar by a lot, maybe a foot. The home team jumpers begin to sit down. Rick Hanks is over by the football goalpost, reading a book. A few minutes later, after the other jumpers have begun to settle down, he appears to be advising his teammates on their approach to the bar and to the take-off area. Each boy stands under the bar and swings his leg up toward it. Some boys do this many times, too many times. It is clear they are trying to appear to know what they are doing, but they seem nervous. Rick Hanks gets a tape measure from one of the coaches and with the help of a teammate stretches it from the near side of the crossbar, out several feet into the grass infield. He sticks an ice pick on a measured spot and winds up the tape. One of the other guys returns it to the coach. Rick Hanks stands motionless at the spot. He goes over every inch of the ground leading to the take-off spot — for twenty minutes. He tries out his steps, and then gets the tape measure and measures it all over again. He seems to be staring at the bar. He drops his head and with the first step of his first warm-up jump, everything in the stands, on the field, in the universe stops. Rick Hanks takes nine even steps, smooth and relaxed, with absolute purpose and ease. He does not stop at the take-off spot. His run and take-off combine in a single explosive instant. He shoots lightly into the San Diego sunlight, rises up, passes above the bar immediately, continues rising, rolls slowly hovering high in the air for what seems to be four heartbeats, and slowly descends into the sawdust. He brushes himself off as he returns to his book.

I am sure the girls responded in some manner. I know I heard a couple of hoots from the stands, a smattering of applause, and a grown man yelled something. I am sure that anyone who saw Rick jump that day was happy and inspired to see a boy eventually jump 6'10". But for me the world had not begun to turn yet. I was riveted to the boy reading on the lawn, lying on one side, propped on an elbow, his chin in his hand, his twitching foot the only indication of energy. A boy who knew something. A not-so-special boy who knew how to hover in the air, and do something so beautiful and so dramatic that he could let it speak for him.

"YOU'RE ON..."

THE STAKES ARE ALWAYS SO HIGH. From the very beginning I thought it must be a complex combination of guts, glory, luck, and resolve. But I was looking too hard. If it had been a snake, it would have bit me. All the stakes are high, it shouldn't have thrown me off. As usual, I guess, I wanted it simplified.

It turned out to be more difficult than simply "Keep your eye on the ball." An old Indian used to drink behind our Little League Park. A home run was a lost ball. I was still ignoring the warning track in those days. After bouncing my head off the chain-link fence with a miracle disguised as the third out stuck in my glove, I lay still on the grass for an eternity. I knew a dramatic moment when I felt one. Slowly I raised my glove above my prostrate body. My dugout, of course, became a Vienna choir of cheers. Ecstatic, and bounding toward my team, I heard the Indian's voice pulling me down to earth, growling, "Relax." I told him to speak to me in English. His laughing fit lasted the next two extra innings. We lost.

For the next few days, the Indian was determined to teach me to hit. He made his own assumptions, I guess. He thought I'd be motivated by his words, had a direction to begin with, and really wanted to hit the ball in the first place. I didn't.

My field of glory was out there. Not in some box with a fat man in black breathing down my neck, pointing out which ball I could have hit. I lived in the field, in the unpredictable moments of defense. I didn't want anything served up, I didn't want to think about a trick pitch. My life was never gonna be a count of three or four.

But the huge face with the purple alcoholic lips kept insisting, "Keep your eye on the ball." I knew it was the wrong advice for me. With a nervous system resounding like a perpetually rung tuning fork, I became a strike-out king. I started swinging the Louisville 31 about the time the dust popped out of the catcher's mitt. I wasn't gonna look harder, I wasn't gonna look at all.

The Indian must have known that. He had to. I was born to live above the letters and below the knee. Out of the strike zone. His advice just turned me on my heels and sent me walking, emptying the Red Hots down my throat, thinking in a whisper . . . speak to me in English.

I liked that Indian, I think he was telling me about something he had once but didn't own anymore. It took me a long time to understand it. But now, to this very day, every time a fastball hisses at my heart, I can hear his voice echoing. "Take your base."

Clarity

It rains accidentally, or it rains on purpose. It rains, we know that for sure. At weird intervals, for a moment, or for a couple of celestial days, I'd get it all. I could see it all plain, I'd be absolved of all these sins, I'd have the blessing of cognizance and capacity. I'd be living right then and there. But it evaporates. It leaves no trail. When it's gone, you feel left behind, on fire, in the glare, wishing that clarity would drop out of the sky and soak your long hair, and wash your burning face.

Next Fall

Sex does the same thing. Hours where whatever ground your feet are planted on, the rest of your body is wrapped in the confusing immersion of hers and yours. Warm rapids rolling and bouncing into a flat placid space, revolving slowly in a fainting spin toward the lip of the next fall. Old women whisper about it, saying to anyone who'll listen, that it's just like youth, one day it just doesn't come back. It's gone, except in annoying dreams that make the fabric of their clothes irritate them here, here and here. They look away, and their fingers draw light circles on their soft cheeks, they get up and walk into another room.

The magic of a principled universe has us on our knees anyway, there's no need to bend down. We stand in our gain, and walk to our loss. There's nothing to remember and only ourselves to forget.

BLACKROAD

WHEN THERE'S NOTHING LEFT OF America to sell, try a piece of blacktop. Just go right out there in the heat of the summer and kick off a hunk or two by the side of the road. Take it back to your doorway, your park bench, your abandoned car. It'll give you something productive to do while you wait for the rest of your life in the two-day-long line, once a month, every month, for the maybe-it-works-maybe-it-doesn't anti-AIDS vaccine. And if you can't pay for your vaccine again this month, you can use a chunk of asphalt to help you take the change off the other homeless people you used to step over every day.

You see the beauty of it? It's versatile. Bust out a piece of your car's rearview mirror. Get the light just right and it's as good as a microscope. Now just sit down and get a good long look at that gritty piece of oily shit, that smelly piece of America, that black hunk.

What you have there is the hottest-selling item in the world today. You just need a little imagination. You'll want to catalog the things of value in each piece. And it is rich, and just by association, you are too. Look close. You are holding American nostalgia right there in your hand. You've got product and you can sell it.

Go ahead, collar any fool. Show him the tiny pieces

of roadkill and hit-and-run. Little scraps of flesh and hair, feathers and blood — every damn thing that walks, crawls, swims, or flies on this rancid continent is stuck to that tar baby. Minerals? Well, you can pick out a bit of rusting natural resource in any piece; it's standard. Just follow the wasted trail of any romantic redneck who aimed a Bud can at the "Dangerous Curve" sign ahead.

Give your prospective buyer a taste of the shit-splash and piss from the abolitionists and Negroes who were out of place, out of time, out of luck and, with unanswered prayers, hanging right here above this very road. There's probably a faint trace of the marshmallow sandwich from the happy picnic under the kicking feet above.

You can stick a piece next to your pigeon's ear and let him hear the tires screeching out of control from five thousand prom nights. You'll hear the abruptly ending pleas of the cheerleader's last ride. There's Janis, singing about a drifter who decided to squirt and scram instead of riding along with some trucker trying to remember another song. You can tell that pinched-faced woman trying to sell her kids off to rich folks for a good price that she's already rich if she's holding a piece marked with the treads of the weight of Elvis as he spun the Cadillac around for one more peanut-butter-honey-and-fried-banana sandwich.

Now that you've got the woman's attention, close the deal. Remind her of the poor boys who jostled shoulder-to-shoulder to Fort Fucking This or That, going to boot camp and getting brainwashed and gung-ho, blistering their knees praying for a chance to kill a Commie for Christ. Sink the hook. Mention those forlorn, lonely flag-draped coffins hiding the addresses stapled to those boys' big toes, as they wind slowly down these black roads back to Momma and Poppa. While Brother and Sis watch the television wondering if Cronkite's box score really matters much anymore.

Remind the techie types that pieces of the space shuttle

passed along these roads, big rigs pulling part by part, rutting the asphalt, warning lights flashing to premature takeoff, while coked-out scientists perfected the fuel mixture. If your mark seems patriotic, you got him in the bag. Just mention all the politicians who have been rolling down these roads for the past fifty years, checking their maps for the next shopping mall, sitting behind tinted windows with their trousers and BVDs around their ankles deciding which lie has that statesman-like ring. All those millions of moronic hopefuls racing for the parking lot, smacking their sugar-rushing kids, waiting in the heat like sardines to see a little bit of the history your client is holding in his filthy hand right now. Roads are huge in American politics. Turn to the left, turn to the right. Kennedy got his occipital bone slapped on Elm Street like a slung piece of cantaloupe. You can sell it.

Entertainment? Lennon answered a cop in the back seat as he departed the Dakota for parts unknown, while rain-singing tires spun a last verse of "A Day in the Life." You can sell this. You have the foresight to see the value in this black asphalt, from this long, long dark road. A petroleum product. Everything America has to offer. How do I know? I'm glad you asked.

I saw it myself. I saw a clumsy generation of American dinosaurs dying right here in the middle of the road. Wrinkled knees with ten times the weight of an elephant thudded down on pinkish-raw skin. Scraping for one last time on the hot black grit. I'd been waiting a long time for it. I knew it was coming. I watched as the old giants slowly lifted their fevered heads, saw their eyes go wild with helpless rage. Mouths opening in senile, uncomprehending groans. I could make out their pale faces suspended high in the brown skies, eyes like dim search lights, cataract-blind and tearful. They wobbled over, cursing useless threats, but they coughed up our own young blood. Infecting us. Until we became the same dinosaur ourselves, when the echo of the long hairless necks beating obscenely on the asphalt had time enough to turn into our own nostalgia.

Death shuffled to the east, shuffled to the west, and over us again. We countered clockwise in a slow, dark circle of power, throbbing to the black bass line of resurrection. We ran blindly on the soft shoulder, screeched around the corner of our ever-present dreams; in a flash, the melted schoolgirl became a white shadow negative.

Clutching our worthless icons, we fought over channels, tried to oppress the world, lost our souls along the highway, became just a fearful guilty hitchhiker, screamed each other's names, and jumped eagerly into the fire.

Ask anyone who was there.

MY FATHER HOWLED IN HIS SLEEP

MY FATHER'S HANDS WERE STILL SHAKING, his lips moved in silent sentences, his red eyes blurred with the tears of his stolen youth. His language was obscured in the mirthless sound of his gut laugh, and slurred with another Pabst Blue Ribbon. His eyes squinted behind the smoke of another Lucky Strike, his mouth softening from a hard snarl to a weak broken smile in the moments he thought I wasn't looking. I was looking. I saw a heartbroken boy who walked like a man.

Snatched off his father's farm by the events of history, he marched willingly under the rumbling thunderheads and into the sunset slash of brutality. My father allowed himself to be trained like a dog to kill, and in that process lost more than he could afford to lose. My father emerged from the nightmare fractured, his soul in pieces.

My father returned to us hollow-eyed, death in a shell of skin, obscured by the ill-fitting uniform. My father lived in a junkyard of human wreckage and tried to make the best of it. My father tore his neck raw against the invisible chain of manhood twisted too tightly, cutting off his inspiration. My father was a dog of war.

JOYCE

A SINGLE AIRSTREAM TRAILER SAT shining in the envy of the white trash inhabitants of this U.S. military camp. It was the trailer Joyce lived in with her older brother, David, their mother and their troubled father. There was a newly laid asphalt road that led through overgrown forests, ending in a series of shorter roads and four or five rows of pocked, scraped trailers surrounded by marshland and meadow.

On a drizzly morning, in one of those meadows, twenty children were watching some older boys shooting arrows straight up above their heads. David, a broken-toothed ten-year-old, was bent over backward pulling his bowstring, aiming for the sky. The bow vibrated under the tension, and the striped, feathered, steel-tipped arrow launched into the mists above us, immediately invisible in the low clouds.

We stood small in the field, our faces upward, eyes squinted against the filtered sun, silent. Suddenly one of us shouted, and we scattered. The arrow spun downward and embedded itself deeply into the soft earth. Wiping our runny noses, and shivering in our soaking pant legs and shoes, we converged on the arrow like a flock of birds. An older boy pulled the arrow out of the ground, marking the depth it had sunk with his thumb on the shaft. Each older boy took his turn in the contest of whose arrow would drive deeper.

Joyce and I were five years old. I had just had my birthday; Joyce had hers at Christmas. I was completely enthralled with the older kids as they once again displayed a power and privilege beyond ours. We were charged with an element of danger. We knew that for a few brief seconds we had no idea where the arrow was falling, or where it would punch into the ground. The older girls took it on themselves to guide the younger kids out of the path of the descending arrow.

As with most of our games, this one began to shift to increasing risk. I watched the older boys rewarded with cheering and backslapping congratulations for standing under the arrow as it descended, delaying their move to safety as the arrow whispered downward on them. I realized the right to remove the arrow was bestowed on the boy who stood nearest the shaft when it hit the earth. I looked at Joyce, slipped my hand from the hand of the older girl between us, and waited for David to launch the next one.

Another arrow jumped skyward. As it began its climb, an angry adult voice yanked our collective spirit down from the disappearing arrow to the oppression and threat of our parents. The older children looked to the approaching voice. The bow was flung on the grass, the launcher running toward the edge of the woods as his father gained speed and fury behind him. Other hungover adult voices screamed confusing and conflicting directions.

"Stay where you are, Joyce."

"David, you little son of a bitch, STOP or I'll. . . ." "Come here. No. NO!! Stay right there."

My eyes strained for the dot to appear above me. Frozen, heart pounding, face skyward, the arrow falling above me. I could hear a faint, growing whistle and whisper. I felt a feathered breath blow on my face, heard a soft thud and the beautiful arrow stood vertical at my feet, its wet feathers shining at my waist.

I stared. It had just been so high, so invisible, moving

so fast, and now it was within my grasp. I reached for the smooth, polished shaft. My fingers brushed the red and yellow feathers. I began to pull. I got down on my knees, put both hands on the shaft and slowly it began to slide out of the earth.

I felt a rough hand push me aside. I heard a crack and saw our bow in two pieces, twisting awkwardly on its string in the air. My friend's red-faced father jerked the arrow out of the ground and snapped it over his khaki-trousered knee. I heard a boy saying, "David's gonna get it." Joyce's voice was crying, "Run, David!" and "No, Daddy!" in an even tempo.

The meadow was emptying with stern scoldings, an occasional slap, and tears. My friends' arms were being jerked, little feet were bouncing in the air beside the stamping strides of enraged parents heading back to the trailers. I sat there stunned, with the crying protests of my friends filling the air, feeling the familiar sense of guilt at another thing I couldn't understand.

One of the oldest girls, who made cupcakes of mud for the little girls' pretend tea parties and usually let me wear her old doll's blanket as a cape, took my hand. She was smiling, with her warm hand on the top of my head, saying, "Time to go home."

A few months later, my mother and I were visiting the Airstream. Joyce was inside watching cartoons. David had brand-new sneakers right out of the box. They smelled great and he was singing to himself under his breath, "Paul Parrot, Paul Parrot, the shoes you ought to buy, they make your feet run faster, as fast as I can fly." He went outside and sat on the stairs leading to the trailer door. Unsure of myself, I sat on the stair above him. Behind the screen door our mothers sat drinking coffee. Joyce was playing in a chair, watching Bluto make improper advances on Olive Oyl. I watched David and tried to retain as much of his big-boy ways as I could. I watched with envy as he tied his own shoe. I saw him clear his throat like the men and spit a rolling little ball into the dust beside the stairs. I asked where he was going.

"Jake's."

I asked, "Could I go?"

He gave the expected answer. "No."

I asked the obvious question. "Why not?"

He gave the only answer. "Because you're too little."

He called into the trailer, "Ma, I'm going to Jake's."

He jumped off the stairs and ran out of the yard, imitating to perfection an internal combustion engine of tremendous horsepower, and buzzed down the dusty lane and around the front of the trailer. I followed, watching as little explosions of dirt jumped behind his feet with each stride. It was the first time I was conscious of running. This led to hours of practice running and looking over my shoulder at the tufts of dirt flying behind me.

God and country. Joyce and I took the yellow church bus to Sunday school off base. I enjoyed the clean clothes, Graham crackers, metallic-tasting orange juice, and coloring books. Jesus and sheep, more Jesus and sheep. Lights and bushels. Burning bushes. Little Moses floating in his basket. The teacher looked like Peggy Lee, who was at that time singing "Fever" on the Hit Parade. I thought my teacher was Peggy Lee and I began to associate Sunday school with early stirrings of the erotic.

One early August morning, several parents found themselves sitting under canvas awnings, drinking iced coffee and escaping the oven-like trailers. We'd heard the rumor of a plan to caravan cars to the lake in the afternoon and then to a drive-in movie. The word spread from the woods and yard to yard, until the trailers were streaming with picnic baskets being carried to cars. Suntan lotion was smeared over tiny backs and older kids stood in impatient knots as families prepared for the outing. It was the second time in the summer we were heading toward pine needles, cool shade, hot sun, muddy shores, hot dogs — all to be followed with the miraculous treat of a drive-in. In an hour, six carloads were ready.

There was a delay in getting under way. The problem was Joyce. We sat silently, sweating in the cars as, one by one, someone went to the Airstream, opened and closed the door and soon reemerged, smiling, shrugging, and shaking their heads. First her mother, then her father, then David, then a neighbor. Then calls from drivers and honking horns. Joyce had locked herself in the bathroom. Just as her father was telling the rest that they'd catch up, my mom disappeared into the trailer. Joyce's embarrassed mother stood by the stairs; her father sat behind the wheel popping a beer with his "church key." A couple of minutes later, my mother came out holding Joyce's hand and smiling. Joyce's chin was quivering and one fist was rubbing an eye.

"She wants to talk to you," Mom said to me. Joyce walked to our Oldsmobile and faced me. I said, "Joyce, let's go." She looked at me and seemed very far away.

I tried again. "Don't ya wanna go?"

With a shamed look on her face and a hint of anger in her voice, she said, "I don't love Jesus."

I was shocked. Of course we loved Jesus. We learned that in Sunday school. And He loved us. But more importantly, Jesus had nothing to do with this trip to the lake. I stared at her. She stared at me. I reached out of the window and she extended her hand.

"C'mon, Joyce."

She looked crushed. It was the first time I saw that look that told me I did not understand something very important.

Mom walked her to her parents' car. Mom stuck her head into the driver's window, her chin resting on her folded arms. Three or four men leaning against the car, drinking beer, listened to what she was saying. Then they exploded in laughter. My mom pulled her head back out and reached one arm inside to pat Joyce on the shoulder. The others took turns hugging and patting Joyce through the window, but her expression never changed. She continued staring at me from a million miles away.

Mom walked over to our car and got into the front seat next to Dad. She was saying, as she slid her bulky hips over the seat, "Joyce had a little problem with Jesus. She doesn't like him watching her go to the bathroom."

Dad laughed a single cough, and switched on the ignition. He turned his shoulder so he faced me, sitting alone in the back seat, as he reversed down the dusty lane, saying, "Jesus."

As we passed her, Joyce looked white and more like a painting frozen on a wall than my friend in a car. Her eyes remained on me for a second, and then shifted to the car floor. I thought she looked scared.

On the drive to the lake, the assorted Fairlanes and Plymouths were filled with kids — except ours, since I always threw up in the car. We parked on a huge grass lot facing the lake. My father said disgustedly, "Go wash off."

I weaved my nauseated way to the water's edge, followed closely by Joyce. I walked into the water, submerged, waded to the shore and sat next to her. I stuck my hands in the warm brown mud. She was sitting with her knees drawn up under her chin. We watched her brother lead a pack of bodies blasting full speed into the shallows and stroking out to the raft anchored in the middle of the lake with a riot of older kids lying around, diving and dunking each other. They were followed a few seconds later by a cascade of whooping fathers.

"How come you didn't want to come?" She shrugged. I waited. Nothing. I said, "Jesus sees everything, but He doesn't care." She said, "But I do."

We sat there a minute more in silence. Then she said, "And at night I see Him looking at me through the roof when I'm trying to sleep."

I said, "He looks after us. He loves children." She said, "Why?" I didn't know so I didn't say anything.

We quit talking and began to play. We played hard through the long afternoon and into the early evening. The only interruption was the period just after lunch when we watched the older kids sitting alone, smoking cigarettes at a picnic table, passing the hour that would keep us from drowning from the cramps in the water. The sun got lower in the surrounding hills and our parents were running low on beer, so we packed up a little early and made our way toward the Lakeside Drive-in.

We stopped at a Dairy Queen next to a Piggly Wiggly and got ice cream for us and booze for them. At the drive-in we waited in a long line filled with carloads of teenagers and families. We felt a little superior to some of the younger kids since we were still wearing our bathing suits and they were in their pajamas.

There was a playground under the huge movie screen: monkey bars, swings, teeter-totters, all made of candy-striped pipes and set in sand. While we waited for dark, we played with the kids we knew and challenged the ones we didn't. I was getting real excited. It was turning darker and darker. We were with the older kids and no adults were watching us.

Suddenly the lights blinked on and off rapidly. One hundred kids swooped in a sprint toward their cars. Row after row of elevated blinking lights stretched out before us. I was ecstatic. I couldn't feel my body. I was swept up in a wave of kids. To my left Joyce's blond hair was streaming behind her, her legs churning gracefully beside me. I saw kids running ahead of us, being drawn back to our side and then vanishing behind us. We were flying, aware of each other and euphoric in effortless speed. David passed us in a T-shirted, sunburned animal burst, followed by a wake of struggling friends. Joyce and I held our own. Two men were leaning against the side of a car, smoking. As they watched the flock of kids fly by, I heard one say to the other, in a voice with warmth, amusement, and admiration, "Jesus, look at those kids run."

My energy doubled and my strides barely hit the ground. My arms cut through the warm summer night. I felt a bursting pride and love of my own life, and for what I would later understand as my generation. The older kids crammed into one of the Fairlanes. The huge Plymouth settled under the weight of the men. The women spread out in the other Fairlane. Joyce, David, and I shared a Chevy with the three oldest girls. Our Oldsmobile sat empty. We watched the first war movie and fell asleep during the second, film explosions and Asian screams giving way to exhausted dreams. A long time later, we heard voices gently untangling us in the back seats and carrying us to our own cars. Our parents were stumbling out of the cars they shared. We heard loud voices and laughter as Joyce's father backed over one of the speaker stands. Joyce's mother and father yelled at each other for a few seconds, until my mother cursed them and everyone laughed. Our fathers gunned their engines, and we squealed and rocked our way out of the drive-in and onto the black strip of asphalt leading to our colony on the Indian reservation in the woods.

The next morning I woke up and found my father sitting with several adults and two Military Police. My mother was at the stove making coffee and voices were very low. I walked down the hallway and out the screen door. No car was parked in front of the Airstream. It was quiet as a tomb. One of the kids standing in a knot in front of the shining silver home waved me over secretly.

"Did ya hear what happened to Joyce?"

My heart hit a huge beat and froze as she said, "Last night she got killed in her dad's car. He hit a tree. David broke his arm and his leg and he's in the hospital. So's his mom. His dad is in jail."

None of the kids on that base ever went to Sunday school again. And our parents never even mentioned it.

THE WIVES TOOK TURNS

THE WIFE OF A SHELL-SHOCK VICTIM in the trailer park is usually young, and a long way from home. Exhausted, often publicly abused and battered, she tries to keep alive enough spiritually to love some of her several kids as much as possible. Which is not easy. The father's influence over her first son is poisonous. She watches her son agonize, from infancy on, as he is taught to reject the substance of her affection. Affection has no place on a battlefield. If she interferes, she is punished for weakening the boy.

Despite her efforts, including the beatings she must endure when she takes a stand in the boy's interest, she loses contact with him as he struggles to catch up on the trail of his father's violent footsteps. She watches helplessly as her son gradually develops a deep seething rage, which takes the place of the love he feels, but is forced to deny her. A confusing rage that will be submerged, yet extended to his sisters, and eventually to all women. If she has a second son, he will be lost to her even quicker than the first.

She turns to her daughter, whom she finds struggling not to repeat her mother's bleak existence. They argue constantly, confused by the need they have for each other, and the self-loathing they feel as their love becomes a mockery in this world ruled by the Army. Eventually the wife accepts her fate, shuffling within the trailer in a semi-stupor of silent compliant slavery. She is heartbroken as she watches the blind desperation of her daughter grow into a perverted attraction for men with the same essential qualities as her own brother and father, beginning her journey toward her own enslavement, and perpetuating the cycle.

In childhood the siblings develop a lifelong communion of fear. They are kept apart by the associations of submerged horror and forgotten cruelty. They are bound by their blood and the memory of their flickering souls, long ago extinguished in the airless childhood of those trailers.

They are afraid to see their mother take another beating. Afraid to take another beating themselves. Afraid of the temporary quiet that in a moment can explode in another unpredictable scene of Father's hysterical, blind, hallucinating, medicated panic. Afraid of the catatonia that fills the low ceiling of the trailer like a storm cloud. They creep around, watching Father as he sits on the edge of his bed in the dark, far end of the tunnel, saying nothing, hearing nothing, responding to nothing.

The trailer stinks of terror when Father begins his sixteen-hour confession, filled with the struggling revelations of his broken soul. He tortures his wife with his self-deprecations. Why is she so afraid? Because she knows that in any instant she will see the flip side of her husband's illness. The deprecations will become accusations, the confessions will become denials, the denials will become rationalizations. His rumbling voice will storm in the close confines of the metal tube, and threats and weird plots will hiss into his wife's face. Father will change from a pliant and hopeful invalid into a monster of cold, hard, hopeless cruelty. Father will make the dependents suffer. Then the military man will make the wife and children feel a little bit of the fear and pain and rage that is at the heart of his regimented insane world. They'll learn well — because he'll teach them.

The wife will take her turn, in her own desperate need. You'll see her in a scarf, hiding the lumpy cheeks and jawline. Almost glamorous in her sunglasses hiding her bloody eyes. She goes to the hospital to arrange an appointment with the base doctor, the highest in command. She tells him she can't take any more, and asks if they can please take her husband back on the ward. Sometimes they do. But usually the request has to come from her husband or his superior officer, because this is an important decision, a man's decision.

Sometimes the husband discovers the wife's visit and then the wife is hospitalized for a couple of days. The children remain buried under sheets in their bunks, forcing themselves to sleep with high temperatures, unable to set their feet on their father's linoleum floor. They dream of dinosaurs mating in blood and mud under black skies as their drunken father careens against the thin trailer walls muttering, "What did I do — oh baby — what did I do to you? I'm sorry — I'm so sorry. You BITCH! You CASTRATING whore."

Normally the doctor just feigns a sympathetic voice and tells the wife the old story. How her husband is in bad shape from the war, and that she just can't understand what he has been through. How much he needs her support, and that he'll be better when he gets back his confidence in himself and the world again. The doctor might even read her husband's war record, and he embellishes it a little. The confused wife wants to believe that her husband is a war hero, that somehow all this slaughter is not in vain. She makes an effort to believe the lie that his sacrifice somehow belittles her own. She starts feeling proud of her man, and guilty about complaining after all he's been through.

Slowly she reaches for her handbag, as she begins to see the image of the young man she married. She walks down the steps of the hospital, adjusts her scarf and sunglasses, and fights bravely the flow of her tears.

She returns home, chilled to the bone in her cold nervous sweat, seeing an old photograph of her husband before her eyes — the farmboy from Lawrence, Kansas, with the funny grin, the 4H president from Tacoma, or the football hero from Amarillo. She'll decide to face another day, and another night. Besides, where could she go with all those kids?

Epitaph

She walks onto the trailer stair and grabs the cold metal handle. Her breath gasps in her throat as she steps into the dark, into the tomb, into the stench of Jim Beam and beer. She hears a voice like the growl of a dog, somewhere in the darkest corner: "Where the fuck have you been?"

NAVAJO

I HAD THE FRONT SEAT to myself, windows down, hot air exploding in loud gusts propelling little tornados of paper and dirt around me. The landscape was hot as hell and repeated itself over and over and over.

She was sleeping — taking the back seat on one hip, jet-black hair blasting in the wind, swirling around her head, all over her face. She was so tired she couldn't feel a thing. With her Navajo eyes closed, she looked Japanese, beautiful as all get out.

The car I was driving was exactly the kind I had always hoped to drive — a real gas-guzzler, with a broken headlight, oversize tires in the rear, and a mass of tangled wires hanging under the dashboard, rumbling along the absolutely abandoned highway. Nothing worked except the gas gauge, and it read empty.

Her dog was thirsty. I twisted over the back seat and felt around with my free hand until I was scratching behind the dog's long, pointed ear. We approached a Texaco station with a faded Pegasus heading forty-five degrees skyward on a round tin shield.

The car growled as I downshifted. The gravel from the roadside rose in a dusty cloud. I drove past the station, slowed down to around sixty and spun a bootlegger turn back into my own dust cloud, filling the windows with brown grit. The girl rocked against the back seat, still sound asleep. The dog tried to get his footing and thumped into the front seat twice. I idled the car into the station's garage and parked it in the empty shade. The dust cloud blew slowly down the road outside. I sat there in the dark, adjusting my eyes and feeling the cool air, thinking of the sun, blinding hot outside of the tin shack, and my wife.

I opened the car door and kissed the air loudly a couple of times until the dizzy dog pressed unsteady front paws on the greasy concrete. The dog followed me around until I found a bucket and filled it with water. The dog drank in sloppy loud slaps.

I went around the corner of the shack and took a long piss. The car door latch opened and slammed shut. Her voice was cooing to her dog. I began to make out her words. "Where'd he go? Huh? Where'd he go?"

I shook off the last drops and buttoned my pants. She wound around the corner, pulling her waist-length black hair off the side of her face. She rubbed one eye with a small silver-ringed fist, breathed in and out deeply, put her hands in the back of her jeans and settled her weight on one leg, getting her balance in her rough-out boots.

"Where are we?" she demanded with a smile.

I shrugged. "Dunno."

"Good. The less you know the better."

"That's what they tell me." Her teeth gleamed behind dry lips.

We stood awhile looking out across four hundred miles of glaring desert, ending in heat-wave-rippling, reddish mountains.

"We're lost, then," she finally muttered. I knew that was a way of referring to how we felt about each other. I knew not to respond. A minute or two passed.

"Almost lost. We're heading south. We'll cross a main

road before too long. We can be in those hills tonight, or in some beach parking lot by tomorrow morning." My words sounded like a speech and I felt embarrassed. I hoped she wouldn't put me down.

She nodded and said, "Let's go to the beach."

She picked up a stone and dented a fresh beer can lying about forty yards away. I didn't move. She did it again, same beer can. I wiped my nose and covered my smile, in a self-conscious movie-cowboy kind of way.

She leaned under my face and looked up into my eyes, saying in a mocking tone, "I'm magic."

I told her I knew that already, with the same tone I would use later to ask the ancient man behind the motel office desk if he had a room.

She tossed a stick and the dog chased after it. He brought it back wagging his tail with pride.

She looked at me and said, "Just like you."

"True love," I said, sniffing the air.

DOG PARTY

WELL A LONG TIME AGO, when I was young, the other kids and I were pretty much left to ourselves — not much supervision or anything. We were all pretending we were happy, watching *Leave It To Beaver* and *Ozzie and Harriet* but feeling this gnawing loneliness. And this anger. Like it wasn't supposed to be like this, like we were getting tricked. We were always fighting and our fathers always talked about the war. Until we began to feel like targets or something.

There was a boy living on our street. He had this thing with dogs, ya know? (Pause.) He had an inordinate attraction to them. None of us knew why. We knew he loved them, but still. . . . He was a strange boy with a strange laugh, a fourth grader with bleeding bite marks and scratches all over his arms. We'd see him following an old lady's cocker spaniel or feeding somebody's mutt through a fence. Calling and crooning — anybody's dog. He'd devote his whole weekend to one dog. We'd need another kid to play outfield, or we'd be alone and want to play catch. Nope. He's got no time. (Girl leaves the stage.) He'd be waiting for Fido. He'd just wait. He was inexhaustible. The dogs knew what was on his mind. They'd hide. The kid knew they knew, and that made it better for him. He'd wait for hours until they made their false move. They'd get hungry and take the bait, or they'd finally give in to the hope against hope that the boy wouldn't really do it. They were wrong. He was quick. He'd grab them and he'd say, "You fool — I'm going to drown you, Fido." He called every dog Fido, don't ask me why.

For a couple of months he did it in secret. But by then we knew he had an odd devotion to dogs. He had witnessed their desperation, he'd watch their losing cause. He weighed each dog's pain threshold. He knew what they could take, he was impressed. He'd stroke them, hold them in his arms as they shook with fear. He'd whisper to them. Then he'd take them to a big fifty-five-gallon drum that his father brought home from the Army base, and drown them. Normally we used the drums for trash cans. I remember he was always so happy on Wednesdays. The trash trucks emptied the cans on Wednesday. (Sound of trash trucks stops.) He called it "Anything Can Happen Day."

He'd drag the garden hose to the black drums, greasy pieces of who-the-hell-knows-what floating with lettuce and tomato skins. He'd be talking real softly to these desperate, writhing, wimpering dogs. Somehow he'd get one into the spinning water. You don't know how long it takes for a Labrador to drown. You don't measure it in minutes. Eternity is more like it. Eternal moments. They fight like hell. They fight to stay out of hell, swimming that pathetic pointless upright paddle, nose bleeding from the broom handle he used to push them under, pinning them to the bottom. Panic. Wildest eyes you'll ever see. Then, just when they were on the other side, as soon as their bodies stopped struggling and only twitched, he'd rescue them. He'd pull them out of the barrel. He'd hold them upside down. Pink water draining out of their mouth and nose. Then it looked like a little light would go on behind their eyes. He'd look relieved and he'd start to cry, saying, "See? There it is!" He'd be smiling at them as they began to figure out where they were. He'd lie down beside them on the ground. They'd be too weak to move. He'd pet them and put his arms around them.

The dogs would think that the boy had saved them, although they would always have a fear of the green garden hose and the barrel. And on Wednesdays after that summer, the whole street would howl when the trash trucks turned the corner. You could see that the dogs sensed something else. Belief, I guess.

The dogs wanted to believe that the boy had saved them. It was easier than facing what the boy had really done. So they let their memory start from the moment they saw his smiling face. The dogs loved him. Really. They followed him everywhere. If you ever saw him, he'd be with a couple of dogs. All by himself, with a couple of dogs trailing behind him.

I asked the boy, "What did you have to do that for?" He looked at me like I was stupid. He said, "I'm looking for love, something bigger than my life."

DASHBOARD

"What the fuck should I be trying to write lines for?" He wiped the running nostril awkwardly with the heel of his hand. His drunken eyes focused on the grimy visor over the filthy dashboard. The 1949 Ford truck bounced over a series of potholes. The drunk's eyelids took a second and a half to raise and lower over his wet red eyes. He turned to the driver. "I can't even play guitar." He thought this remark was very funny. He managed a slack smile to show the driver he got his own joke.

"Can't sing, either. Wish I could, but. . . ." He shook his head with sloppy emphasis, "I can't."

His shoulders twisted to his side window. He stuck his head outside the cabin, looking backward down the road. He pulled his head in again, swung himself back around, and faced the dashboard. He stared coldly for a long moment, then examined the floor of the truck cabin, muttering, "I know that fuckin' bitch."

Looking into his rearview mirror, the driver caught a long-legged girl stumbling in her blue jeans and red jacket. Her boots kicked up small stones and dust. The driver downshifted, let up on the gas, backfiring the truck, pressed his sweaty palm on the steering wheel and spun it counterclockwise from ten to two o'clock. The drunk's weight pressed on his door. Afraid his passenger would fall out, the driver grabbed a handful of sweaty yellow T-shirt and yanked against the centrifugal force.

The driver straightened the wheel, ground the gears into third, saying "Fuck," and began to accelerate. The truck jumped forward, lost some of its traction on the dirt road and slid from the far right shoulder to the far left. A here-comes-a-rowdy-farm-boy cloud of brown dust billowed behind the tailgate. Irrigation ditches sat deep on either side of the road and cattails began waving from side to side in the brown air as the truck continued to gain speed.

The driver punched into fourth gear. The truck did what it had going into third. The accelerator remained flat on the floor. "Stand on the maafucker, Lyle!" the drunk hooted.

Lyle asked the drunk who the girl was. "The biggest slut in El Cajon," muttered the drunk, his high spirits disturbed by something. "Ya fuck her?" inquired Lyle. "Yeah, sure, once — me an' about twenty other guys."

The driver smiled to himself. He straightened his elbows back from the steering wheel, pressed his weight against the back seat and hit the brakes with one serious jolt. The drunk didn't have a chance. He had been looking at the buttons on his Levi's. Completely vulnerable, he flew forward. His skull jammed into the corner where the windshield met the dashboard.

During this micro-second, he was thinking clearly. He heard the voice in his head say "dashboard." His memory provided a total recollection of his aunt's farm in Oklahoma. He hadn't seen the place in fifteen years. He remembered her grating voice whining, "Clifford, you be careful on that swing. . . ." He could feel the warm summer wind blowing across his aunt's front yard. He could feel the gravity and release of the rope swing he was pulling against. He could see the blue sky and his little-boy knees, bare and skinned. He saw a dirty white tape bandage on his left big toe, which he held just a little bit higher than his other dirt-encrusted foot, both pointing directly into the sky. He heard his aunt cough, clear her throat, and finish her warning, ". . . or you'll just dash your little brains out."

Clifford's head wobbled on his broken neck. His arms flapped awkwardly; a giant blood blister formed like a bruised peach over the mushy crown of his head. His ear hit the wind-wing support bar and sent blood splattering out the window and over the back of the bench seat. He shit his pants, in a single convulsive explosion; a huge volume of piss firehosed down his pant leg. His legs slid to the left along the floor, knocking Lyle's feet off the pedals. His paralyzed body flopped lengthwise on the floor.

Lyle tried frantically to kick the heavy legs off the brake and accelerator pedals. He screamed when he realized the truck was describing a slow arc with the front of the hood falling. He tried to remember the position of the wheel, but it didn't matter. The truck, in a solid bounce, crammed into the ditch on the left side of the road. Lyle's forehead sent a shower of broken glass into the air. His head popped through the pre-safety-plate glass windshield and snapped off on the bottom of the jagged hole. His head bounced once on the fender near the left headlight, right next to the spot wiped clean by the jeans of the girl he thought he loved, and had just seen in his rearview mirror for the second time this morning.

The girl paused as she noticed an abrupt end to the brown cloud of dust leading diagonally across the field to her left.

She wondered what the boys in the truck were stopping for. She shrugged and kept stumbling down the road.

BOY IN THE AIR 2

YOU WOULD HAVE TO HAVE been in that stadium, and heard the echo every time the gun went off. You'd have to have been in the bottom, on the black asphalt with the white lines setting the limits of the lanes and the beginnings and the ends. You'd have to have been sensitive to the irony of the black surface and the ruled white lines — and somehow linked it all with an appreciation and awe of the threat to you, and the promise to all of black athletic talent.

You'd have to have been there twenty-five years ago when cities ignited, fists were clenched in love and in hate, and at the same goddamn time. You'd have to have red hair, be thin with milk-white skin tinted orange from the hot spring sun of this border town in the southwestern corner between the Mexican border and the blue Pacific.

You'd have to be thirteen years old and dreaming of a national record in the running broad jump as they called it in those days. You'd have to be consumed with the knowledge that some kid in New Jersey had jumped 19 feet 3 inches. You'd have to accept that you were the unchallenged best jumper out of thousands of kids, except black ones, by jumping just over 17 feet. You'd listen to Keith Richards, or some other Delta blues imitator, and understand as you heard "King Bee," that the line could be crossed in expression, but the mystery of color would never change. You'd have heard of another white rocker who just had to be named Tripp. Arnold Tripp who had been king of it all just ten years ago. Tripp the fastest boy in San Diego whose career was dumped at the state meet, when the coaches raced him on a torn hamstring — because they wanted someone to beat the niggers. They had their Tarzan. You'd have to hate both of the words, Tarzan as much as nigger. You'd still have to bring your white skin with you to the starting line, and snort in contempt at the attitudes of both colors when the resentment came from the blacks, and racist encouragement was offered from the whites.

You'd have to be in a stadium that echoed not only with the sound of pistol shots, but also with the sound of girls' voices high and wild with humor and sexual anticipation as they waited for Louis Rey to take his next jump. You'd have to be sitting on the grass in the blazing sun at ten o'clock on a May morning looking indirectly at and listening intently to the conversation directed at a boy your own age, who came from a world with ten times the life and death of your own. Sitting there on the grass listening to the most beautiful girls in the world, gleaming white teeth, almond eyes, dark tanned deep black skin, tight skirts, white angel blouses that had heavy breasts bursting light and perfect under buttons that split and revealed black skin — and those shoes.

You'd see Louis Rey (no one ever called him just Rey, or just Louis, because he was Louis Rey). Thin and muscular with large bugging eyes and a snarl for a mouth when he wasn't smiling and hair that was becoming an Afro, skin oiled to a shine and every bit the urban Masai warrior walking proud and defiant, dominant and beautiful, and better than you at what you wanted to be best at more than anything in the world. You'd watch him intently because you had enough of it yourself to know what a genius looked like, but not what one acted like, as you waited for your next jump. You'd watch the girls in the stands who were at one moment on the coolest nonchalant trip, unconcerned and casual, and the next instant spreading their legs right in the twentieth row laughing and telling Louis Rey they had something for him. Louis Rey was smiling and promising all of them a ride in his brother's car. Sharing the laugh when one of the girls asked which brother's car it would be this time since he had taken them for at least ten rides this spring in different cars and he only had three brothers. The laugh peaked when it was noted that one of his brothers was only six. Louis Rey just smiled and took his place at the end of the runway, as the entire stadium watched him. He raised his hand lightly and told the official at the take-off board, "Scratch," and jogged off across the field to talk to some older guys in trench coats with James Brown conks who seemed certain to be packing revolvers.

You'd take the lead hitting 18'10" on your next jump and there would be a spattering of applause coming from the white section high in the shade of the stadium. The announcer would declare that with one jump to go you were less than 6" from the long-standing national record. You'd be wishing he never said that. You would steal a look at Louis Rey who never flinched at the announcement, but looked at the knot of white spectators as they called encouragement down to you. Ten minutes later Louis Rey would accelerate to the board, hitting an approach speed that was simply faster than you could ever hope to run. He'd transfer that black velocity into a neat thud and plant into a vertical lift that suspended Louis Rey in the air for a beat and another beat, and your own internal timing would be feeling your body drop because any other boy in the world would have to be dropping by now. But Louis Rey would be holding his apex because he had come in with such speed and power that he was still hovering. The stadium full of people began to sense that something was happening, but not KNOWING like you did, and the energy would cause the universal turning of a few hundred heads focusing on the boy in the air who for this instant was stopping time. Sailing above the sand, freezing your reality, taking your breath away and pissing you off in the highest sense of compliment imaginable. Gradually he wound downward and blasted the sand in a spray that surged from under his body, which bounced silently with heavy impact at a distance that was just weird. Plain weird.

"Foul," the official yelled as the red flag snapped into the air. You'd say under your breath, "Yeah, he did foul," as you jogged lightly and with more speed and spring in your legs than you ever felt before toward the hole out in the sand. It was sad, it was just the slightest foul. You'd hear your voice demanding of the official to "Measure it anyway," because you had to know. The official didn't need much prompting. Louis Rey was on the grass holding his head with tears streaming down his face, the stadium silent. Just you and the official moving in slow motion, and your voice still echoing "Measure it anyway." As they did, Louis Rey's body started shaking like he was expecting to endure a beating, and he did when he heard the official, "Jesus Christ, 22 feet, 3 inches." Louis Rey stood up and looked at you. You said, "You'll have other days Louis." Louis Rey thinking you were being mean said, "Shut up, you white motherfucker." You just stood there and said, "Nice jump anyway." He stared at you, and the girls started yelling, "Fuck him up Louis," because if they couldn't see a record they could at least hope for a fight. Louis Rey said quietly only to me, "I already did." And I smiled. And he smiled.

SPHINX

IF YOU WERE ROASTING in the desert, twenty-five miles from the nearest gas station, standing under the sun, shielding your eyes and watching a little dot making its way toward you, you would be struck by a major and a minor element. The major element would be the heat, and the fact that the solitary dot out there in the shimmering horizon is a junior high school boy. The minor element, the question: Why?

Pulling focus on the long lens of your imagination, you see him sweating in his shorts and T-shirt, crunching over the decomposed granite under his boots. Facing the blasting sun hanging low on the horizon, his three canteens riding the small of his back in the shade.

His boots are aptly named desert boots. They are perfect: tough tan leather, ankle high, laced in four holes on the arch to prevent hot sand and stones from falling inside, flexible thick gum soles. The boy loves those desert boots. The boots are almost the answer to our question.

Eddie feels trapped in the culture of Southern California. He is tired of the billboards offering him his own masculinity through tobaccco products. He hates the promises of confirmation of his sexuality and desirability from sports car ads on T.V. He is insulted by the assurance that he earns power and validity through the possession of this product or that, by the distorted and grotesque subliminal images promising him manhood, sex, heroism. He mistrusts the easy rites of passage supplied by his culture. He knows the commercial influences are wrong, threatening something akin to what used to be sacred.

He couldn't have put any of this into words. He feels it, with the unique clarity and purest wisdom of adolescence. He had begun to think there was nothing he could do about it. The cultural bombardment was sneaky, constant, unavoidable. It took a gradual and relentless toll on his spirit.

Months earlier he had heard some embarrassed, uneasy laughter from his friends, and a faint voice calling him back to the school yard. "Eddie, Eddie. What the fuck, Eddie. What are ya starin' at?" He was focused on his feet, and the feet of seven of his friends all standing in a circle. Five of those friends, including Eddie, were wearing desert boots. These boots were not used in the desert, and they suddenly seemed to him part of a uniform for pretenders. If he could have taken them off his feet and thrown them into the bushes surrounding the quad he would have. Instead he stared, stunned.

He felt like a complete fraud. A fraud who hung around with other frauds, being fraudulent. He thought of a lyric from a new song by one of his favorite bands . . . "and he can't be a man 'cause he doesn't smoke the same cigarette as me."

The bell for class rang, scattering his friends in four directions. He lagged behind, sleepwalking his way to his math class, feeling contaminated by what a few minutes earlier had seemed like just a kids' collective sense of style. He wandered to his seat late, his face blank, unconcerned as Mrs. Fields eyed him over her glasses while marking him tardy again. His heart began pounding wildly. He understood clearly, as each thought possessed him, that he was already on his way to the desert. He stuck his feet out in the aisle and smiled.

The next weekend via Greyhound and his thumb, he was out there. He loved it. He loved it so much he kept it a secret. Once every month for the next six months, right into the teeth of summer his boots became Desert Boots. Capital D, capital B. He progressed from walking out and back in an hour or two, to elaborate treks often to fourteen hours, each time feeling his spirit gaining strength as he lost sight of civilization. In the last two months he started out in the dark before dawn, heading out for a point to be reached before nightfall.

The sense of accomplishment upon reaching his destination was extended and reflected upon during the ride in the Greyhound back to San Diego, prolonged during his silent, noncommittal rides as a hitchhiker from the downtown bus terminal to the eastern section of town. Waving thanks and closing the door on the stranger driving, he'd cut across orangegroved back yards and along the floors of domesticated canyons, making his way up to his front steps. He'd swing open the screen door saying, "Hi Ma, 'say Dad," and head for his bedroom.

Surging with secret pride at his accomplishment, and relishing the exhausting toll it exacted, he'd examine the dust on his boots, the sunburned skin, the burnt-straw shock of hair, the salt-caked clothes. He'd open his bedroom window, take off his shorts, pull off the T-shirt and slip off those scarred, durable boots. Yanking the cool sheets back on his bed, he lay in the darkened room looking out into a world which now had boundaries no one who knew him could imagine.

He'd see the tops of the apartments sitting in the canyon that bordered his back yard. He'd listen with amused contempt to the faint calling and laughing from the miniature golf course which sat — phony and fake, unreal and gaudy — at the end of his street. The yelps and hollers would grow fainter. The sounds of the people playing and flirting on the plastic grass and trick fairways would subside entirely. His breathing would change into a slow shallow rhythm, dropping like a stone down a well into deep sleep, splashing slowly into the sweet carnal dreams of early manhood.

After these weekends he relished coming back to school, standing with his buddies in the circle, looking down at these boots and the boots of his friends and saying nothing.

There he is, a tiny dot making his seventh desert excursion, swinging along in a comfortable walking rhythm, confident that he will reach his destination. He stops, fumbles with the strap attached to the canteens, twists the top off one, and takes a long swallow. He turns an about-face in the direction from which he's come. The expanse of desert stretches flat, rippling in the growing heat. The peaks jutting in the far distance seem to Eddie as close as they appeared six hours ago. A gust of furnace wind blows over his face.

As though this were a silent signal, he turns and begins walking again. He has broken his rhythm during this forty-second stop. He will struggle out of harmony. The heat will bear down on him for several long minutes before his stride becomes the metronome that permits his mantric mindless peace. His heart palpitates at the restart. His skin flushes unbearably hot. Sweat gushes off his face. Khaki shorts find a new way to bind and hold his balls, rubbing a deeper blister between his legs.

Still in stride, he reaches into his front pocket and takes out a small sandwich bag. His fingers wiggle in the plastic and remove a melted glob of Vaseline. His hand slips under his waistband. He stops, spreads his legs, and smears the goo around his crotch. The boots crunch along once again, searching for the harmonic drum of his steps on the desert floor. The heat has swollen his penis. He feels awkward as it flexes and flops until it finds its spot, riding the rhythm between the hot wet shorts and his bare Vaselined leg.

He begins to think of his best friend's mother down the

street. Beautiful, warm disposition, a light, insightful sense of humor. He imagines her flat-roofed stucco tract home. He sees her on her couch. Lying on her side in the dark with the curtains pulled against the afternoon sun. He sees her ankles crossed and her body stretched out. Her palm is resting behind her sweating neck, revealing a black patch of armpit next to her face. Her breasts are outlined in the transparent, sweat-soaked, white cotton blouse. She slowly lifts her hips and shifts her weight toward the outside of the couch. Her eyes are closed. She's nearly asleep, wide-hipped, heavy-breasted, peaceful.

The fan, which always sits on the parquet floor during hot weather, buzzes left to right, an admiring machine repeating its once-over from head to toe. Repeating toe to head, head to toe, over and over. The breeze hits her thighs, flowing up the stream of her loose dress, following the indented line to the V under her stomach, fluttering her dress, trembling in the V, and continuing. It buzzes over the stomach, up along her breasts, giving her nipples a pulsation of cool against the white wet cloth, causing a slight blush and tightness.

The fan continues up the curves of her thin muscular neck and stops on her face to reverse direction. A few sweat-joined strands of jet-black hair reverberate along her cheek for a second. Asleep. Her face turns like a dark flower to the cool moon of the fan's breeze. Her lips kiss the fan's invisible pressure, her tongue sliding slowly along her upper lip, pulling cool drops of sweat into her mouth. The fan's buzz changes to a deeper tone and travels down her body.

Eddie stumbles, unconscious of the variation of his cadence, on and on, over and around the knee-high brush, zigzagging along the frying desert floor. "Where am I? I'm here and I'm OK . . . still have a canteen and a half of water . . . about four or five hours to the gas station . . . it's only . . . four-thirty . . . shit . . . but . . . hell, the headlights on the road work pretty good . . . like last time . . . full moon up at eight . . .

plenty of time . . . I'm not scared, am I?" His heart pounds slightly. He swallows and waits for panic. Nothing. "No." He checks his bearings, turning in a slow circle, finding all the landmarks exactly where he wants them to be. "Four-thirty-two . . . four or five hours. . . ." His heart races. He inhales the hot air deeply, blows it out and inhales again, blows it out fast and inhales again.

"Fuck that. Who the fuck cares what time it is or what the fuck time I get there? . . . I got the fucking direction and I don't need to waste my fucking energy getting all the fuck worked up over fucking nothing. Fuck it. I ain't scared and I'm not going to start getting fucking scared by wondering what the fuck time it is, or when the fuck I'm getting where the fuck I'm going." You'd have heard him laughing at himself if you had happened to be in the middle of the Mojave in August 1964. "I'm not scared, I'm OK. Now where was I? Oh, yeah."

He sees her again. It was the time he came to her house last week. It was really hot that day. Good thing he wasn't out here then, 106 in San Diego. That'd be somewhere like 120 out here. Anyway, he went into her house in the late afternoon. The house was asleep, everything completely still. He trailed the absence of sound out to the back yard patio, found the woman's husband and their kids passed out in the heat, lying on mattresses they had dragged outside into the shade.

He could hear pipes and faucets sputter from the bathroom shower inside the house, settling into a high-pressure rain. The woman gasped for breath as she stepped into the shower. He argued with himself as he involuntarily walked back into the house. His silent steps wound from the patio along the corridor between the bedrooms and the bathroom. From the amplified splash and the sound of the spray and the bare feet squeaking against the wet porcelain, he determined that the bathroom door remained wide open. He could hear the water storming over her body and exploding in wet impact on the floor of the tub. Taking a breath, he turned the corner of the corridor and faced the bathroom. Cold steamless water ran over her silhouette, streams of water raced in clear webs on the inside of the shower curtain. The shadow bent at the waist and long arms stretched downward, breasts falling easily under shoulders, head down, hair hanging like a black waterfall.

She stood up, arms pulling the mane of hair up and over her shoulders. Her face was tilted upward, her mouth open. The jet of water blasting against her neck. Cool air swirled from the bathroom door.

She twisted the faucet shut. Eddie slipped out of the doorway and waited. Hearing her yank the shower curtain aside, he timed his voice to say, "Robert? . . ." with perfect innocence, and turned the corner. Her eyes met his. She was mid-stride, one leg suspended over the rim of the tub. She made no effort to cover herself, but froze there like a photograph, her eyes driving into his, betraying a mixture of curiosity and amusement.

She stood there, skin gleaming, holding his eyes prisoner with a magnetic power within her gaze. He could see nothing of her but a terrifying and increasing depth behind her eyes. He felt his body go weightless in panic as he realized he was far beyond his depth.

At that instant she smiled and reached smoothly for a towel and hugged it front of herself. She glanced out of the side of her eye, letting slip for an instant something that felt to Eddie like understanding and forgiveness, unsettling him even more and informing him immediately who held all the power. Her attitude shamed him, as though in these frozen instants he could see the real meaning of his mistake.

It was as though she had expected, even recognized, the inevitability of this contact but was disappointed in what Eddie had done with it. Without a word, she told him he had gone about it entirely wrong, and although she would not use the word, he knew "fool" was the only one appropriate. His face burned, his eyes dropped down, unfocused. Still holding her image, almost but not quite registering his boots on the wooden floor, he said, "Oh, I'm sorry."

Her voice held a curious tone, coming from deeper in her chest, ironic and more real than it had ever sounded to him before. It made him imagine the way she would sound giving simple directions to a stranger who had lost his way. A matter-of-fact voice that in some way labeled him an equal. It seemed final and strangely welcome, spoken under her breath. A code, a frightening challenge, a whispered riddle. "Oh, yeah, sure, you are."

SHERRY BABY

E<small>LEVEN-THIRTY, A MOONLESS NIGHT</small>. E<small>MPTY</small> streets in sub-urbia. The tenth day of a heat wave. The Santa Ana gusts hot and dry, ninety-two degrees. Eddie Burnett is urinating under a street lamp on the middle of an asphalt road. It's a tradition with him this summer. Standing in one spot, he turns a slow circle. His record is four revolutions, he calls them "piss rings." He does this almost every night on the way home from his girlfriend's house. The rings stain the road for several days. Each night a new overlapping ring, until he gets five. He's doing this to commemorate the 1964 Summer Olympic Games.

His girlfriend's house? Not really. That is, it's an un-requited love. Sherry likes him, but on the social level he's considered much too goony for her. Eddie does not quite get it. He gets his hair cut by his mother, and dresses from the Navy PX, with no sense of style, and worse, no interest in it. The social situation means much less to Sherry than the sense that Eddie doesn't trust something about himself. She puzzles at his obvious feeling of inferiority, despite qualities that should make him confident. She wishes Eddie would find that place that gives most of the other boys the ground they stand on. He seems to have lost that place, or had it sto-len. Sherry's curiosity and attraction comes from the feeling that Eddie knows where that place is, needs it, and thinks it's worthless at the same time. He speaks in a code, using images that create unwholesome feelings in Sherry. They appeal to something essential inside of herself that she fears most. Just about everything he has to say makes Sherry laugh, or seems faintly intimidating, as though he knew some bitter secret.

Eddie is especially happy tonight, though. Earlier today Sherry passed her Coke bottle to him. When he passed it back, she just finished it off without a second glance. Right in front of her friends. Didn't check for backwash or anything. Didn't even wipe the lip of the bottle. To Eddie and to the other kids, this gesture spoke of intimacy.

Sherry's hair is summer blond, her eyes are gray. She smells stunningly innocent. She's ripe and it's all operating, pulsating just under the surface. Eddie is in full-throttle, aching adolescent love.

Mornings they meet at the beach. She rides with a girl-friend's mother or older brother. Eddie thumbs out with a couple of the guys, making a heroic beach entrance from the far reaches of thirty miles of inland freeway.

Sherry knows she drives them all crazy. She sees it as their problem and has zero patience with any boy who brings it up. The boys her own age can speak of almost nothing else in the minutes that follow seeing her. Men pull over in their cars to holler their promises to her. She sends them off stammering insults in her general direction, with about the same effect on Sherry as if they were bouncing off a nearby lamppost. Nothing disturbs her self-possession. For this quality Eddie adores her. Her beauty is only secondary.

He is fascinated to discover that her self-possession is not the result of insensitivity or a callous stupidity, but is fueled by her tremendous intelligence and fierce courage.

Tonight, as Eddie finishes off the last piss ring, he hears Sherry's voice from the phone call that afternoon. Minutes earlier he had been in her front room keeping her company as she ironed clothes for the entire family. He hears her soft, trusting voice as she sobs tearful-hateful-father misunderstandings. Sherry is being punished for being out too late the night before with Eddie, and for coming home with grass stains on her white shorts.

Eddie had walked her home. They were only a few minutes late. He made her laugh at something. There was an intoxicating jasmine bush hovering over their heads. Suddenly a wrestling match exploded. Sherry and Eddie struggled against each other on the warm, wet lawn. A blue light shone out of the window of some stranger's house as they sat inside watching Ed Sullivan on T.V.

When Sherry's father inevitably forbade her to see Eddie, he spent his nights, wings clipped, perched on the rims of the canyons of his childhood, looking down into an expanse of darkness.

He had already lost his direction. That summer he didn't go to movies, or hang out with his friends. He didn't go to the beach, or read, or learn to do anything new. He was overwhelmed. He needed Sherry.

He dragged around the streets at night, trying to dodge the ultraconservative, ultramilitary San Diego police department. Eddie had already been introduced to the San Diego police. It had occurred on a sidewalk two summers earlier.

Cops pull up in their cruiser. Cops jump out. Cops tell Eddie to stand still. Cops throw him facedown, pin his arms, shove his face into the concrete, twist his wrists, ratchet on the cuffs. Cops throw him in the cruiser, banging his head into the doorjamb as they toss him into the back seat. They drive him someplace, and tell him to get out. They walk him to a screen door, where a woman with a purple swollen face and a bloody cloth held over her mouth says, "No, that's not him."

Cops take off the handcuffs. They try to tell Eddie they're sorry, but add that he "answered the lady's description." Eddie looks at the short redheaded one, with stubble like rust on his chin. Immediately Eddie understands something about the genetics of outlaws. He senses something that is not in his favor, in fact quite the opposite. It's as though from that moment on, he saw the line drawn in front of his feet. Something they think makes him wrong, and he knows makes him right. He looks at the cop and smiles, "That's alright, I'll always answer the description." The rusty face contorts at an equation, the face cannot find the sum. The cop takes his stand behind authority: his weight settles on his spread feet, his pelvis shifts forward and this conversation is over. The other cop offers Eddie a ride home. He looks like his feelings are hurt when Eddie replies, "No, thanks."

After that initial meeting, it seemed the cops felt that they should find something he had done to justify their mistake. They picked him up and drove him home a lot. Parked squad car rumbling in front of his house, neighbors opening curtains watching his parents' place.

In response, Eddie committed as much malicious mischief as he possibly could for the next year and a half. Specifically motivated in his contest with the cops, generally motivated by the silent, stucco, lawn-sprinkler existence of San Diego. The contest was a tie. Eddie didn't get caught, but he remained stuck within the quiet, soulless, white-pebbled roofs, all contained by the cops. But by the time he met, and lost, Sherry, he was leaving the community alone, and wasting his time by himself.

Sherry was in a car with her big brother and one of his friends. Eddie was on foot carrying a couple bags of groceries home. He felt something was wrong before he turned around to see the smirking faces on the boys, and heard the enthusiastic shouting of his name called out of the car window. He managed an awkward acknowledging jerk of his head above the bags in the general direction of Sherry as she passed out of sight, sitting in the front seat between two football heroes.

He finally dropped the bags on the kitchen table and

said, "I'm taking a walk" to his mother, who tried to stop him but gave up as the screen door swung closed.

She may have only wondered why Eddie would want to take a walk in 102-degree heat immediately after carrying two full bags of groceries a half mile. Maybe she wanted to offer him an iced coffee, or ask him why he got in so late last night, or would Sherry like to come to dinner some night, and she hadn't seen much of Sherry lately . . . was anything wrong?

Eddie was walking in the dehydrating, asphalt-melting, cornea-frying, lip-cracking summer weather of interior San Diego. His head ached, it buzzed with fatigue. He made himself go look at the tire tracks on the shoulder of the road leading from Food Basket. He was slouched more than ever, his face parallel to the mushy black road. He was not moving across the busy intersection fast enough for the man driving the station wagon.

Eddie is in the middle of the crosswalk, directly in front of the station wagon's two-tone baby-shit-brown hood. He can smell the suffering fan belt's burning skin. He hears the wheezing radiator.The windshield reflects a blinding glare. HONK! HONK! HOOOONNNNKKK! Eddie is stunned. He stands there, then turns and faces the guy driving, who emanates a tremendous amount of loathing. He starts to walk again. HOOOOONNNNNNKKKKK!

Eddie gets to the far right headlight and turns an about-face, crossing the front of the hood again. The man starts yelling shit at Eddie. He sticks his American-man war-hero head out of his car and spews more shit at him. Eddie makes another about-face and crosses in front of the car again. The door swings open. The man clomps his backache out of the seat. His hard soles hit the pavement; his sweaty shirt is stuck to his pear-shaped body. He swaggers toward Eddie with balled fists.

Eddie is supposed to run. But he is pissed. The man grabs for the boy's T-shirt and tries to stretch it within the grasp of his other hand. Eddie cannot believe that this fat fuck thinks he is going to treat him like a child. It seems almost funny that the man thinks he can yell and try to overpower him with his adult-size bulk. Eddie jerks loose of the man's awkward grabbing. The man's fingernails tear into Eddie's arm. In an instant, Eddie has hit him — hard. The shot is planted on the side of the man's crew-cut. The man is already tilted downward, from just that one quick pop. Disgusted, Eddie belts him again. The man hits the pavement. Eddie leans down, lines up the spot where the jawline meets the neck under the ear, and passes. Blam, he hits him in the forehead. Just because the man doesn't have basic respect for anyone; because he honks at barefoot kids in hot crosswalks going too slow. He honks, honks, honks, at disillusioned, nothing-to-live-for, nothing-to-die-for kids. He puts his hands on people he doesn't know. The man wants to intimidate other people, too busy ignoring his own kids, who are staring at Eddie in terror.

Daddy's kids are crying. Boy, are they crying. Screaming. Daddy is lying on the ground trying to get his burning elbows off the furnace-hot grit. Daddy is flopping around with his equilibrium fucked up from the knots on his head. The kids are under ten, two little girls and the youngest a boy. They keep repeating, "Daddy, Daddy, Daddy," in sobbing, breathless screams. Eddie has a vacant feeling, as though there is nothing left of himself. If he'd put it in words, it would have had something to do with nature, what he had done, and the way he felt about those kids felt unnatural.

The wife is sitting in the honey seat. While Dear is getting up on his knees, Eddie sees the wife's wide eyes. He knows that he has humiliated her husband. Her desperate expression tells Eddie that he has given her husband problems he will not overcome, and those problems will extend to her and her innocent kids. That although she will never express anything but hatred to Eddie, at the same moment she is pleading with him to do something. It is his responsibility because he is the one standing. Eddie's remorse at the sound of the shrieking children, and the sexual tilt in the woman's unspoken plea, is more than he can handle this morning. Eddie walks over to the curb and sits down. He realizes the man's behavior is not an isolated incident, and his wife probably hates him as much as Eddie does. But the kids.

Dear staggers to the car and parks it across the street. He's yelling brave things now, since it is apparent Eddie is down for the count. The blustering pear is just that kind of guy. Then Honey starts yelling about the police and runs into Speedee Mart.

The stock boy, a friend from elementary school, comes running out in his green apron. He squats down next to Eddie on one knee, surveying the commotion building on the corner. "You better get the hell outta here, Eddie. They already called the cops." Eddie mumbles, "That's good." He focuses on a gum wrapper between his dirty, callused feet. His heart is exploding in fear and anger. The fear is climbing and the anger is falling. He wishes they would just drive away. He knows they won't.

The cops come. Dear stands there, the center of self-righteous attention. The cops stand nearby, regarding Eddie like a rabid dog. Eddie overhears Honey, who evidently has read Newsweek, because she is certain that Eddie is on "pot" or he would have run away. Dear picks up his cue and makes it clear in a loud voice to all the bystanders that people on "pot" have more strength than normal, and that is the reason he didn't kick the kid's butt. They start speaking in quiet voices suggesting that Eddie is winding down from some high and is falling into a stupor. The kids have quieted down. Eddie sits there smelling the wrapper. He'd bet it was Juicy Fruit — wrong, it was spearmint. Slight smile in the corner of Eddie's mouth. Sentence inside his head — "Just not my day." The man stands next to the big guys with the guns, nodding his head in some social bond. Eddie looks at Honey, who is smug with the knowledge that she has, probably for the thousandth time, gotten Dear his balls back.

But as the black-and-white pulls away with a silent Eddie in the back seat, it's because Eddie wants the kids to see the police take the bad guy away.

BUCEPHALUS

I WAS FIFTEEN. I'D JUST gotten out of Juvy, and my parents were pretty upset. I was starting my first year in high school and I was hoping to do something right. My father told me I was trying out for the school football team. As usual, I wasn't in a position to argue with him. I knew I'd never make the team anyway. So there I was on September 5, 1964, at nine-thirty a.m., sitting in the locker room of Wilson High School, the pride of interscholastic sports in San Diego, California.

I had a helmet that didn't fit right, way too loose. It looked stupid. My neck was too thin, my eyes too big, my face too narrow. The idea of intimidating anyone in the locker room was laughable. I sat in front of my locker with tunnel vision. Putting on the gear I was having an anxiety attack, before I ever got near the football field. I sat there surrounded by last year's championship players, thinking, "Dad would just love this." The linemen were acting big and brutish, defensive linemen especially. The linebackers were the characteristic psychopaths everyone imagines linebackers to be. There was a cluster of pretty-boy stars, undoubtedly the quarterbacks, running backs and receivers. They were all smiling, telling jokes, happy to have another year of glory, admiration, and sex beginning again.

I sat there in my underwear and socks with the huge

helmet wobbling on my head, a ridiculous stranger. These other guys looked like giants; thick cords ran up and down their wide brown necks. Whiskers collected beads of sweat. They looked at me kind of funny. Each pair of eyes would dart at me; each pair assessed me as nothing — that bugged me. I lifted the helmet off my head and put it on the floor as nonchalantly as possible — I had noticed that no one else was wearing his. I reached down for one of my cleated football shoes. At that instant, a huge foot sent it spinning along the concrete floor. I got so nervous I nearly fainted. My brain struggled frantically to determine if this was intentional or accidental. What challenge or warning should I declare? How could I get out of this without looking more absurd than I felt, which was very absurd? Without looking up, I crouched down, staring at the floor, and stretched a few small steps, reaching for my shoe. I could see a thousand tails on a thousand dogs tucked under a thousand chicken-shit dog butts.

A thick-wristed hand intercepted the shoe and handed it back, saying, "Sorry, Red, here ya go." "Thanks," I peeped without looking up. Red. I hated to be called Red. This guy didn't know my name, sees my red hair, red freckles, red nose, and assumes my fucking name is Red. Plus, I knew that if he had intentionally kicked my shoe again, I would have chickened out.

I hid my burning face and pretended to need something in my locker. I dove way in, smelling at least eight years of athletic tradition at Wilson High School. My thoughts echoed, "This is not a good start."

My father never taught me a thing. He hardly ever said anything to me. He never put his hand on my shoulder, never extended it in a handshake, never even slapped me with it. He saved that for my mother. It was clear that he thought I didn't exist, wasn't even worth the bother.

He was a hero. He was compromised by his war experiences, but he still walked with the stride of a leader of men. He drank too much, and he was pretty fucked up when I was younger. He was a sergeant-at-arms with cannonball biceps. He used an "Aw-shucks" style of humor that stung like hell but was really funny anyway. He was always making me laugh and hurting me at the same time. He had rock-a-billy hair and sloped powerful shoulders, stood six foot four, and smelled sort of randy with smoke and beer. He always got smiles from the women that knew him, and furtive glances and a smile from any who didn't. He accepted this as his due and kept walking. He never walked next to me or my mother. He had an old M-1 in his closet with a chunk kicked out of the stock near the grip where an Italian's bullet had ricocheted. He had a glass eye. He cracked his knuckles, belched his beer and watched lots of football on T.V., and was drunk all the time.

We were going into the second hour of tryouts. The grass was shining. The ground was soft; the sprinklers had been on early that morning. The sun shone with surreal heat directly above. We'd heard speeches from coaches and listened to stars of last year's team urging us to win again. With the team in a tight knot in the center of the field, upperclassmen were impressing younger boys with references to parties and dances that followed last season's games — the emphasis was on "pussy." I looked at my feet. I'd never so much as held a girl's hand. The father of the only girl I had a chance with wouldn't let me see her. I began to hate these stars with their girlfriends, their own cars and their friends to eat lunch with.

The sidelines were deep with kids. Several parents walked up and down talking easily, fathers with chests expanded in vicarious pride. A ring of girls stood on the thirty-yard line. They were dressed casual, in revealing hot-weather clothes; they had tanned silky skin. They seemed to be having a subliminal conversation from the waist down with some of the older boys, secretive and tentative. As far as I could tell, this looked like the big time. We'd been told that we were going to close out the practice with "contact drills." I had heard "men from boys" muttered at least twenty times in reference to these contact drills. We had been racing each other by positions earlier, and I had always been pretty fast. The stars from last year's team seemed a little upset when I kept winning the races. Some of the guys were friendly about it, but they already knew they were slow. The ones that thought they were fast were pissed. I knew the coaches liked speed, and they began to pay more attention to me. The stars didn't like that much, either. I felt the tide turning against me.

A fat red-faced coach screamed, "ALRIGHT — on the thirty YARD LINE." The two stars beside me started making television-sounding war cries. I got disgusted and jogged over to where they were lining up. This is what they had been waiting for. I noticed how much bigger the other players were. I also noticed the pairs of eyes that stared at me, and the knots of players looking my direction and talking quietly among themselves. A coach came over and asked me what position I was trying out for. I just said, "Defense." Two guys made derisive sounds. I looked at them; they looked at me. I didn't like them; they didn't like me.

Two days earlier I had been sitting in the front room with my dad, the curtains drawn. He was watching a team from his home state of Texas playing the rival state, Oklahoma. My mother came from Oklahoma. As a result, she was subjected to merciless teasing from my dad. Especially when he'd been drinking. We were the Okies. I was born in El Paso. He was born north and a hell of a lot closer to Oklahoma than I was, but to him I was the "goddamn Okie."

There he was, sitting in the dark watching the football game — silent, emotionless, intent. His hips and back would jump involuntarily as he watched the athletes smashing into each other. He popped numerous beers, which were in a neat row beside the Lazyboy chair and were removed silently by my mother at odd intervals.

I sat down in a chair near him, watching him and hoping he would want to talk to me about trying out for the team. He was a big star halfback in high school. Trophies, scrapbooks, the whole bit. I didn't care if he got drunk and told me about his five-touchdown night again. But he didn't say anything. The game on T.V. was pretty good. The lead changed hands several times, the players were making great runs, the hitting was vicious. Sometimes the camera would pan the stadium packed with delirium and pretty girls. Oklahoma won. Dad stood up and glared at me, spun a tight circle, sat back down and said, "Goddamn it, goddamn Okies, every one of 'em halfbreed morons."

They started interviewing Number 43 from Oklahoma. When the kid said where he lived, my dad said, "Just down the road from your mother." The T.V. showed three plays the kid made, an incredible run with an interception and two hits near the goal line on the Texas halfback that had my dad saying, "Oh, man." The Oklahoma coach put his arm over the shoulder of Number 43, who looked like he was in elementary school, kinda skinny, with a big ol' grin. The coach said a couple of nice things about all the players on his team and then, referring to the kid who was now dodging a few towels his teammates were throwing at him because he was on T.V., said, "It ain't the size of the dog in the fight, it's the size of the fight in the dog."

My dad looked over at me, and his hand switched off the T.V. "Didja hear that? Truer words were never spoken." Then he walked out to the front yard. I didn't follow him. I went down the street to see some friends who came from Texas and Oklahoma too and were proud of it. I tried out the thing the coach said on the boys and it went over with them like a new motto.

I was pulling off my jersey, it was stuck to my pads with sweat. I was grass-stained, scraped up and laughing to myself because I couldn't believe how good I felt. Every time I lined up for my turn during the contact drills I could hear my father, "Didja hear that. . . ?" I'd watch the players' faces as they came swaggering up to the line and I saw that look change to fear the next time. I saw many faces alter and self-doubt cloud innocent eyes. I kept feeling an impact on them that they obviously knew nothing about. Before too long they were trying to protect themselves instead of trying to run over me. That made it worse for them. I just did what I was supposed to do, like I'd seen the kid do on T.V. In the locker room I kept how I felt to myself. I wasn't saying anything to anyone. I wasn't putting my head in my locker either.

Someone I didn't know was helping me out of my jersey; when I turned to thank him, he was gone. My eyes searched the room, and any eyes that met mine looked down at the floor. I wanted to ask them what they were afraid of, but I knew it would be a long season, and in a few weeks they would see me as a teammate instead of someone who was going to knock their dicks in the dirt every practice.

The red-faced coach yelled out the practice times for tomorrow's tryouts. Then he looked at me. "Way to go out there, Red. Where do you come from ?"

I said, "Oklahoma."

BEST TIME OF THE DAY

THE HOT AIR IS BUILDING outside of Wanda Monroe's house. Inside, the hint of a breeze flows in drafts over the living room's parquet floor, carrying with it the smell of Bruce's floor wax, and causing the dust mice under the furniture to swirl in silent tiny tornados. A Gibson is leaning in one corner of the room. A television is surrounded by a couch, a worn Lazyboy and a rocking chair. Behind the couch is a large dining table with mismatched chairs: two aluminum, one wooden, a couple of stools and a broken high chair.

Sitting on the table are condiments: salt and pepper shakers, mustard and ketchup squeeze bottles, a large pour-type sugar container and a paper napkin dispenser. Everything that you would find in an all-night roadside diner. The floor is littered with newspapers. On a coffee table nearest the couch rests an empty cereal bowl beside a huge ashtray heaped with butts. A dusty old fan sits in one corner. On the floor beside the rocking chair, an ancient Zenith radio buzzes.

Wanda Monroe walks into the living room and stops, looking out the screen door into the twilight. Her hair is thick and black, shoulder length. Her eyes are also black, her skin is brown, her lips full. She has wide full hips, a narrow waist, long muscular legs, huge hands, and firm breasts that have weight. She is a thirty-five-year-old exhausted mother of five. Her hands are pressed into the small of her back. She emits a slight groan as her pelvis sways forward. Tentatively one hand rises to her face until one long finger sweeps the sweat from her forehead and flicks the drops onto the tiny squares of the screen. She stares out the door, her eyes losing focus. Slowly the hands that seem to have a purpose of their own in their slow and constant movements press into her back again. Her eyes clear for a second. Timed with the slow tilting of her head they again lose focus and stare into the floor. The hand lifts slowly to her lips, her little finger flicks like a slow switchblade, and the long sharp nail traces the indentation between her bicuspid and an incisor. She stares out, wondering for the ten thousandth time how she got here. In this early transition into night, the years from her youth and the present become blurred. She closes her eyes and listens to the voices in the neighborhood, calling children home for dinner or delaying a request in the interest of some other chore. "Be there in a second. . . . I've just got this last section to wax." Calls back and forth across the street. "Janet, is Jack over there ?" "No, he and Eddie and the dogs were heading for the canyon last I saw them. That was about two hours ago." "If you see them, tell Jack that his dinner is cold. Hey — oh, never mind, I'll tell you tomorrow."

Wanda can listen and hear her own mother calling her from a time when she was a lot happier and a lot less lonely back in Oklahoma. Her eyes closed, Wanda calls up all the sights of the street she grew up on. Darkness sets on that remembered street and she sees the headlights of her older brother's Plymouth jumping down the road leading to their home. She sees the face of her brother's best friend asking her if she didn't want to come along with them into town. Her heart hammers inside her chest. She hears her brother's friend urging her, "Yeah, Wanda c'mon. We'll let ya sing." How she had felt herself split in two, a scared shy daughter, fearful of the mere idea of going into a place like that, and the other side thinking, "Shit yeah, I'll sing alright, I'll sing until you won't ever hear anything else . . . but my singing." She went. She had her first husband three months later, her first child six months after that. Rock-a-bye baby. Wanda heard the voices inside of the liquor store, she remembered the look in his eyes when he came running out, heard herself saying . . . "Oh, my God no." She saw the gun in his hand, and his laughing face. Saw her brother stumble over the confused farmer in the doorway. Heard the car doors slam after the tires had already begun screeching. Felt his hands press her onto the floor of the back seat and heard her brother saying . . . "Get down, Lyle, here it comes." She remembered the muffled explosions and the sound like a beer opener popping into the trunk of the car. She remembered the kiss he gave her when they crossed the state line and he whispered "Welcome to the Lone Star State." She knew right then and there she'd never see her mother again.

The buzzing radio annoys her. She walks over to the rocking chair, slumps into its cushions and adjusts the radio to the Top 40, hoping to hear Brenda Lee. Instead, the weather report, "Expect temperatures to increase over the next three days as the seasonal Santa Ana winds are expected to drive temperatures above 100 degrees." Something makes her laugh her frequent good-natured chuckle, and the fingers of her hands pull through her long hair.

Eddie Burnett knocks softly against the screen door with one knuckle. Before Wanda can reply, he walks into the room. The knocking serves as a formality, giving him permission to proceed as though he were one of the family. Which in nearly every respect he is, and has been since he was seven years old. Eddie is wearing black pointed shoes with white socks, Levi's and a poorly ironed button-down shirt. His hair is not behaving. Instead of the sleek order it held for a few seconds as he left the bathroom mirror, it has reverted to an explosion of orange haystack. Eddie seems mildly concerned with this condition and attempts to plaster it into some sort of part, but each gesture becomes increasingly halfhearted.

"Hey, Wanda."

"Hi, Eddie."

"Boys here?"

"Nobody's here."

"Oh."

Eddie sits down on the couch, passing up the Cosmopolitan for a Saturday Evening Post. He is feeling absolutely confused. Normally he would be saying, "Uh, see ya." and be out the screen door. He finds himself sitting here in the front room with Wanda and nobody else home. He looks at the Cosmopolitan.

"Shucks, I was hopin' to get a ride to the game. Don't matter though, really."

Eddie pauses for a few seconds and blurts out a comment that surprises him.

"I'm not ready to play tonight. It's just. . . ."

Wanda leans back into the chair and crosses her feet on the coffee table. Her loose cotton dress slips up her leg for an instant, and she gently pulls it over her knee. She sees the breath catch in Eddie's chest. It surprises her when she deliberately readjusts her feet and allows the dress to slip up her leg again. Eddie pinches a nostril with his thumb and forefinger, his eye darting in her direction. His neck feels funny. What was he saying?

"Well, Eddie . . . the boys tell me you've been just tearin' it up in practice. Don't tell them I told you."

Eddie knows the boys would never acknowledge their admiration to his face but inside it makes him feel great, just thinking of them telling Wanda of his exploits. He thought he sensed a feeling of pride in them when they sat together at lunch even though the guys on the team and even some seniors saved him a place. But hell, what could he talk about with those guys? And the Monroe boys, well, they know more about what is really happening than any of those snobs, anyway.

"That's not what I mean. I mean, yeah, sure I can play and all — and I want to play. But . . ."

Wanda is feeling more than the normal tension in Eddie tonight. She thinks she can recognize the feeling — something from her memory. It bothers her.

"They just now left."

"Well, maybe I'll walk. Don't want to ask my Dad. He's going to the game."

She looks at Eddie as he cracks his knuckles. So that's it. I don't blame him. Wanda shudders at the thought of Eddie's father hooting his drunken head off in front of a few thousand PTA types. It surprises Wanda that Eddie's father could actually get it together to leave the house and arrive anyplace.

"Really?"

"Yeah, saw him with Buster and his moron brother coming out of the liquor store, hollering about seeing me tonight."

Eddie tells himself that he doesn't care what his father does. Everyone is going to find out what he's like sooner or later anyway. But he doesn't believe himself. He feels trapped. Maybe he — ah, hell, he has to play. What would he say to the coaches?

"He's proud of you Eddie."

"Yeah, he thinks he's playin' . . . uh, can I use the phone?"

"Sure."

Eddie dials home.

"Hey, Ma. Dad there? Oh. So how ya doin'? No, I'm not excited. . . . The boys — yeah, was gonna get a ride. Naw, don't worry about it. He was? Yeah, I know. It's OK. How 'bout you? OK. I'll be back late. Sherry's. No, now that I'm playin' her dad loves me. Yeah, her too. Milk and cookies, the whole nine yards. Weird, huh? He's with Buster, I guess.

I'll call ya from Sherry's. Yeah. Yeah, we'll win. Both. Defense and offense. No. It's better. If I thought I was gonna get hurt I wouldn't be playin', Ma. Don't worry. He'll be alright. Yeah, sure. Thanks, Ma. See ya in the morning. I will. Bye."

Wanda has been watching Eddie intently. She cannot see anything about him that should make him an unusual athlete. He's kinda skinny in fact. There is something inside that has always been there, and although he could get a little out of control sometimes, it didn't seem to be anything he could use. He wasn't as tough as her sons. Not even close. But her sons wouldn't mess with Eddie either. The kid had a crazy streak. But he didn't get it from his mother or father. Unless . . . his father. No. He wasn't like his dad. Took after his mother, sorta. She felt so strange when she asked herself, "I wonder what this boy is gonna be like in bed?" It was a direction she didn't want to go. But as soon as she'd thought it, she knew it was the direction she was going. She knew it was the direction she had been going for the last few months, maybe couple of years even if she didn't want to admit it.

In the next instant she saw herself getting into her brother's car on the way to town to sing. She heard the farmboys hollering again for another song. She remembered the way she felt. How it had been the best feeling, and the most dreadful feeling at the same time. How late that night beneath the trees next door she had spread out the blanket stolen from her sleeping house with a final sense of determination to make sure the feelings from that stage would last up inside of her until morning. And they had, and then some. She didn't think she would like it, but she did. She was as good at it as she was at singing. Almost like there was no difference. Just take a deep breath and let what was going to happen, happen. Just find the power you're born with, and then stay out of the way. She knew when she felt his body stretching into a hard panting straining animal that he was going to let loose inside her. And she didn't care. And she cried at the knowledge that she didn't care, that she had finally left herself behind. And become something else. A woman. It was time. That's all. It didn't turn out so bad. She looked at Eddie.

"Eddie, the boys were telling me this morning that you could jump across this room."

"How big's the room?"

"I don't know."

Eddie stands against the far wall and begins counting, measuring one foot in front of the other.

"I find this a little hard to believe."

Eddie stops and looks up saying, "I get a running start."

"Well, yes. I know that Eddie. I didn't think you were from Mars."

"Oklahoma."

"I thought you were born in El Paso."

"I was, but that's not where I come from."

"What does he mean by that?" thought Wanda. "15 . . . 16 . . . 17 . . . 18 . . . "

"What'd ya jump?"

"Twenty-one feet."

"19 . . . 20 . . . 21 . . . Yeah, guess so."

Eddie looked at Wanda and tried not to be reminded of Sherry when he caught the look on Wanda's face. He refused to believe that the look was nearly the same as the look Sherry had just before she pulled him close to her. He knew it was the same look.

"Looks pretty far in here. Kinda hard for me to believe, too." He noticed that his voice had a strange quivering sound around its edges. Wanda started to get up with an empty coffee cup.

"Another kid jumped 22. Here, I'll get it." Eddie takes the empty coffee cup and walks into the kitchen. Wanda calls over her shoulder to Eddie, who rattles the coffee pot on the stove and runs fresh water from the sink.

"The boys are going to the beach tomorrow, you going?"

"Yeah, storm surf — huge. Still 'red tide,' though."

Red tide, thought Wanda. "What's red tide?"

"I dunno — some kinda plankton, I think. Makes the water smell kinda funny. It gets dark-colored. When you get out you feel sticky. Most people don't like it. At night when the surf breaks, it shines. It glows in the dark. Really beautiful."

"Never heard of it. Glows in the dark?"

"Yep."

Wanda saw Eddie standing at the foot of her bed glowing in the dark, and the blood on her skin and blanket under the tree in Oklahoma.

"If you don't get going, you're gonna miss the game. Sherry'll be fit to be tied."

Eddie returns to the living room and stands behind Wanda. He is thinking of Sherry's father and his own father sitting there in the stands cheering away. He wishes they would outlaw parents at these games. If she could, though, he'd like his mother to come. But that would be too much. His father only acts worse when she's there.

"I wish it was just a game, not this big show. It just doesn't matter. Even Sherry doesn't get it. She always wants me to see things like everyone else. Sometimes I get sick of Sherry."

"Really, I thought you guys were in love."

Wanda draws out "in love" in a Gomer Pyle imitation. When she sees Eddie's expression she drops the teasing and states seriously, "The boys say you're crazy about her, and I think she's real cute . . . sweet."

"That's right. She is. Perfect."

"That's not what I meant and you know it." Wanda couldn't miss the sense of frustration in Eddie's voice. Wanda knows Sherry comes from a family that aspires to be above the rest of the neighborhood. She's always thought it romantic that Sherry and Eddie were together. It seemed so natural and so absolutely wrong at the same time.

"Her father kicked me out of the house two weeks ago. Tonight he's my best friend."

"Well, I've kicked you out of my house a couple times as I remember and tonight I'm your best friend."

"It's different."

"How?"

"It just is. . . . "

"Eddie, we're all just people you know."

"What do you mean?"

"We're fallible. Sometimes, we do things we know we shouldn't because something tells us we have to."

Eddie felt his feet lifting off the floor. The room began to pound and he was afraid. He couldn't move. Wanda's eyes were looking right through him again like they did during the heat wave last summer.

Eddie looked like he was hypnotized. Wanda's voice was softer and lower, "You're going to need fallible people your whole life, Eddie, because there aren't any other kind . . . and you are the kind of person who will need to have people. It's hard to explain. In fact it is something you learn that can't be explained . . . you have to learn it by yourself, with someone else."

The street lamp over the Monroes' front yard popped on, casting a striped shadow from the venetian blinds across the floor, and over Wanda's legs. Eddie stood in the center of the room in the dark looking toward Wanda's shadowy figure in the rocking chair. She finished her coffee. Eddie walked to the screen door.

"Eddie, will you turn on the sprinkler?" The screen door swung open and Eddie walked out. Wanda smiled to herself and made her decision. If the boy left for the game, then fine. If he came back in here, then fine. It was up to him.

The rain-bird began its staccato blasts. Reversed itself and repeated its blasts. Reversed itself and repeated its blasts, again. Brenda Lee came up on the radio. Eddie walked through the screen door.

"Eddie, have you and Sherry gone all the way?" Her voice had the same quivering sound Eddie's had had earlier. He remembered Wanda's voice saying, fallible.

"No, we haven't."

"Have you ever wanted to?"

"Yes."

"Do you want to?" He watched the rocking chair shift forward and saw Wanda's figure looming in the dark. He was frozen. He felt like he was getting sick. She moved closer toward him, until he could see her face clearly inches away. She looked like she was summoning up courage. The moment it scared Eddie to see her under that kind of strain, her face relaxed into a smile. Her fingers touched Eddie's rigid hands, hanging stiffly at his side. The touch felt like an electrical storm. Her hair brushed the side of his face, her cheek pressed against his jaw. Her voice joined Brenda Lee's ". . . please accept my a-pol-ogy . . . I was too young . . . and I was to blind to see. . . ." The song ended. Wanda's arms were around Eddie's chest, her breasts pressing lightly against his shirt.

The inside of one of her legs bumped the outside of his thigh. She smiled up at him and said, "Thanks for the dance, Eddie." Eddie who felt as though he had gotten older and stronger in the past two minutes said, "You're welcome, Wanda." She didn't move. Eddie couldn't stop thinking that a woman was holding him, a woman he had always desired and had always thought was above and beyond him. He couldn't understand what was happening, but her dark face and easy smile were guiding him someplace. He fought off thoughts of the boys, and her husband, and tried desperately to find some type of omen, some sense that the time here was right, and the consequences would not destroy him. A hot breeze from the desert rattled the screen door and blew over them. "Santa Ana," thought Eddie.

"I love this time of day, Eddie. Don't you? I've always thought this was the best time of day."

"It is."

"I'm going to kiss you, Eddie. Is that alright?"

"Yes."

Wanda's lips had more weight, more depth, more demand than any lips Eddie had ever felt. Wanda felt Eddie's lips hesitate, and then join hers. She pulled away slowly, and then kissed him again. There was less hesitation this time. They met, and the intensity increased. She pulled slowly away again. In the next instant their lips touched, her tongue ran over his lips, and his mouth parted slightly. Eddie leaned back, a thin silver thread hung suspended between their lips, snapped and slapped wet against Eddie's chin. Wanda's fingers reached up and wiped his lip and chin, whispering, "Sometimes it's hard to keep our dignity at times like these." Eddie smiled, "What are we gonna do, Wanda?" "I think we're going to go to bed, Eddie." Eddie's heart pounded so hard he thought he'd faint. "What are we gonna do after that?" "I'm going to drive you to the game." "And after that." "You're gonna play football." They smiled in unison. "And after that?" "Nothing, because the first time is just once. This is your first time. . . ." Wanda's words faded as Eddie realized it was his first time, and that he was in the beginning of his first time, and they were not going to stop here, and that soon he would be lying naked in bed with this woman, and he would be inside of her, and all the images he had ever had would become images he would never forget. ". . . Eddie . . . it is your first time isn't it?" "Yes." "It should be with someone you care a lot about, and someone who cares a lot about you, someone you trust . . . the first time is only. . . ." She lifted her face and kissed him again, her mouth warmer and somehow more pliable, as though it were more alive. ". . . Just once, and that is all. I promise you, once. Once. And we'll never mention it. We'll never let on that it ever happened, not in front of anyone, and not even when we are alone. I promise. Do you promise?" Eddie couldn't believe that it could be happening. A hotter breeze blew in the door spinning the newspaper along the floor, dogs started barking. "It's the only way it could be, Wanda." Wanda breathed the words "That's right" into his face. She took his hand and led him in the dark toward her bedroom.

The phone rang. Wanda reached over the rocking chair, still holding Eddie's hand and picked up the receiver. Eddie knew it was his mother. "Well, hi. Yeah, he's here. Couldn't hook up for a ride. I thought I'd take him." Her voice sounded exactly like it always did, nothing hidden, nothing deceptive, natural, comfortable. Eddie felt her squeeze his hand as she said, "Why don't we pick you up in about an hour? . . . Yeah, you do? Oh, great, I'd like to take a shower and change and we'll pick you up at quarter to eight. Great. I know Eddie will be glad you're going. You want to speak to him? Alright." Eddie heard the electrical duplication of his mother's voice in the telephone saying "See ya" as Wanda put the phone on the hook. "OK, Eddie?" Her eyes looked bright, at their easygoing, good-natured best. Eddie put his hand in her hair and let the black strands untangle slowly as he slid them from her forehead, over her ear, and down the back of her neck. It had been something he had wanted to do every time he saw her loving hands caressing one of the boys. The tender expression her face held as she touched her children was now on her face and he had brought it to her. His whole body responded, his groin pounded and began to ache. The black eyes closed and her body arched like a cat. Eddie shuddered slightly, and Wanda sensing it, opened her eyes. "C'mon Eddie." Her voice had a final tone, a purpose, a warm determination. As they walked by the rocker Eddie put one hand on the chair and pushed it gently. They disappeared into the shadow toward her room. As the rocker tilted back and forth, back and forth, in and out of the striped shadows of the venetian blinds, to the music of the rain-bird, the rattling screen door, the hot wind outside and a woman's voice singing on the radio.

A T-SHIRT, PHEROMONES, AND GRIEF

"WELL, IT'S UP TO YOU, always was. . . ." The boy could hear the drawling voice hanging in the air. The big man had been dead now for almost two months. The boy was crying, not from the beating he had just endured as much as from the aching in his chest. The boy felt he could never get the air he needed again, as though he would never breathe free like he could a couple of months ago.

He kept hearing the adage "rug pulled out from under him." He felt ashamed. He hadn't been able to put up more than a half-hearted effort at the defense of the big man's name. He had put on a show of fighting back, but his heart wasn't in it and it made him feel like a liar. The jeering and the laughing and the names he was called were still echoing in his head as he started to cry again. He hid his face in his elbow and watched the spit and tears congeal and drip from his open, sobbing mouth, landing on the gray cement, making patterns as it dropped and shook from his sobbing chest.

". . . Always will be," continued the big man's drawl. The boy could see the invisible smile following the remembered words. He cried harder. The sobbing sounded deep and foreign, a shaking, breaking call to a couple of months ago.

Abruptly the boy rose to his feet. With both hands flat

against his face, he smeared away the wet and slipped his fingers into his hair, combing the long strands flat. Not crying any longer, but still sobbing because his body couldn't stop, he walked over to the big man's tool box. He pulled it open by the chrome handle and it opened like a tackle box. The big man's wife began playing the piano in the front room. She stopped. The boy started saying to himself, "Don't stop, keep playing . . . keep playing." There was a pause, and then she started playing again. He closed his eyes, wishing she would play forever. He was relieved that she wouldn't come out and find him with the big man's belongings.

Around the corner of the house and out in the street the boy could hear sounds. The other boys were out there arguing about something. It was the standard declaration of dominance, not a real dispute. There could be no real dispute. There could be no opposition to that voice. It belonged to the ultimate victor. The boy's feelings weren't as hard against the victor as they were against the victor's friends — the boys who would egg the victor on, who would make the victor think, in his stupidity, that his show of force and brutality was admirable, who would use the boy as a sacrifice until the next time the victor felt threatened and would pound, kick, and beat his next victim.

For the past couple of months all of the victor's anger and stupid, huge violence had been directed at the boy. The boy was tired and feeling an essential part of his coming manhood suffering and dying and cringing. He would renew his resolve daily, trying to stand upright against the demoralization of his heart, which had been breaking since the big man died. He quietly moved the tools around in the box, freeing the white T-shirt stuffed into one corner.

He held the T-shirt out at arm's length. It stretched out in front of him and its bottom seam nearly touched the cement. He tried to see the big man inside the flat material. It was useless.

There was a time once when the boy had promised to take care of the big man's dogs. The boy had shown up every day except one, and the big man found out somehow. The boy had taken the long way home from school winding through the canyons avoiding the route the victor and his friends might take. When he got home it was almost dark and his mother wouldn't let him leave the house until morning. When the big man asked the boy about it, the boy lied. "Boy, I'm going to tell you something and you'd better remember it. You'll be better off putting your faith in what you know is on earth, instead of what might be in heaven. You are on your own. Nobody gets to heaven holding hands and no one can help you get there. Most people fail to realize that what goes on up there, is determined by what goes on down here. If you give your word, like you did to me, then you have to do everything you can to keep it. It's hard, and you'll have to face it every day. The devil always gives you a good reason to do wrong. Keep your word, boy. It's one of the most important things you've got. And if someone loves you, and I love you, then you never have to lie to them. And if someone hates you, then never let them make you make less of yourself."

The big man took several deep breaths, broke into a sweat and then looked at the boy and smiled. "The weight you're willing to put on your shoulders here on earth gives you the strength to climb up to those pearly gates when the time comes." The last thing he told him before he turned and walked into his house was "Listen to your own voice. Not your fears, or your feelings, good or bad. Listen to what's in your heart and do what it tells you."

The boy never really understood what the big man meant most of the time. The words seemed crazy. It was the big man who made sense, not his words. The big man always seemed to be trying to help him cross a bridge that could never be crossed. The big man always seemed to be answering, in one way or another, almost by riddles, the only question the boy ever wanted answered: How could a skinny, awkward kid ever hope to become a man? "Boy, what are you talking about? Now I have heard everything. How am I gonna become a man? Silliest shit I ever heard. You are a boy, so you are going to become a man. What kind of man? Maybe that's the question. That's a little more important. You're a boy now, so you'll be a man soon enough. You've been given a brain and a body and a heart, right? Well, if you've been given these things then they are yours to use. To use. Don't worry about having it or not. Hell, you might have been given it by mistake. Just put it to use. Nothing else counts. Not what you or anyone else says, thinks, or even does to you. Now hand me that crescent wrench so I can put it to use and see if I can fix this damn thing before dark."

The boy knew in the world of boys he wasn't much; in the world of men, he appeared to be doomed. Everything the big man did or said seemed to indicate that the boy's opinion of himself was wrong, nearly always summed up with a statement like "Time will tell." It terrified the boy to hear the big man say things like that, or "Don't worry so much. Ya know ninety-nine percent of the things folks worry about never even happens." It was especially upsetting to hear the big man mention love, as though it was a real thing and would someday play a large part in the boy's life. The boy took the T-shirt and pressed it against his face. He could smell the big man. He didn't notice that the piano had stopped its music, or that the curtains to the big man's back room were being parted by the big man's wife. He didn't see the puzzled look on her face as she watched the boy breathing through the shirt. Her husband of forty years was gone. The boy was trying to contact his departed soul through the shirt. She knew the boy meant no harm, and she understood the indulgence of pain his action represented. She also knew it was wrong, contrary to life, would weaken him. She watched the boy carefully put the shirt back into the tool box, push the box into the patio corner, turn silently and climb over the fence and disappear.

The boy was challenged as soon as he hit the street. He tried to walk past the catcalls and the derisively chucked bottle caps and curses. The ultimate victor began to cross the street, cutting him off. The boy's heart pounded; he tried to walk imperceptibly faster. He heard the words again, "nigger lover." He heard them ten thousand times. The big man's front door was hidden in the shade; the old woman was watching. She saw the boy stop. She saw the victor walk toward him faster and hit him on the ear. She saw the boy's hand go up, and saw him cringe and cower as the next blow landed on his face, the other boys surrounding him in a half circle. She saw the boy respond to a comment from one of the other boys and watched them fall to the ground, twisting and swinging. The fight was brief. She saw the boy standing over the other boy. But the triumph of her husband's defender was short-lived. The victor waited a second and then pounded the boy down next to his opponent, who then took to his feet and began kicking as the victor continued to land thudding punches to the boy's head.

The boy lay on the ground, humiliated and silent. The boys and the victor wandered slowly back to the curb, pausing momentarily for a stray kick, another punch, another spat epithet. The wife of the big man walked out to the back patio and removed the T-shirt from the tool box. She washed it that night, folded it neatly and placed it on the window sill in the back window. A couple of days later the boy crept across the neighbor's yard, climbed the fence, and kneeled over the tool box. The woman walked quietly out of the back door. She looked at the boy. "Eddie, this shirt don't fit you yet, but it must be yours." She handed it to the boy, turned around and walked back into her house.

JENNY

EDDIE'S MOTHER AND FATHER WERE preoccupied with the card game that was now into its fifth night. There had been the usual passing out, hysteria, vomiting, and hilarity among the nine players. Tequila was fueling a three-night run of luck by a one-legged neighbor wearing a straw hat and a loincloth. The others were amazed and enraged at the drunk's ridiculous streak. Each player came with $200, in one-dollar bills, most of it presently under the cushion of the stool the straw-hatted man sat on, too crazy with the streak to sleep, and unwilling to slow down the pace. Eddie and his friend Robert wondered how long it was going to be before one of them killed him. It was Mexico after all. The game had started with Eddie's aunt Ellen taking most of the hands. But when her husband went back to San Diego, because he had to work, she was seduced by her friend Lois's brother and she lost her inertia. It had to happen, as far as Eddie could tell. Lois's brother had a legendary cock, Ellen looked good in a bathing suit, real good, and her husband liked Lois's brother a lot anyway, and was careless despite Ellen's wandering eye. Eddie watched her walking bow-legged out to the beach at about dawn the night she gave up her streak, furious as hell about the shitty hands she was getting.

The heat was off the next afternoon and the card game

was picking up energy, all players present. The guy with the straw hat was rubbing it in as Eddie watched the tequila bottle being passed between his uncles, "Gotta stay in the game. That's the secret, Ellen." "Just deal you one-legged idiot." The man laughed and raised the ante as the table groaned and Lois's brother told Ellen to "Shut up." Ellen said "Shut me up." The man with the straw hat said "Yeah, Bill, shut her up." Eddie's mother said "Not this again." Eddie's father said "I'm out," and headed for his tent. Eddie loved it when they got like that.

Eddie saw three horses coming over a sand dune to the north of the encampment so he started walking in that direction. Robert and two Mexican kids had been riding for a couple of hours, hunting rabbits inland. Eddie heard a shrill whistle and saw Raul lifting a pile of gray things in the air above his head. Eddie began a slow lope as they kicked their heels into the ribs of the exhausted nags. The horses shifted their weight back as the boys slid up their necks. A couple of minutes later Eddie was looking up at the three boys sitting bareback on their mounts, Robert cradling his .22, Arturo looking bored, and tiny Raul wearing a string of bloody dead rabbits over one shoulder. Robert said he'd help with the horses for a few minutes and then meet Eddie to catch the glass off. Surf tonight was nothing to get excited about. Yesterday was the day. Raul split the rabbits with Eddie, and the horsemen rode back inland. Eddie walked back to the camp.

Two station wagons loaded with surfboards blasted down the dirt road toward the camp from the highway, raising a dust cloud forty feet in the air, skidding, spinning and bouncing along at about fifty miles an hour. The entire camp containing about twenty families started hollering at them. The car continued blasting its way into camp. Eddie stood mid-stride watching the cars and noticing the girls inside.

The station wagons spun to a halt. Doors swung open. Girls jumped out. Doors slammed shut. Brief partings were exchanged. "Later," "See ya." The station wagons blew out the road they'd come in on, and five girls walked toward a palm-covered pavilion, carrying a cooler, a record player, and a box of 45s. Five angels walked toward the pavilion. Eddie immediately envied the boys driving those station wagons. MSA? Wind and Sea? Didn't matter. The girls knew who they were, knew what they had, and knew what they were doing. A couple of campers came up to register complaints about the dust, the racket and the dangerous driving, pointing to little kids playing two-hundred yards distant. The girls walked along until one of them said, "Yeah, we know. They always drive like that." In the distance the station wagons headed south on the regular roadway at a controlled speed. The girls walked under the rustling palm leaves, sat against the support pillars and fell immediately to sleep. Eddie lingered around the card game with his eye on the pavilion. Bill asked him why he didn't go over and say hi. Eddie said he had to get the rabbits ready for dinner. "Why? Robert shot 'em, let him skin 'em." Eddie shrugged, "I bet they'd get three at the most." Ellen staring at her cards shot a look at Eddie's mother. "Runs in the family, I guess." Eddie's mother made a sniggering sound and muttered, "Stupid bet, place is hopping with bunnies." Eddie picked up the rabbits, walked over to the side of one camper and said, "He only had six shots." Bill said, "Well, go on over there and get something bloody." Eddie's mother settled further in her chair. Ellen said, "Oh, Bill . . . you nasty man." The man with the straw hat drawled, "The only blood anybody'll get from bunnies around here are from the kind with long ears," and shot a glance at the pavilion. Eddie tore the skin down the rabbits' backs, cut their guts out, lopped their heads off, and tried to ignore the sound of his father puking behind the tent. The card game mumbled on.

With his ankles in the cool water and his hands leaving a bloody trail in the foam Eddie could just see the top of the palm fronds from the pavilion. Robert walked up carrying one fin. "Fuck, man. Did you see the girls at the pavilion?" "Nope." "Unbeleeevvable." "Some surfers dropped them off about twenty minutes ago." "Bullshit." "Let's check it out." "Ok, let's cool off first." The whining sound of a spinning reel sang behind them as a line with a lead sinker and three hooks baited with mussels flew above them and out beyond the surfline. The boys began running into the surf slowly, hurdling each shelf of white water, until waist deep they submerged. In an instant they pulled the fins over a foot, and like otters stroked out into the surf. The waves to the outside were pretty good size and of perfect shape. Robert got most of the rides. Eddie was preoccuppied with the girls in the pavilion. As each swell rose, he'd turn, hoping not to see station wagons. "Robert, c'mon . . . let's go in."

A minute later they were banging the water out of their ears and heading toward the card game. They heard yelling coming from the table. Wordlessly they turned at an angle that led directly toward the silent pavilion. Eddie, looking at his brown feet, mumbled, "Fuck that shit." "Eddie . . . ," the sound in Robert's voice said, " Look at that." Eddie looked up and saw an angel in a pair of Levi's walking in the shade carrying a record player. The boys walked to a broken-down rusted truck hulk sitting to one side of a cement slab that began sending music over the campsite. The boys climbed into the rusted cabin, Robert got his cigarettes from under the dashboard and lit up. The boys watched the girls dancing together between their propped-up feet on the rusted dash. Robert and Eddie sat in silence, occasionally double-taking each other as one or another of the girls moved in perfect, casual, almost bored, timing. Robert exhaled a cloud saying, "Oh, my God." Eddie shook his head.

The girls had already attracted plenty of attention on their arrival, but since the main water source for the camp was a spigot on one side of the pavilion, the campers had plenty of reason to nose around. Their dancing had drawn a crowd. The elderly couple that Eddie and Robert liked were the first ones there. They had immediately found it possible to talk to the girls, and the old man was given a beer from the cooler. The old man said something that made one of the girls laugh when she extended the beer. As her body language responded to the laugh, she pulled the little old man under her arm, hugged him, and beamed the most beautiful smile the boys had ever seen. "Oh, my God. She's . . ." words failed Robert. The stack of records dropped one by one, and one or another of the girls would dance easily and casually, while one of them leafed through a magazine. Eddie was watching her. She had long straight waist-length hair that gave credence to the term flaxen. The eyes following the pages were blue. She had a cleft lip which, it immediately seemed, held absolutely no consequence to her. She sat with her knees hugged up against her chest, her jeans straining with their contents — a perfect butt. She and her friends were of that infuriating age just beyond the range of Eddie and Robert. They must have been fourteen or fifteen to the boys' twelve. The youngest kids in the campground had joined the oldest, and the most beautiful. Two of the girls were dancing with kids about six years old. Another record dropped, a song Eddie had never heard before. The song was from a girl group and began with a chorus, "Wah, whaa, wah, oooh, wah, tusi. . . ." The five girls began to dance in earnest with each other, the little kids pairing off in participation on the periphery. Eddie and Robert may have breathed three times each in the next three minutes. Their eyes may have only jutted half an inch out of their sockets. Their jaws bounced on their gulping Adam's apples. Eddie watched the girl put the magazine aside and slowly shuffle across the smooth cement floor, singing with the record. The girls sounded as though they had made the record, adding to the sound in perfect harmony, and raising their voices higher as they realized the covered cement floor gave them a reverberating amplification.

A little boy was raised above the head of Eddie's favorite, and spun in a slow circle looking down at the girl's smiling face, her lip pulling her mouth slightly off to one side, and her eyes bringing a contagious grin on the little boy's face, who was already plainly, and totally, in love. Eddie envied the boy in the air, and felt almost ashamed at the envy. He felt uncomfortable identifying with the little boy, who was getting the ride of a lifetime, but couldn't help himself. The song ended. The girl ran over to the record player and put the needle back on the record and clicked the switch. By this time Eddie and Robert had climbed out of the truck like zombies and walked mesmerized to the side of the elderly couple. The little bald man tilting back the beer, gave Eddie a wink. His wife clasped Robert's arm in her skinny blue-veined hands and said, "Oh, dear. Aren't they wonderful?" Robert managed to say, "Yeah." The music carried the girls to within a few feet of the two motionless adolescents and the elderly couple. The blonde girl had her back to Eddie and he watched the end of her ponytail flick in time with the bass. The old man cleared his throat just as the blonde girl turned to smile in his direction. The old man's voice at Eddie's left said, "Do you want to dance?" Eddie felt the old man's shaky hands push him onto the cement in front of the girl. Eddie stood frozen. The man's wife laughed. The girl closed the distance between Eddie and herself, and took his hands in hers. Eddie was gone, absolutely and entirely in sync with the girl. If he had had the slightest chance to think, had not been entirely mesmerized he undoubtedly would have stiffened to a board and died of embarrassment. There was no reason for him to be able to move with her, there was no reason for him to adopt the male version of her female interpretation. There was no precedent in his life for catching rhythm with his body, and there was no evidence to anybody watching that he hadn't done this a thousand times. Only the blonde girl knew, and maybe the little boy who earlier had had a similar feeling as he spun above this angel's head, riding on her outstretched arms, safe in the air. The music stopped. One of the girls pulled the plug on the record player, the records were gathered, put in the box. Another beer was tossed to the elderly man, who snatched it one-handed out of the air. The station wagons appeared from out of nowhere. A tall boy of about sixteen, and another boy of just a couple of precious years more than Eddie by his side. The younger boy called out "Jenny . . . ," and the blond girl ran over to him and was spun once in his arms. She climbed up his broad brown arms and whispered something into his ear. The girl ran out to the station wagon. The boy grabbed the cooler and they disappeared into the back seat. They spun around in a dust cloud and the girl's long arm extended out of the window and waved goodbye to the elderly couple. The boy beside her grinned out of the window and revealed two tin front teeth. The instant they saw that shining silver smile Robert and Eddie said at the same time, "Jimmy Blackwell." That said it all, the coolest and most famous surfer in San Diego. The station wagon blasted down the road, turned on its lights and the red dots disappeared down the dusty road. As Eddie began to walk back to the card game, he noticed the little boy looking at him. Eddie winked at him, saying "Fun, huh?" Robert mumbled, "Shit, Eddie, Fred-A-fucking-Staire." "Yeah, twinkle toes," sighed Eddie. As they watched the white headlights turn south on the main road leading deeper into Mexico, they realized they'd have a lot to think about that night.

Here He Comes . . .

It turned out there were a lot of nights to think about Jenny, because in the next five years her path and Eddie's crossed frequently. When Eddie hit the huge boom-town Junior High School that fall, he saw her walking past his wood shop class on her way home with a girlfriend. Ninth graders free by the sixth period, seventh graders with two more to go. He stared out the window watching the girls shifting their notebooks and laughing. The shop teacher growled "Burnett," and Eddie returned to his scale drawing of the wagon wheel lamp they would be making that semester. A few seconds later the teacher barked "Buurnnett!" Eddie looked up to see the class of boys smiling at him and turned red realizing he must have been singing "Cathy's Clown" a little too loudly under his breath.

Swish!

In the early spring Eddie and Robert had gone to watch the league high school basketball championships and watched Jimmy sink 42 points, most of them rafter-high bombs from the outside, as the gymnasium went nuts. Eddie asked around about Jenny and was told she was down at a communal beach house keeping company with a blues quartet that was playing later that night downtown. When the final buzzer sounded as his winning shot exploded the net, Jimmy blasted out of the gym exit for parts unknown, to the astonishment of the spectators. Next Monday at school Robert's older sister told them that Jimmy had sat in with the quartet playing sax until three in the morning. Furthermore, and to his credit, Jimmy was going to be kicked out of school again and off the team forever because he ditched school to go up to L.A. and sit in on a recording session! Robert's sister walked across the street to the high school and Robert and Eddie stood there awestruck, contemplating the cool lives of Jenny and Jimmy.

Dying Swan

Eddie was completing a crucifix swan dive, propelled with a force sounding like a choral roar sliding down a glassy wall, heading for the welcome imprisonment of a closed-out 8' wave next to Crystal Pier. The object was to be overwhelmed. He was seeking, day in and day out, the awe that catches the breath, before the lungs fill with dread and delight, under the surface on the edge of the Pacific Rim, cooperating zen-style, spun and twisted, trying to maintain a tight fetal grip, while the washing machine tried to pull him apart. He shuddered at his own ecstatic smile as he ran out of air and his vision turned a dark reddish blue. It seemed the cleanest, most honorable, and most satisfying way to go.

Back in elementary school he had experienced a sensation that was akin to drowning, but it lacked the physical release that would have permitted him to use the experience as a message, a symbol. Instead of screaming inside his head the demand to survive, it felt as though his soul had imploded on its host. He noticed the deformed hand of his third grade teacher. As a third grader does, he registered the desolate-hopeless pain the image transferred, with complete empathy and surprise.

It explained why Jenny was so cool. Jenny lying in the sand talking with her girlfriends about cultural topics beyond Eddie's scope. Books, movies, themes to songs, make-up, fashion, cars, and older brothers. Eddie was dumbstruck recognizing the power of compensation. How what might seem tragic on first sight, might essentially be an asset, even an advantage. Maybe the friendship between Eddie and Jenny was based on something they had in common, some genetic error or difference that was revealed as a scar on Jenny's face, but was hidden somewhere inside Eddie's thoughts or spirit. Dragging himself out of the surf exhausted and spent, the tips of his fins slapping in the water beneath him he thought of Jenny's scarred lip, and his own incapacity to communicate the things he saw and felt.

Jenny was exactly what she was, and it was enough for anyone, even Jenny. Eddie was not anything near to what he was, and it was lacking for everyone, especially Eddie. The sentence ran through his head, "Who's scarred?" Jenny had composure, self-assurance, adamant self-possession enough to lend it to anyone seeming to need it. She got it from a scarred lip, and the courage to face it. Eddie wished he could identify his internal scars, in order to try to find the courage to face them. As Eddie walked into the hot sand toward the towel Jenny was lying on he felt as though he were walking into a sort of church. She was anointed by direct knowledge, knowledge from birth, knowledge she could not escape, and reminded every second that life is not fair. She would have to seduce life, and she did. She held up her end of the bargain. She filled those hours making friends laugh with her regrounding gentle humor, making wisecracks that carried the long shot into a pin-point deflating bull's-eye. She had never in the years they had been friends once stooped to an instant of cruelty. It amazed Eddie. He watched her from a distance and continually fell under her spell. It was as though her words and face attracted him to follow her to a place where the fears weren't imagined, where pain wasn't temporary, to the place where she lived. As he neared the place where Jenny and her friends gathered in the sun, he thought back to that moment in the third grade when he stood transfixed, looking at his teacher's terrified eyes.

He saw the hem of her skirt flicking down the hall, he heard the clickety pattern of her heels reminding him of the weird beat of the wild hen faking an injured retreat leading the predator away from her hidden nestlings. She was carrying her deformed hand inside of her purse, a place that could and did, for the first time, draw Eddie's attention to it. In the classroom she must have felt safe, and therefore the kids felt safe as well, seeing her hand but not registering its difference, or seeing it as a source of shame and pain. Out here she clutched the purse in a give-away that was desperate. Eddie wanted to cry as he saw his teacher turning her back on her own beauty, hiding the portion of herself that made her whole. She was so beautiful, carrying proportions of a movie star with innocence and a complete lack of vanity. Permitting an eight-year-old's face to be buried in her Vargas bosom. Her tiny waist encircled in little-girl-pal arms. Her smile was devastating, inspiring the children to please her. But at that moment in the hall, traveling from this place to that, surrounded by strangers and out in the open, her shoes clicked too fast and her blonde head snapped from side to side, tilted with a studied staunch challenge, her eyes insane and terrified, a tortured smirk taking the place of her smile. Eddie remembered the horror pogo-ing on his guts and bouncing off the base of his brain making him lightheaded and nauseous as he absorbed his teacher's mysterious nightmare.

SLOW DANCING IN '66

THE END OF THE SUMMER brought the next football season. Eddie was walking into an after-game dance nodding thanks to the kids whispering "Nice game," as he moved into the hall looking for Jenny. Junior Osuna walked up and indicated the spot where Jenny was dancing. Eddie wasn't sure if he should go to her immediately or wait a few more minutes. He had a feeling that compelled him to her. Junior nudged him with his elbow. As Eddie looked down at Junior's profile, which was locked in the direction of Jenny, he took the proffered half-pint of Bacardi. He elbowed the boy next to him and the Bacardi passed along the line of boys leaning against the wall in the dark, listening to San Diego's reigning band Sandy and the Classics playing "Hitchhike."

Jenny was dressed in black, with her hair shining in the red and blue light cast from the makeshift stage. She had lost weight in the last week. Never having been anything but thin before, her too skinny arms swung in time with the music. She had a peculiar luminous glow, like a ghost. Her cheeks were sunken and her eyes dark holes in a stoic face. Her head was tilted down and her hair was falling forward from her jawline, helping to hide any expression. Jenny was doing what she always had done every dance Eddie could remember. She was dancing in her inimitable style, and just a little bit better than any kid in the place. But tonight she was dancing alone. The hair on Eddie's neck stood on end.

Jenny could lift the whole room to a sway, and a stop, a turn and a drop, an increase, and a decrease of energy, all this absolutely on time, until every kid in the place was secure and euphoric, giving each other accepted half smiles and furtive glances as they followed her trail along the coolest interpretation of those too cool rhythm and blues.

Tonight Jenny had it all to herself, no one followed her. She tracked the territory of the beat, and the meaning of the beat, and rode the bass all by herself. Any distance along her trail was too close for comfort for anyone dancing with her, except when every fifth or sixth song became a slow ballad. As the first slow notes began, and the elbows in the dark hall lifted under the lights and settled around the necks of each pair of dancers, a different boy would weave his way to Jenny to take his turn in her arms. Eddie observed one of Jimmy's closest friends lose it completely when Jenny managed to give him a kiss and one of the smiles that reminded him of a time that wasn't going to come back. The boy left in a beeline for the side exit with the sound of the push-handle door slamming into the wall outside in the night, while the Classics finished the last chorus of "You'll Lose a Good Thing."

The parents who had volunteered as chaperones for this after-game dance noticed the pall over the floor. There was no laughing, no loud talking or horseplay in the entire gym. The usual three or four hundred kids were packed on the floor and the shoulders and hips dipped and waved in unison song after song, but other than the music, and the low murmur of voices, the place was silent and dark. There had always been tearful exits at these dances, the result of unrequited love, or discovered betrayal of the early teen variety, but tonight struck the five or six parents as something different. They patrolled the perimeters of the hall and spoke quietly to each other in small huddles, sensing something happening but not knowing what it was. A couple of parents made an effort to ask a few kids but none of them, from the most mature and cooperative to the most anxious-to-please sophomore, would give an answer. The parents noticed a distinct coldness from each kid, as the question was posed.

Jenny was followed into the bathroom by four or five friends. The gymnasium seemed to swell in a sigh of collective relief. The room returned to something more normal for a dance during the next few songs, and the voices got a little louder.

Eddie looked at the other boy standing across the girls' bathroom door. "Eddie, ya wanna go next?"

Eddie answered with a nod of his head and the older boy walked over to the open spot next to Junior Osuna. Eddie could hear the girls walking toward the door as the sax began its climb up Harlem Nocturne. Jenny balked at the entrance to the huge cavern, and then seeing Eddie walked quickly toward him. Her face pressed against his neck and her hips drove into him. Her body trembled furiously beneath her black dress. They began their slow dance.

As they held each other tighter she transferred her rage and pain to Eddie until it was trembling into his bones. As Jenny whispered one word into Eddie's ear, instinct told them both that it was a waste, it was wrong, and it was a crime against nature that Jimmy, or anyone had to die in this new war in Vietnam. The inexplicable wisdom of their youth predicted that many more deaths would soon follow Jimmy's. Jenny whispered, "Promise?" And knowing what Jenny was asking, Eddie replied, "Yes, I promise."

HAPPY BIRTHDAY

1967. THE ACCELERATOR PEDAL IS on the floor. Robert Monroe and his younger brother Grant are heading to T.J., Sin City, Aunt Jane, Tijuana. Just a twenty-minute car-flight down Interstate 5. Their mother Wanda has finally succumbed to permanent depression and never leaves her rocking chair. Their older sister from Texas is married, unhappily, with her third kid on the way. Eddie Burnett is driving. Tonight's excursion "South" is to finish off Grant's eighteenth birthday. The Vietnam war is central in these boys' lives. The war has polarized the society in which they live. Lots of rhetoric is tossed around, but the boys know the bottom line, and it's profit over blood, their blood, Vietnamese blood. The practice is now common to cross the border in the trunks of cars driven by an eighteen-year-old friend for a night of drinking, whoring, and, increasingly, confronting Marines from Camp Pendleton sixty miles to the north. Tijuana is no-man's land, patrolled by brown uniformed Federales who throw servicemen and rowdy Americans into the madhouse that serves as a jail. The boys and Marines are found in "off-limit bars," the Federales serve as a natural buffer between them.

Eddie Burnett has changed since you saw him last, constantly furious behind a cold-as-stone facade. His wide-eyed innocent perspective has become a dangerous angry rebellion. He is driving his boyhood friends to the notorious Green Note Bar brothel, a few blocks north of Avenida Revolución. Robert is certifiable, hopped up on huge quantities of speed, tequila, and anything else he can get his hands on. He has "checked out" for hours, now lucid and inspired, and then for days, vicious, irrational, and incredibly paranoid. Grant has been trying in recent months to be a stabilzing force between the outright hostility of Robert and the repressed anger and sadness of Eddie. In recent months they have been wrecking cars at an astonishing rate. They know where they are heading. It's 1:45 a.m. and they are passing through San Ysidro.

Cars are honking and brakes are screeching. Eddie is tailgating a Cadillac, then passing it and slamming on his brakes. He sees an "America Love It or Leave It" decal in the rear window. "Caaadddaaaalaaack . . . Caddaaaalack" repeats Eddie. The window on the passenger side goes down and Robert leans out beyond his hips with Grant grabbing the waistband of his Levi's. "Fuck you . . . Yeah you . . . Love to, you blue-haired old bitch. . . . " Eddie sputters, "Fucking little flag waving in the plastic decal." Eddie jerks the car in front of the enraged Caddy and slams on the brakes again. The car lurches to one side and flies along the cyclone fence for a couple of hundred yards and pulls to a stop. Robert looking in the side rearview mirror comments disapprovingly, "Ah, Eddie that wasn't even close." Eddie, entirely calm and looking for another song on the radio besides "Light My Fire" which he hates, comments off-handedly, "Well, it's the thought that counts."

Robert climbs over the seat and pulls Grant into a head lock singing, "Happy birthday to you, happy birthday to yoooooo, happy birthday dear Graaaaannnnttaaaa, happppy birthdayyy tooooo yoooo. Eighteen! My little brother eighteen. Man-ohman. You are now killin' age little brother, old enough to bleed, old enough to butcher." Robert begins turning his pockets inside out, then he raises a finger in comic recognition, and pulls off his pants. From the front seat, "Robert, what the fuck are ya doin'?" "What am I doin'?, what am I doin'? I am getting high on my brother's killin' age birthday. I happen to have a stash of little bennies up my ass and I think we should indulge before we hit the border." Grant trying to calm Robert down informs him that he is a little too high already. "No such thing. Never happen. That is to say it is all relative, little relative. Uh sorry, that was bad. But inside this tin-foil package that has remained stuffed under my young warm balls are at least fifteen little white pills." Eddie tries to get the word to Grant to get the pills out of Robert's hands. "Grant. . . ." Robert starts laughing, "Oh yeah, Grant, what are you gonna do? Hey, do you think Indians got high? They did. They were the stoniest mother-fuckers in the world." Grant trying to slow Robert down a little. "Those Indians are dead, Robert." "That is what the white man wants you to think, they're still around — some-place." Robert opens his mouth over the mound of pills in his palm. Grant pulls on his arm and Robert jerks violently away. "Hey!! Now relax. There are up to twenty little whites melting in my hand presently. I will take them all immedi-ately, or I will split them with my best friend Eddie. How's that? I am willing to share. Hey. Where the fuck is the fuck-ing brew? Who took the brew?" Grant cracks three beer cans open in rapid succession. Robert downing one and reaching for another, "Ahhh yesss. Now then. We drink the brew as befits a wake, which is your birthday, brother, in a manner of speaking, and Eddie, you and I split these bennies." Robert climbs back into the front seat. "Open the old mouth Eddie. Stick out the old tongue." Eddie opens his mouth, and sticks out his tongue. "Good. Now then. One for you, one for me, one for you, one for me." This procedure continues with Ed-die laughing as the whites pile onto his tongue, and Robert chews his. "Watch the fucking road there, Burnett. OK, one

for you, one for me. . . . Fuck! Dropped one. Hold it a second.
Ah, here it is, one more for me." They start laughing. Eddie
swallows his tongue full, washing it down with a hit of beer,
checking the rearview mirror. Robert finishes the rest. Grant
mumbles from the rear window, his elbow hanging out in the
wind, his head resting on his shoulder and the air blasting in
his face, "Happy now?" "Yeah, for the time being," responds
Robert in an entirely different and devastated tone. Silence
in the car for several minutes. Robert looks out at the land-
mark electrical plant near the highway and mutters, "Crazy
Horse. What a great fuckin' name."

BOY IN THE AIR 3

HE WAS WALKING PAST A CHURCH that stood on a corner, painted brown and doing nothing and nobody any good. He resented that church, felt at odds with it, because he had been in headlong pursuit of forbidden kicks, and flirting with foreboding consequences. Strolling along the streets surrounding his campus, full of the rewards of athletic life, strong as a cat, fast as anything, daring, mean and violent. He was getting stoned as he walked along with his buddy, who he didn't know at the time was into rape. They were passing a fat joint between them as night was falling. The last light of the sun had left the spring air warm and intoxicating. His buddy had an evil atmosphere that made Eddie feel secure, because he sensed that he had the worst-case scenario walking right beside him, so there was nothing to imagine that could be worse. Eddie had begun running dope across the border and part of his reward for those nocturnal labors was an endless supply of drugs. So, Eddie was walking along, keeping his secret, and his buddy keeping his, when he said to Eddie, "Uh, there's a cop behind us."

In 1969 in San Diego you were on your way to jail for a joint. Eddie had just been busted again, and was out on a hard-to-get-in-this-case Own Recognizance bond. Some local sports fanatic had come to his aid, willing to pay any weird price to tell his friends he was "helping" the star. Eddie was very glad to be out. He hated jail. He turned slowly, as he swallowed the joint, and adjusted the baggie under his nuts, expecting to see the much feared cruiser down the block. To his dismay the car was right beside him. Two cops looking out of the window, one saying, "Hey, get in the car. I want to talk to you."

Eddie stood there with his hair down to his shoulders in sunburnt coils they call "dreads" today, shirtless, with those late teenage constantly worked-out muscles slapped on his bones, baggy defiant Levi's under the heels of his Adidas. Eyes blood red, angry mouth snarling "What did you say?" The delivery dripping with the disrespectful inflection that ends the sentence with an unspoken meaning that says, "Fool." The car stopped and the cop began to move his arm on the door to get out. Eddie leaned off the curb and pressed his weight against the car door. His buddy was frozen in his tracks. Eddie put his face close to the face of the cop, who for a second was taken by surprise and had failed to grab a handful of Eddie's hair. Eddie repeated in increasing volume word by word, "I-ain't-getting-in-no-fucking-car."

Eddie took off straight down the road. It surprised him when the cop who was driving nearly had the tires lit in reverse by the time Eddie had cleared the rear bumper by twenty yards. The car beside him was rocking wildly to the left and right screeching black smoke.

Across an intersection another cop car was making a two-wheel turn through a red light. Another one peeled out from behind the church. Set up. For what? Eddie realized they had been surrounded and his determination to escape doubled. He ran out into the middle of the street and drew two cars toward him, then reversed and blasted across the church parking lot. The car from the intersection approached, siren blasting, lights spinning, gaining speed to head him off.

At the end of the parking lot was a cliff that dropped into

a deep brush canyon. The car was heading straight at him, the intersection point would be the edge of the cliff. The cops hit the brakes, the screeching stretched for ten seconds of sliding burning rubber. The car was just barely under control, and Eddie's legs were spinning in the headlights. He saw the black canyon looming beneath him. Step by step he approached the lip of the rim without the slightest drop in speed. The car spun in a circle of smoke and dirt. Eddie planted his left foot on the edge of the cliff, and jumped up and out, full speed above the canyon. Eddie hung briefly in the suddenly silent night air. He felt the cops' frustration and awe behind him, knowing they were hoping like hell he'd break his sixty-foot drop on a concrete corner, or a pile of cement blocks, or with a trimmed branch between his legs. As Eddie began to drop he repeated to himself, "If I can move, I can get away."

As he gained speed he began to expect some awful end to this flight. It was plain that the cops were going to have to conclude that Eddie was willing to go to any length to avoid their smug arrest, the humiliating ride downtown, to say nothing of their resisting-arrest excuse to beat him without regret or explanation. He was falling faster, the speed of the run and the blast of the takeoff overcome by an increasing speed in the dark, just as dark brush appeared under him, Wham. A leg-collapsing, back-jarring, teeth-gnashing, neck-snapping, impact. Eddie immediately relaxed and began assessing the damage. Ankles intact, back unbroken, eyes unpoked, wrists and elbows skinless but functional. He was on his feet crashing a trail down into the depths of the canyon floor. Flashlights pointed beams from the cliff edge, searching in vain. Eddie heard the cops mumbling, and saw more headlights converge on the rim. Twenty-five minutes later he was in his room at the beach. They caught his buddy though, got him identified and convicted on four counts of rape and aggravated assault. Gave him three years. Eddie never saw him again.

WINGED SHOES AND A SHIELD

INSIDE THE CAMPER, THE STREETLIGHT lends a silver glow to the reeking blue waves of marijuana smoke hanging over the bunk. The ice pick rattles the silverware drawer in response to the figure jerking under the blanket. The rhythm accelerates into a brief moment of frenzy and the figure unfolds, rising to his knees before the window. He freezes a second and then punches the curtain with four jolts of semen, adding to the wet weight hanging on the thin white cotton. The voice, caught in the strain of the effort, sputters, "Four."

Eddie squints at his watch which reads 2:30 a.m. Still coming on. Perfect. He takes another tab. He wipes the sweat from the back of his neck, feeling an increase in fear and anger as he calculates the three and a half hours that remain until dawn. He examines the curtain as he wonders if, at this pace, he will splatter that curtain two or three more times before the cock crows, so to speak.

If these past sixty seconds were a video installation in some chic art spot, the viewer would see that a classic warrior-boy-statue — Perseus standing on a corpse holding a woman's severed head at arm's length — has somehow come to life, revived and cleaned of the dust of centuries and — drenched in sweat induced by alcohol, speed, hysteria and acid — has made the long journey to jack off in a camper parked around the corner from the U.S. Armed Forces Induction Center on Wilshire Boulevard in 1971. The boy stands barefooted in the camper, buttoning his Levi's with one hand over his exhausted dick and cracking another Colt .45 open with the other. Finished with the buttons and half the Colt, he wets his five fingers with the sweat of his forehead, places the tips into a pile of "white crosses," raises the hand with a pill or two stuck to the end of each finger, and inserts each into his mouth. He takes a mouthful of Colt and waits, letting the chalky pills foam into a acrid-tasting mess that seems to bring an electric charge to his mouth's dental work. He swallows. He flicks a match beneath the joint pressed between his lips and the burst of flame reveals the insane red eyes of Eddie Burnett. Insane is the right word — self-induced, circumstantial, or a product of amplified empathy. The boy is out of his mind. His eyes change from a bulging hysterical stare into snake-slits of thought. True sailing is dead.

The gods have snuck into hell for a while to lie in the arms of senseless blood lust, groaning and writhing in a top-and-bottom scene that is beyond comprehension. And let's leave it that way, huh? Besides, as far as Eddie can tell, they're having a real good time.

Eddie feels his muscles swell from his chest up, his heart suddenly pounding in what seems like an empty cavity. Whoa — beginning to rush pretty heavy, Eddie. So he does what he always does when he rushes. He uses the opportunity to knock out another fifty or sixty pushups. Might as well stay in training.

2:32. Eddie thinks he hears the groaning of the souls in flames in Vietnam. He knows outraged spirits are still breathing and are contorted in isolation, sucking in any possible air that does not carry the stench of napalm and My Lai.

The tiny camper fills with shields and appendages laced in leather. Bodies press around him, and what has been the silver light of the streetlamp becomes a roaring din of carnage. Metal clangs against metal as the ringing echo fills with the grunts of exertion from hundreds of men dying together in a grisly human ball of horror. Men anchored together in a chain of desperate terror are thrown down, link by link, into an inescapable pit.

Eddie looks to his left and sees a small man, thick-set and whimpering, with snot and tears dripping from his face. The man in front of him shifts his weight constantly, revealing the end of the line — the place that shakes and convulses in an orgy of hand-to-hand death. The man on his right rises on his toes in an effort to see into the coming hell. Catching a glimpse, he screams in rage and despair. The men behind Eddie press their weight, constantly inching him forward.

Eddie thinks about the oncoming hell and the irony that he is moving toward it. Eddie's arms hold a small shield and a short, thick, blunt sword. His vision is obstructed by a nose piece that runs off the front of his helmet. His shins are covered in pounded metal. His mouth is wide open and he is screaming, as he realizes he is less than eight men deep from the front of the stage, where the concentrated effort is a tangled climax of souls departing this bloody earth. He looks to the left side of the swinging, moving mass and sees a blade rise and fall, rise and fall with flesh and blood splattering and spraying in its path. A single man is going berserk, killing one man after another as though they are under a spell and are commanded to cooperate.

Eddie knows in a single flash what he has to do. He locks eyes on the monster who shows no sign of slowing down as he continues to mow down the men before him. Eddie's only chance is somehow to kill that man, who has, at that instant, with a single cracking stroke, lifted the cranium of a man and sent it flying into the ranks beside him. Eddie looks for signs of fatigue in the warrior and the signs are there at last. He watches the arms dropping and the chest heaving. Eddie's hope to live hinges on reaching the man before he can pull back behind the line and recover.

Two men before Eddie fall suddenly. The first is knocked off his feet in surprise with the sweep of one of the man's legs, which catches him under the ankle and spins him onto the ground where his spine is severed with a deft chop behind the neck. The second cannot withstand the press of his shield and slides sideways, exposing his ribs, which are cleaved from bottom to top in a single two-handed stroke.

The warrior slips in the mud and guts, nearly recovers, then lands heavily, pinning his own sword in the mud beneath him. Eddie realizes that the warrior will die at his hands, and not because of his planning or his skill, but because of — what? Fate? Luck?

The men beside Eddie charge into the silver light of the streetlamp after the retreating tangle of hysteria and disappear. Eddie looks at the camper floor and sees blood running in a stream under the door and out into the street. He opens his eyes. Medusa. Perseus holding Medusa's severed head. Eddie parts the curtains and strikes a match. He looks at his reflection, he sees the source of his self-hatred. Something female inside of him, distorted and repressed for centuries because of his shame of it. Hated since the instant he saw the light of day. Over the years the undeniable female self — the half he felt he had to hide — has been transformed into his own enemy within, and is becoming the enemy to all those without. His life and this world was a battlefield. Aries has nothing to do with it. It is Medusa, living right under the surface, once innocent and beautiful, but warped into a force that knows nothing but hatred. Eddie stares, as he has stared countless times searching for her. He brings her into focus and stares motionless as though he had been turned to stone. Looking right into his own eyes, his long hair hanging in coils to his shoulders, twisted into tangles falling over his face like snakes.

Eddie cracks another Colt, inhales a burning cloud into his raw lungs, holds his breath, and thinks: Something has got to be done about her. Eddie lies back on the bunk, blowing another cloud to the ceiling, thinking, "Good thing I'm a Gemini, and a good thing I know Athena. That's all I have to tell them." Eddie laughs out loud at that one, and washes down a few more whites with another can of Colt.

Seven hours later he is ushered out of the induction center, excused by the psychologist on the grounds that he is too insane for the U.S. Army.

1972

No words came out of his mouth. She thought it was much better that way. He'd knock on her door, or maybe just say her name in the telephone. She knew what he meant. He'd show up in the next five minutes, the next few hours, the next week. "Save me for a second baby. Put me in the shower. Feed me. Get me out of this." She was good to Eddie, always fed him first.

Running in every sense of the word. Magnified gray crystals shining in the beach-fog headlight reflection. Sticky salt-air streets sliding his bald tires. Eddie hasn't blinked once in forty minutes. A fragrant pound is under the seat, who knows what is in the trunk. The speed limits are only suggestions that go unheeded. He pulls up on her lawn. Her clothes cling perfectly, she wears only vintage cotton dresses, forties style. She whispers when she talks at all. Her bare feet even whisper on the kitchen floor. She's a tactile girl. She always fed him first.

Five hours later. Fucked. Fucked. Fucked. He's so fucking fucked. What a fucker. He makes Eddie weigh every fucking brick, while he drives too slowly around the same streets of Tecate. It is taking an extra hour. They'll get noticed. Eddie starts reporting lies to him. He knows. Makes him weigh every brick again. Fucker.

Red light. Pulled over. Knew it. Eddie doesn't hear voices. Not Spanish, nothing. This is taking too long. What the hell is going on? He has seen the same Federale pass the front window three times already. What is he waiting for? Hey, maybe he's alone. "Shut up." "You, shut up." The driver sits there in the front seat, both hands visible on the wheel. The great brown makes another slow pass by the windshield. He's checking his note pad. Why isn't he pulling his gun and getting them out of the truck and laying them on the ground beside the road? Will he look back here? Of course he will. Eddie hears the doorknob rattle.

The fucker in front is frozen in fear, he is out of plans. He's not calm and sitting there, he's frozen. Eddie hears an echo in his head turning into desperate action, "I am not spending twelve YEARS in a Mexican PRISON." Fuck this. He opens the silverware drawer and pulls out an ice pick. The door opens. The Federale's hat pokes in the door, followed by a flashlight. The weight of the camper tilts as the Federale steps in. Eddie grabs him by the skin of his neck. The grime squeezes under his finger nails. The ice pick is punched through the back of the brown-shirted shoulder. The Federale thrashes with surprising power. Eddie has expected it, and hangs on tighter getting a handful of hair and skin. The ice pick slams into the shoulder again, and then again. The Federale is confused, fumbling for his gun. Eddie is furious, "Stupid motherfucker. You should have thought of that before you came in here." Eddie has him on the floor, with one knee pinned on the pistol in the holster, one hand gripping his hair and smashing his face into the linoleum floor. Eddie thinks his knuckles will pop out of their sockets. The man is struggling for his life. Eddie wishes he could convey to him that he is not trying to kill him. But that is impossible. He is screaming. Eddie is screaming. The fucker in the front seat is screaming. Eddie has done it this time. It's a runaway. Make or break. Eddie feels vindicated in the fact that at least he is doing something. He's not sitting up there in the front seat with his carefully weighed twelve-year sentences scattered all over the camper. The engine starts up. In seconds they are rolling. The camper door swinging crazily, banging the man's kicking legs. They are picking up nighttime-Mexican-smuggler speed. More speed. "He's gotta go." Eddie begins to change his position. The Federale gets the idea and grips the side of the cabinet. He makes a move for the gun. This leaves one hand with which to grip the cabinet and his legs are bouncing further out of the camper door. Eddie kicks him behind the ear. The Federale's body sags as he makes the decision to hit the asphalt rather than endure another kick. "Lo siento, Adi-fucking-os," and the man slides out the door into the dark. "Fuck you." "What do you mean? What the fuck could I do? You want to go to prison?" "Not for murder." "He's not dead." The two hysterics exchange a series of "Fuck yous." They start laughing. They keep laughing and Eddie sticks his head into the front seat. The man driving looks directly at him. Their eyes are four inches apart and they are laughing insanely. Inside of Eddie's head he is telling the man that he is the boss now. Without a word the maniacal face is answering, "Yes, I know you are, Eddie, for now." Eddie's red speed eyes are driving a hole into the driver's brain, his face a fun-house-mirror contortion telling him, "You will do what I tell you." The man's laughter is subsiding. He's trying to calm down. He checks the road. In the windshield reflection Eddie sees the Federale's blood on half his face. He looks down at his hands and sees they are red. He wipes them in his hair. He says nothing more and pulls his head back into the camper like a dog coming out of a hole. He croaks, "It was him or us." It is so absurd they start laughing all over again. Eddie announces the plan they have already agreed upon, to make it his plan now. "Let's stash and switch and get back over the border." The driver nods his head, and casually locates the .45 under his seat with one hand. "How fast were you going?" The man shrugs disgustedly. His voice from the front seat echoes like the sound from a storm drain, sounds reminding Eddie of an emergency room gurney, or a voice from a nightmare. "What difference does it make?" Eddie feels something evil becoming aroused, as though a capacity for power he does not want is taking over, as though something wrong in him is the boss. He knows he has finally, completely, turned his back on himself when he says, "None, none at all."

Another six miles up the road they switch cars. Eddie sees the man going out the camper door again. He lights another joint. He's getting so tired — exhausted, and much too loaded to get anything resembling sleep. But he knows that he is asleep right now. Eddie stumbles out of the truck and holds out his hand to the man. "I'll drive." "No, you won't." "Yes, I will." The man hands over the keys. Eddie slides behind the wheel of the Porsche.

It's Le Mans over the Tecate hills. They gain speed as they approach the burning bales on either side of the road. The little shack has two Federale cars parked in front. They pass through at over a hundred miles an hour, a .45 weighing heavily in the wind out of each window. They fire off weird explosions that the car outruns immediately. Come and get us. Come and get us. Come and get us. By dawn they are in a third car holding nothing but cancelled bullfight tickets and what look like severe gringo hangovers. They pass the border with the guard giving them a casual wave. Back to Mars.

Unable to sleep, Eddie wants to see her. They go walking along the lawns surrounding Mission Bay. Her eyes are cool blue, icy. The smile is normal, the eyes are cold. Eddie sees it coming. He tries to get her to talk about it. She won't. Suddenly it's out. She's leaving for France. Eddie can't believe it, but something makes him cry. As he cries for this girl that means so little to him, he wonders how wigged out he must be. He doesn't love her. He doesn't love anything. Is that it? She purrs, "Poor baby," in a practiced tone that would seem sincere to a square, and should be an insult to Eddie. He doesn't even care. He keeps sniveling. "Fuck, what am I turning into?" She asks for his speed when they climb the beach house stairs into her studio, assuring him that she'll give it to him as soon as he wakes up. Yes, she knows how he gets. She'll be there, because she has to pack anyway. They go to bed. After the first time she asks him to take a shower. Eddie doesn't blame her. Before he finishes the next, he feels himself falling asleep, her beautiful vague body sliding away. She's sitting in a chair when he wakes up on Tuesday around dusk. Her feet whisper across the floor. Warm fresh-squeezed orange juice, a handful of bennies, and she tells him she'll miss him. He'd better go though, her father is coming to take her to the airport. Going down the stairs he's glad that it's over. A man gets out of a Lincoln Continental and passes Eddie at the foot of the stairs. He looks at Eddie, he looks at him again. Eddie says, "Yes, I am." The man says, "I thought so." Eddie walks back to his apartment behind the low-life beer hall that he thought was dangerous and interesting when he moved there two years ago, and now just smells like piss in the sun.

The next morning Eddie knows the man is dead as soon as he steps out of his door. Lying there motionless with the beach damp in little dots in his hair. Who needs to see his face? Bottle Chicano fought Red-freak last night and won. Bottle Chicano banged Red-freak's head too many times. Red-freak managed to get his headache and temper tantrum just this far, to the front door of Eddie's house in Old Mission. Eddie steps over him. It is now beyond his code to care about things like violent death. Fuck him, Eddie's roommate can call the cops. Eddie walks down the beach noticing the perfect sets rolling in, but he's a little hungover, and the speed makes him cold as hell in the water.

That night Eddie's with a new girl and yes, he is fronting a little. His Levi's drag down too large. He wears a red waiter's jacket and no shirt. Eddie looks like a baboon with a huge head of tangled hair. A month ago he was at the Olympic trials, faking an injury when he couldn't get any higher on the speed he had left, and had nothing in reserve. Besides, he had himself convinced that the whole deal was a joke, supported by the kind of people that believed in the war, and his life contained the true life of the outlaw which meant he was really the winner. The predominant voice in his head kept telling him he was an asshole and would soon be dead, and fuck you, anyway. The new girl is rich, from Marin. She is tall, skinny, with the narrow rib cage and medium breasts that Eddie likes. Her mouth is huge and she smiles rarely, the lips are enough. Her infrequent smile is like punctuation, timed perfectly with an ironic observation. It was hard to say who hated themself more, the girl with the money, or the boy suspended over the ground awaiting the next fall. They were young, they took what they had in common and tried to call it love, or attraction, or some fucking thing. It didn't matter, they drank themselves to sleep and hated each other after they fucked, because it used to mean something with someone else and meant nothing now. But she'd let Eddie do anything, and she wanted him to. Eddie imitated her upperclass attitudes and style. She convinced him he was a coward, or he'd be dead already. But they walked like the proudest people on earth. The public must never know. And the public was aware of them. Wherever they went they carried a certain on-time charisma. The midnight rambler and a beautiful stray cat.

A Hell's Angel grabs his cock and groans at her as they walk past. Eddie is nuts to do this, so it is perfect. He walks back to him and says, "C'mere." The Angel stands stock-still. Eddie slaps his face, calls him ". . . a fuckin' punk." Eddie has been eating steroids and speed for several weeks, strong and crazy. The Angel is no match. The Angel's face is pouring blood in seconds. Eddie scares himself as he goes absolutely wild, transformed into an angry body, but sitting back with ice-cold emotions. It's as though Eddie is just above their heads watching two animals fighting in the street, but at the same time he feels his fists cracking the face of the Angel, turning it to mush. Eddie picks him up and runs with him. Wondering, what am I going to do next? He spins and throws the helpless Angel in front of a carload of tourists, as the near unconcious body bounces off the fender and lies there, Eddie screams he's not hurt and starts kicking him. He wonders, in the semi-quiet part of his brain, if he is going to kill him, surprised that he wants to kill him. The girl is holding and doesn't want the cops, she grabs Eddie's arm and pulls him off. Eddie wants to leave before any other Angels see this. They drive up to Del Mar and pick at their food on a deck overlooking the setting sun, drinking tequila and feeling aroused.

For the next six weeks, Eddie is pursued by Angels. He sleeps in a new place every night, his cars are broken into, his bed is set on fire, his new girl gets raped and leaves town.

Eddie moves to Logan Heights in the riot-burned section of the ghetto. He is not wanted there, he looks like trouble. Nevertheless there are a series of parties, the house is a clearing room for speed and marijuana. Eddie beats his roommate's dog. He stays in the house for two days with the cowering dog lying in the kitchen. Eddie scalds his hands in the sink. He cries and wonders what he has become. He stops crying. He sits. He cries some more. He knows he is just too pissed. He goes down the list, naming everything but himself.

He's got another run to make tomorrow. Back at the hovel at the beach he stays up drinking, smoking dope, lifting weights and listening to "Gimme Shelter" over and over again. He's half hoping this will be the time and he can take a few with him. Scared into a stinking cold sweat, the volume of everything much too loud.

To his surprise, when he's sitting on the cliff five miles north of the campground where he first saw Jenny ten years earlier, he misses his mother. He misses her the whole time he waits; he misses her like a little boy. He sits on the cliff waiting for the speedboat, mindlessly packaging the bricks, setting the net, watching for the flashlight signals, hoping the Federales haven't learned the spot and signal . . . to lure him out there, to shoot him in the water and let him bloat, and be found by some surf fisherman like the guy before him. The white light blinks about a hundred yards off shore. Eddie will never let go of the load, he knows the only respect anyone has left for him comes from those that can respect craziness. If he drowns they'll find the net with him. He takes the gaffer tape and weaves his fingers into the net, a handhold he can't let go. He jumps. Eddie, and a net of two hundred bricks wrapped in plastic, drops down the black cliff and splashes next to the rocks below. Coming to the surface and slamming into the rocks under the force of angry white water, Eddie looks at the boat, recognizes it and swims toward it, dragging his load, laughing.

He hasn't been in his old house since his father told him he'd turn him in to the FBI if he could tell them where to find him. His mother looks at him like he's a ghost. She stands there by the door, nodding her head: Yes. Yes. This is what you've become. She knew it all the time. Yes. Yes. This is you. THIS is NOT me. I am temporarily living this. I am partial; this is NOT the whole story. It is what I have to DO, not what I have BECOME. Can't you see that? No, she can't. She nods her head — cold as ice, unfeeling. Yes. Yes. Look at yourself. Eddie tells her, "I missed you." She says, "That's good, now leave." As he leaves, he hears her crying, heading for her bedroom.

He winds up delivering some dope to a fraternity house that is holding some afternoon party. The frat boys think Eddie is some kind of romantic figure, they get some vicarious rush out of being close to him. They promote him to some of the girls in an effort to keep him around. Besides, Eddie gets good drugs. There are some great-looking girls there, some of them curious about Eddie, most of them pushovers for anything he'd tell them. They're too young to see through the outlaw front, never guessing he'd just been put down by his mother. Eddie talks to a few of them looking for some sign of decadence in their faces, some giveaway that his being with them would not be the low mark of their lives. No luck. His soul is in a drought and the mark is even lower than he thought.

Just before he leaves, a guy walks up. Eddie knows the guy is a narc and tells him so. Eddie feels something gaining strength, feels an expansion of some wrongheaded need, blames it on the narc, tells him if he sees him again, he'll kill him. Eddie swallows a lump, knowing that he really means it and that he really will. Eddie knows that he has finally given up. It is a weird perverse freedom finally getting to that place. To have that power, not over the narc, over himself. Eddie knows he'll throw it all away now, at the drop of a hat. He'll stand in the moat and yell "Fuck the King." Eddie spends a little more time convincing the narc, who needs no convincing. The narc can see it in Eddie's eyes, smells it coming through his skin. The narc is never seen around again.

Eddie likes the fear he brings where ever he goes. Because Eddie has realized he is entirely powerless. Empty. Dead already. Just breathing. The war rages on, the killing reverberates just over the heads of the whole world, no one escapes it. The war makes a lie of anyone still breathing, no one deserves to breathe, no one can stop the killing, and until the killing stops everyone and everything is rotting like a corpse in the sun. Eddie feels it as a total humiliation; if this is what it's about, then someone oughta kill him now and get it over with. Let 'em try. It's all cheap, blood spent for nothing.

The last run was closer than any — won't be long now. He's rolling joints for a few friends. Smiling in secret amazement at the physics of simply not caring, and how that seems to break the odds wide open. Despite everything, Eddie is still breathing. The room is full of young long-haired friends, some of them radical-left professors, a pimp and two prostitutes, kids from the neighborhood, a buddy and three new girls and another narc. Eddie has been sloppy. He doesn't realize the long-haired rat-faced guy is a narc until six cops carrying shotguns walk through the screen door, and the sound of a helicopter begins whopping over the house. The cops ask whose Galaxy is parked down the street. Eddie says, "Mine." Well, it is being used to hold up gas stations. "It is?" Yes. "When?" At night, around two or three in the morning. "Yeah?" Yeah. "That's when I come home from the job I have, parking cars in Mission Valley." Silence. "That's a bad time to be driving." That's right. "It's a bad car to be driving." Silence. "I won't be driving that car anymore. In fact, I'll be leaving town. Tonight, this afternoon." "That's a good idea." They leave, the narc leaves with them. One cop lingers behind. He's a skinny guy looking and sounding like Hank Williams. He looks so pissed, like he's going to start crying. He tells Eddie, "If I ever catch you again with drugs. . . ." He stops and his Adam's apple jumps up and down his throat as he regains his composure. His voice gains control and Eddie recognizes his face from someplace. He finishes emphatically, "If I ever see you again, I'm going to send you straight to the place where scum like you belong." Eddie smiles at him. The cop catches his breath and tries to get outside. He can't, and slams the door shut. Eddie's heart flies through the roof. He fights off the desire to placate the enraged Okie. The cop's face is shaking under the skin. His eyes are looking at Eddie with a kind of panic. Eddie wonders if the cop knows that the barrel of the shotgun is traveling toward Eddie's chest. Eddie knows that another instant of insolence will drive the cop over the edge, he thinks "Fuck it — him or me." Eddie sucks his teeth and smiles again. The cop seems to lift off the floor, but he begins to back out the door. Eddie sees him killing him in a raid, or for any excuse. Eddie locks his eyes on the cop, who is staring back promising Eddie silently that he will do what he says he will do. Eddie says, "I don't care, I don't give a fuck."

Eddie drives up to Marin, north of San Francisco that night, listening to "Stairway To Heaven" between static on the radio. Oddly, he turns off the exit and makes it to 29th and California to visit a woman he'd met who he has been thinking about a lot. He wants to see her again and get her off his mind. Just see her, sleep with her, talk to her and see that she's another girl, someone else he can leave, and won't need. He makes it to her house, she lets him in, he never leaves.

WHAT'D YA SAY?

THE NEXT TIME EDDIE SAID "I don't give a fuck," and thought he meant it was to his wife. Despite, and because of, his love for his wife and his daughter — he resented them and regarded himself as a coward for his attachments to them. His external world was no longer a battlefield. His simple freedom to risk life or death was changed to stupid domestic quarrels and self-hatred. Unable to express himself as a husband or father he plunged into a darker and darker depression.

The shades of the bedroom were drawn against the warm sun beating on the window. His wife walked into the room holding a picture of Eddie when he was a fifth grader. "Look at him. Look at that eager face. What has become of you? What do you want to do with your life?" It wasn't a cop cradling a shotgun this time, it was his beautiful wife of twelve years. Eddie felt the same emotion as he had when the shotgun slowly turned toward his chest, foolishly he told the same lie, the one he still thought he believed, "I don't give a fuck." In three weeks she was gone, and he blamed her.

What'd ya say? Sorry. Why do I live in the desert? You want to know that, huh. Why I live in the desert? I started living out here, a little while after, a long time ago, when. . . .

I'd been driving all night, in a very dark, very solitary car. You can feel alone that way. I was driving, I was real tired, strained. I started seeing things. It was the last few minutes of night, right before dawn.

I saw a floor-to-ceiling off-white curtain blowing rhythmically in the sunlight. The windows were open and the breeze felt as though I were actually in the room. But I wasn't, I was still in the car. Then I heard a bird calling from a distance, a long distance. I could see the bird stop, stare around, then flip its head up and call out a combination of a song and a cry. The bird was perched on a tall century plant. Each time it sang, it bounced gently on the branch.

I heard murmuring. Then a single loud laugh from the cool shady side of the room. A woman's laugh. I heard kisses softly exchanged. First one, then another. I heard more murmuring, a kiss and a sound in my wife's throat, a deeply satisfied rumble. Mary was walking to the window. The curtains licked her legs, swung around her and clung to her briefly. The curtain seemed transparent, Mary an apparition.

She is beautiful. Radiant. She is happy. Delirious. She is the same and entirely different. Transformed. She stands in an unfamiliar posture of security and strength, drawn from her lover, given to her lover, given to herself. She is free. Feeling at last a time where she belongs, a place she loves, a self to love. The exhilaration of being where she is, where it had seemed for so long impossible to be.

Mary stares out the window. Her brown eyes languish, deeply relaxed, alert, encompassing everything. The still of the morning, the permanence of the desert. She believes what is in front of her, what she can see. She teases herself, thinking that the woman on the bed behind her is not really there. Her heart pounds for a second. She turns and her eyes meet the eyes of another woman. The woman smiles, and smiles again. The impulse of a warm electric twitch throbs between their legs. The look in each other's eyes. Mary remembers taking her lover in her arms, her legs in her legs, her mouth in her mouth. In a post-orgasm choreography, they inhale, they exhale, they smile. Beautiful mirror images.

A knock on the door. The maid. "Come in." Comfortable together in their nakedness, they laugh at the absurdity of covering themselves in this room, their room.

I walk in. The room becomes a swirling centrifuge of emotion. I start to shake, I lose my voice. I suddenly become tired, defeated, desperate.

I look at Mary. I tell her, "I'm sorry. I had to see you. I had to see the reality. The images were so strong that I thought the reality would be better." The reality is not better. I feel foolish. The women come to my aid. They prop me up with their compassionate faces. They register my pain. They want me to be strong. My desperation is a foreign echo to them and it is amplified by a series of dull explosions in my chest.

"I'm sorry, I gotta go," I say. Mary stands silent by the curtain, almost invisible in the light. She is illuminated in the curtain. She is veiled by the bright sunlight. I cannot move to her. I will break down in a useless series of pleads and sobs.

From the bed, from my wife's lover's lips to my ears, a sound from deep in her chest. "Do you want to talk?" she asks like she means it. I can see she regrets the question. Without saying a word she is telling me, "No. Go. Leave now. You don't belong here."

"No, I can't talk. I had to come here. It's like an amputation. Nobody really believes it even after it happens. It makes you sick and fevered not to believe something like that, not until they pull the sheets down, and you see what you have to see to believe it."

Five miles up the road, I see into the room again. I see Mary crying. The woman gets up from the bed and embraces her saying nothing. The curtains sway, Mary sobs. The woman holds her close. The woman kisses her eyes, her ears, her mouth. They fall into each other.

I can't leave the room. I try to put my thoughts in Mary's head. I want her to think of the twelve years with me. They are gasping. I want their love to have some connection to me. Even if it means she is tearing my fetters to pieces, pulsating through my remembered irritability, my condescending understanding, my denials. I want her to exorcise my demands, my bullying. I want her to smother my injustices, to shudder past my protests. I see her body pressing, pushing, spreading, and convulsing like an elevator screaming past the familiar floors, beyond the roof, into the air.

In a medium faint, she falls asleep, sweat running rivulets down her swollen neck, across her open armpits, spotting the sheets. She moans. She has a dream of when she was a little girl with a very high temperature. Then I go into her dream. I dream of her dreaming of me. From another time. My familiar profile with the scenery changing behind me. She sees me force a smile. In a tone as though she were offering me coffee on a long drive, sitting beside me in the car, invisible a few inches away, I hear Mary's voice say, "Time heals all wounds."

I hear the woman's voice breathe in my love's ear, "That's right."

ROBERT, I KNOW WHEN I'M NOT WANTED...

I WAS PRETTY SCARED EVEN before the lights went out. The party had turned from "soul shakes," and "Cómo estás, amigo?" to "Why don't we send these white boys to the hospital?" We were where we didn't belong, and it was too late to do anything about it. It was our own fault; we'd pulled out some drugs, assuming they would be welcome. They weren't welcome and neither were we.

We'd been trying to make as casual an exit as possible for the last minute or two, but the rapidly accumulating insults and jeers were making it clear that there was a penalty charged against us, and our sentences were going to be worked out informally. But severely.

Chris had his hands stuffed in his pockets as he rocked back and forth on his heels, trying to seem calm, while the expression on his face was telling Robert and me, "I told you guys to just buy a record; you didn't have to mainline your ethnic fix."

Robert got jostled from behind and fell into a large and humorless man with a recently shaved head. His scalp, crisscrossed with old scars, was flaky with scabs and had a crucifix tattoo over one side. He had tattooed tears running from one eye and had lost an ear someplace. The man turned and thumped Robert hard on the chest. Robert backed up, slowly shaking his lowered head as he tossed his hands in the air, saying, "Qué pasa?"

"Qué pasa?" mimicked a girl who had been quite friendly to us in the minutes before we pulled out the blow. In that instant, the entire room had frozen. Here we'd been, the three of us, sitting on the couch with the stupid smiles melting on our faces. Our eightball in its zippered baggie slumped on the coffee table. Twenty cold and disgusted faces staring at the bag, then at each other and then at us with a collective menace that was, as I said before, pretty scary.

I put my hand inside my jacket as though I were carrying a gun, thinking at the time, "This is stupid, they'll think you're going for your badge." They knew we weren't armed; I don't know how. I felt like a fraternity boy whose car had broken down in a "bad" section of town. We rose to our feet in unison. No one else in the room budged, except to raise their heads as their eyes followed us to our full height. Robert reached down, snapped the baggie off the table and put it into his jacket pocket. I almost said, "Welp, I guess we'll be going then, . . ." but before I could get it out of my mouth, the guy with the tattooed tears was introducing himself to Robert.

Everyone was on their feet; the weight of the crowd was pressing in on us. The room began to stink with the smell of fight or flight. I glanced at Chris, who managed another tight-lipped smile as he rolled his eyes heavenward, finally focusing on Robert, who was by now on the other side of the room. Robert's dance partner was trying to break his ribs with frequent and devastating explosions.

No one spoke loudly. There were just the sounds of sarcastic muttering and a rigid mocking attitude combining with the thuds on Robert's chest every five or six seconds. In silence our captors began shifting positions, cutting off any chance for escape and separating us from each other. One guy I knew didn't like me even before the room turned ugly, and a particularly beautiful and belligerent girl, worked their way behind me.

I had picked her out the second I walked in the door. We exchanged smiles before I realized that the pair of eyes I felt pinning me from her left belonged to her boyfriend. Under normal circumstances things would have been cool as long as I never looked at the girl again, and avoided any chance encounters in hallways or bedrooms, or at the refrigerator. She was fairly small, in tight black jeans, wearing cowboy boots. She had on a light-blue cowboy shirt with snap buttons. Her breasts were putting those buttons to the test and the first four from the top had already given up. She had large white teeth and a lovely mouth which smiled in a way that stunned me. It was an entirely sexual smile, a knowing smile. Now her eyes were not smiling; her eyes were cold analysts that missed nothing, and found very little in me to appreciate. She and her boyfriend were on the same wavelength. I had clearly fucked up. The girl poked me in the ribs under my armpit a few times, hissing, "Hey, fock you, man. Hey, fock you, asshole. Hey, fock you, man," in an odd sort of rhythmic chant. The guy was a classic "vato loco": compact, durable, tough, with no nervous system to speak of. He didn't say anything; he was pressing his weight against me so I'd lose my balance and he could use my sudden movement as an excuse to attack. I figured I had much less than a minute. I couldn't think of a thing to do or a thing to say.

Then the lights went out. Somebody grabbed the collar of my jacket. I tucked my chin down firm on my neck to take the blade across my chin and jaw instead of my throat. My mouth suddenly got warm and I swallowed a mouthful of blood. I grabbed the girl and bearhugged her in front of me. She was reaching back over her head, pulling my hair and filling her fingernails with skin she tore off my face. The guy who was cutting me couldn't find the place he was looking for. The girl started howling in Spanish. Her body jumped and twisted in my arms as she absorbed the impact of the knife targeted for my stomach and chest.

I heard Chris shouting instructions to Robert, urging him to get over to the window in the corner of the room. I heard the sound of the windowpane breaking. I was too far away. If I followed I'd be certain to be caught up in the pursuit of my friend. I started to back up, offering no resistance to the bodies shoving past me toward the sound of the breaking glass.

The boyfriend was muttering something to the girl in my arms, but she wasn't responding coherently. While he tried to figure out what was wrong, I kept backing up. The far side of the black room grew quiet. It contained a confusing sound of grunts, thuds and expelled breath. I was sure they had Chris and Robert on the floor. I kept backing up.

Finally all the bodies behind me were gone and I lost my balance with the sudden release of pressure from the moving wall of people. I stumbled backward into the kitchen. The voice of the guy with the knife revealed that he knew something was real wrong, but that voice was going to sound a lot worse when he found out for sure. I held the girl as tightly as I could to prevent her from inhaling enough air to find words. Somehow she managed to get my hand between her teeth as I twisted her head back and sideways. She got loose for a second and inhaled before I rammed the palm of my hand under her chin and twisted her head again. I felt and heard a deep pop in her shoulder, and her body dropped heavily into shock. I let go of her with one hand, propped her up for a second and hit her as hard as I could in the face, pushing her against the doorjamb we had just fallen through.

The kitchen was empty except for the sound of two men breathing hard. I could hear them coming closer and tried to place the sound of their shuffling feet. I was frantically feeling the walls for a door or a window. I thought the thin cool handle might be to the refrigerator, but in my panic I yanked on it before I could stop myself.

The refrigerator light threw a dim rectangle, revealing for a second the red girl in the fetal position in the doorway and two guys blinking at me.

I glimpsed another door in the corner and jumped for it. I pushed with all my strength, but it opened to the inside. Then I pulled on it before I turned the knob. The men started screaming for their friends. As the door finally opened, one of the guys climbed on my back, wrapping his arms around my head. The other guy slid along the floor, hanging on to one of my legs; I kicked backward and dented his forehead with the sharp edge of my boot. I turned sideways and tried to scrape the other man, who should have been a jockey, off on the doorjamb. I tried to finish the man on the floor with one final kick, but my foot swung wide and glanced the side of his face. I lost my balance and rose into the air, and then began falling onto my back, with the guy still clamped around my shoulders. I landed hard and felt the air leave his body, as my weight deflated his chest. I could see his eyes bug out and hear his desperate gasps for air as we lay on the floor. He was tough as hell and his fingers still felt like steel talons on my neck; I began twisting his thumb and fingers in all the directions they weren't suppposed to go, and broke free.

I rolled out the kitchen door, got to my feet and fell down the concrete porch onto the sidewalk. I jumped up, slipped on the wet lawn and made it away from the house by crawling, running on all fours and staggering to a fence. I half-jumped, half-climbed over the chain links, dropping flat on my back into someone's yard. A couple of large pit bulls came streaking at me, barking and growling.

JUMPER

HE ROLLED THE CAR WINDOW down with one hand, drove the car with the other. The sound of the hissing tires on the wet asphalt invigorated him. Being invigorated was not beneficial. Invigorated only meant amplified, and this was the last thing he wanted or needed.

He'd been in an emotional state for months, perhaps years, a state in which slivers of occurrences or actions that remained incomplete would erupt very disconnected feelings in him. The confusion and exhaustion made him feel utterly useless and lost.

These sensations were common; they were the central part of his life, except for a dull, muted sense of panic during increasing anxiety or fatigue. The panic was muted because he had grown accustomed to its clockwork regularity — at intervals three times per night as he slept, and again at dawn. It occurred repeatedly each time throughout the day when he saw a familiar face. It occurred each time his daughter or his wife initiated a conversation with him.

The fear always precipitated a strange series of impressions, some of which were so odd that for a moment they would hold his interest. He would want to construct something out of these images, visions, theories — but being without a sense of who he was, he could not.

He'd made the mistake of trying to communicate these impressions, but for the past few days he had given up. He chose instead to be silent, or he would try to read, in an attempt to arrange the feelings and thoughts into some logical sequence by simply following the writer's sentences across the page. He hoped this would make his struggle less apparent to others.

His wife and daughter began to comment that he seemed remote — "not there." He could not explain. He simply shrugged, hoping that it might pass as a denial. In past attempts to communicate, he had often felt physically ill. As he watched his wife or daughter trying to make sense of his statements, he would be overwhelmed with sadness. He would nod his head in agreement with the rational sense of their views. It was impossible for him to point to the emotional confusion and desperation with which each of their observations struck him. He felt like a short kid riding a huge pretend horse in blinding circles, grabbing for an impossible ring.

He was ashamed as he observed them losing their time and energy in efforts to translate his words and impressions into something that had meaning. He watched them working at finding bogus meanings that offered hope or made simple sense, offered an object lesson or gave some insight. Minutes became hours as he watched one or the other trying to point to a path that might offer relief. He knew there was no relief.

The sound of the hissing tires, the predawn fog, the bridge he was driving over and the cyclone fence above the sidewalk on the outside edge of the rail brought a hallucination.

In front of his eyes he could see the rings of a tree like those at the end of a sawed log. He knew immediately what the image meant. It referred to ego, the core of something real, an ego with surrounding enclosed rings. Each ring represented the time that has surrounded that ego and each ring further from the core was another period of survival. It seemed so pointless.

He pulled his car over and set the emergency brake. He felt mean. He became furious. He thought he would turn out the lights in an attempt to cause a pile-up on the narrow lane. He wanted to add the message of anger to his passing. Feeling that his daughter would have a hard enough time coping with his coming action, he decided that it would prove he loved her if he turned the blinking lights on.

He realized he would have to move fast. He pounced on the cyclone fence, feeling the weight of his body pulling his fingers in the wire diamonds. His feet slipped. He remembered the many times he had hit a fence on a dead run, agile and quick, climbing to the top and dropping off to the other side, into another place where he did not belong. He slipped again. His heart sank. Bungling and awkward, he felt humiliated. He kept climbing, determined to do this, once and for all. He began to blame his slipping and his clumsy effort on the wetness of the fence, his years out of practice, but he was not convinced. Dispirited, he slid down the face of the fence, catching his wedding ring behind the wire, and tearing skin loose from one knuckle. As he sprawled on the concrete at the foot of the fence, he laughed until he cried.

He watched a couple of cars changing lanes as they approached his parked car. He walked in front of his own headlights as they blazed impersonally against his thighs. He swung open the car door, got into the car, and with his heart pounding hard, drove across the bridge.

A helicopter was streaking toward the bridge from the Coast Guard Station a mile away. As the crew saw the car pulling off they radioed up to a Highway Patrol car, "Looks like the jumper has changed his mind. Why don't you guys pull him over and see how he's doing?" The car radioed back, "Will do, thanks, fellas." "No problem."

NEAR THE EQUINOX

THE FLOOR OF THE ROOM must have been made of dry ice. I wondered how powerful the light had to be in order to illuminate it from below. Something down there was burning hot. This dark room filled with ankle-high mist, suggesting hell, seemed like a place I had been before and, worse, like a place I belonged. The cold mists rising in thundering red flashes looked like the stage effect from a production at the Old Globe Theatre near the bell tower in Balboa Park. With that thought, my lips began to form a smile, as another blackout seized me.

I shielded my eyes against the silver glare of an old house trailer. As I moved out of the direct glare, a boy backed down the metal stairs. He was unwinding a steel measuring tape attached to the kitchen faucet inside. He backed up slowly, counting his steps as he went. He ran into the trailer and came out with an old camera. He took close-up shots of every footprint he'd made beside the tape. The camera clicked in the dark nine times. A voice said, "What goes on up there, is determined by what happens down here." Sawdust blew over the footprints, and I blacked out again.

A voice with the confidence and the certainty of adolescence demanded my attention. I couldn't concentrate. A blinding headache moaned slowly and stretched a brutal hand downward into nausea. A face in a pilot's helmet searched the dark water below, his voice was drowned in the sound of the blades beating in the dark. A kid's voice rose above the noise as the copter banked off to the left, shutting off its searchlight. I attempted some kind of denial. The voice wouldn't let me finish. He was saying, "No, you won't. I'll never let you. How high do you think you'll get off your knees like that?"

Dry ice again. The girls and boys were dancing in a slow shuffle, stirring those mists into silent, scorching cyclones which rose to the level of their hips. I heard my own voice: "Where am I?" Warm women's voices mixed laughing, "Oklahoma," "It must be yours," and "Time heals all wounds." I blacked out again.

She always wore those black pumps. Her hips were enveloped in a tight dress. With me in tan corduroy Levi's and a pair of old shoes, the kind with the basset hound in the heel, we wound clockwise in a tight, hot circle. A saxophone rumbled a melody that sounded like the initial moments of sex. Her foot planted between my feet, our weight rocking left and right, back and forth. My heart ached deeper and harder, breathing became impossible. The pain climbed until I feared a nocturnal heart attack. It was soul, not body. Before the images faded, something brushed my lips lightly; I smelled her sweat and skin. Her lipstick tasted vague. My erection began its silent pounding. She whispered, "You didn't keep your promise." I blacked out.

A cat started yeowling in an empty metal storage house. This set off the dogs barking furiously. As the sound grew beyond what the cavernous room could contain, I tried to shut off the hose, thinking it was the source of my nightmare. Outside in the wind-whipped, tall rustling grass, a huge cat coughed a warning. The dogs and everything else alive accelerated into a hysterical retreat. Razor talons pulled down a huge ghost. The grass spun crazily in the wind. The legs of the ghost kicked frantically in the dust before me. The narrator had a boy's voice: "This is not me. This is what I have become." One cat eye stared at me until everything was cold and black again.

My face was hot, my lips salty. The kid who had been speaking was finally revealed leaning against a camper, picking at a bit of athletic tape he had wrapped around one finger. He slouched on his hip, implying an androgyny. He stared up angrily at that thought, then relaxed into an amused sneer. He spat through his teeth and warned, "Don't get me wrong." I knew the look, having used it every minute of my life. He was insolent, standing in the hot sunlight treating a severe sunburn as a matter of course, as though the hot red skin and swollen eyelids had nothing to do with anything.

I was impressed with his self-possession. He'd been dealt a strong hand, or at least had the confident manner that implied he had access to one. He had an attitude of expectation that followed an adherence to some type of code. I couldn't remember it. He stared at me for what seemed like years. During those decades it became apparent that he was locked in a struggle, completely misplaced in the bowels of my own prison. He told me I had introduced his torturers as my guests. I tried to apologize. He laughed and said, "Save it. You'll need it later." He stood there mocking what I had become, while he inhaled honor and exhaled humility. He told me I hadn't listened to anyone but the voices planted in my own head by my own disrespect: "Ya turned on me." At the precise instant I tried to use him as something to envy, continuing to poison what remained of my soul, he interrupted me with a wave of his hand. He turned his head suddenly as though he had heard a summons. I blacked out.

I wanted a drink. I wanted to wear old boots and find a sawdust floor and exchange a glance with a hungry woman. I wanted to find the unspoken promise and set the trap. I wanted to fall. I wanted to burn. It almost doubled me over.

If I couldn't play it, I wanted to hear it. If I couldn't have it, I wanted to see it. If I couldn't do it, I wanted to fake it. It felt like the last twenty years of my life had vanished. The kid's voice: "Weak. You forgot the seasons, you forgot to breathe in the available air." I began to whine in embarrassment. The kid asked me with an incredulous tone, "What happened to you?" I blacked out.

"He's gonna come back." I didn't know if it was a promise or a warning. I began to feel the pain of circulation coming back to frozen limbs. A dreadful and welcome pain. Almost too much to stand. As she continued speaking I opened my eyes to her retreating face. She stood far out in the middle of a dance floor. I walked to her and wrapped my arms around her; the fit seemed perfect. Shadows danced around us, most of them limping and trying to support each other. I could smell blood and disease. I heard muffled sobbing. The mists covered us again. I'd forgotten how beautiful she was. Her face changed gradually from one girl to another, from the girls I had known to the women I wanted to know. The process seemed to take hours. Her body constantly crossed the line and became mine, and pulled away and became her own. I was on the edge of orgasm.

I felt like an imposter, a stand-in, as though I would be discovered any second in a humiliating mistake. She held me tighter and convulsed in my arms. I was afraid to believe that she was still here with me after all this time. I wanted to say something, but I knew it would be stupid. I couldn't find any words. She did. She said, "You're one and the same." She smiled briefly, then leaned further into my ear. Her breath was hot and her sweating face made her words moist as she whispered, "You're making too big a deal outta this." She vanished.

I ran in circles until the dogs were too tired to keep up and howled at me from a distance, enraged that I had escaped. I crept into a grass field as the sun dropped like a stone down a well. I stumbled in the waist-high swirling grass and began to part the field with my hands as the dogs behind me gained ground. Dead white faces at my feet, with blue foaming lips, tried to say my name. I blacked out again. For an hour I heard my father's dog tags jangling as he ran ahead of me.

Pitch black. Dim red light. Close quarters, sulfur, muffled prayers. Felt like a couple hundred degrees. The trick was to keep breathing, in and out, in and out — the slightest pause and I was sure to ignite. I smelled burning hair, it was that close. The kid dragged the chair across my mother's kitchen floor. He sat on the kitchen table and as my eyes adjusted to the dark, his murky form emerged, perched like a statue supporting his head in his hands. I thought of infrared sights and snipers.

He looked up at me. I remembered being eighteen and rushing with the onset of hallucination, how I'd go find a mirror and stare into it, saying, "So that's what you look like." It was him. He grew impatient. "You ignored everything you knew to be true. I wish you'd had more balls. You lost your nerve, forgot all the rhythm and timing, the seasons, stopped counting on your own sense of what to do next. Why did you listen to all of that bullshit, all those times you doubted yourself." He lost control and hammered me in the sternum with his fist. It felt like I was being slaughtered. We coughed blood over the table and bent over in agony.

He paused for a second. We regained our composure. I thought for a minute he wasn't going to finish what he was trying to say. He held that pause the way one who loves you pauses before she tells you she has caught you in a lie. The moments crawled in that strained manner that takes hold when you receive the news of a loved one's death. "We were always afraid, and always will be. But fear alone doesn't make you a coward." He began to calm down. A streetlight went off outside the window. It began to rain. Single early-morning lights went on in the windows of dark houses perched in the surrounding canyons. I walked over to the screen door smelling the rain on the asphalt mixing with the deep green moisture lifting from the lawn, nearly tasting the seductive air from the jasmine tree. A warm wind blew down from the hillside. I heard jeering voices calling me in the distance. Although he didn't raise his voice, but of course he didn't have to, his words drowned out the dark jeers. "They try to make us all declare some kind of war on someone, or something. Your war was on me."

It was as though his hatred vanished when he seemed certain I understood his meaning. We began to gain power. I felt speed and strength returning to my body. I heard the sound of my own voice above the din of the terrified enraged voices screaming conflicting instructions. My fingers became talons clutching my bleeding soul. I was again airborne when he said, "It's the middle of summer, your season. Mine was spring."

let us pray

*Somewhere
between a fight and a dance
is the mystery of our true spirit.
A secret
that can turn moments into a history
fit for human consumption.
To let time nourish instead of erode,
to let time nourish instead of erode,
to let time nourish instead of erode.
To let time nourish instead of erode.*

SPILT MILK

P<small>ELICAN</small> B<small>AY UP ABOVE</small> S<small>AN</small> F<small>RANCISCO</small> is dicey with its visitation rights. I'd drive up from Topanga Canyon to be told the population is locked down and they'd send me home. Like today. I'm playing the Jerry Lee Lewis live at the Hamburg Star Club tape I intended to give Uncle Pete Burnett. A styrofoam cup of brown-water coffee from a Chevron station wedged against my balls. Driving south, thinking about 1961 up in the farm country on the Washington-Canadian border.

My father and mother had just shown up and were getting ready to take me back to Southern California when the feud between the Hoeks and the Burnetts finally got deadly. Like most things that have long-term consequences, it keeps you wondering how it could have happened. I mean, there had been about six other incidents that could have left someone dead. It was a foregone conclusion that something was going to happen someday. And then when it did, you never saw it coming. Things just got out of hand, I guess.

The men in the Hoek family down the road were either moonfaced, perpetually red and sweaty, huge and dumb, or like a cartoon rat, hatchet-faced fucks. They tried to play themselves as practical jokers and bad-asses. Everyone up there knew them. Well, they knew us too, but people didn't spit on the street after we passed, or leave the bar when the Burnett men walked in.

The Hoeks were nine families of nine brothers. We had eight brothers and their families plus four sisters and theirs. Most of the Dutch farms on the Northwestern Canadian border had big families. It wasn't all that unusual.

Two of the Hoek brothers cheated my father's best friend out of a tractor in high school and got the county to quarantine my uncle Ray's herd for six months by spreading a rumor about a sick calf he said he had to kill, one that Uncle Ray sold him. It took two quarantined months of dumping milk and taking blood samples to prove that there was nothing wrong with his herd. If it weren't for his brother Sam, Ray would have lost his farm.

The Hoeks made you feel you'd been insulted. It was in their yellow-stained sneers and smoky breath. The way they'd slink, while their eyes grinned an accusation of stupidity or cowardice at you. They didn't want to get into anything real with my uncles. It was just constant hot air and bullshit. They never really came right out with anything you could build a conflict over. It was sneaky, "good-natured" stuff that just made the world a lot less pleasant. They were universally despised and they reveled in it.

They also had five of the nine brothers on the six-time Washington State Men's Championship Softball Team. They got lots of beer bought for them, and they were able to take advantage of hundreds of hicks who never saw pitching and hitting like theirs, from Yakima to Everett to the Columbia Gorge. They sold unusable aluminum siding, cheated in pool halls and blackmailed a drunk with a wealthy family near Bellingham. The rats played infield, while one of the fat giants pitched and the other one caught.

Mom and I were sitting in the International with Dad eating donuts in front of the thrift store when two Hoeks, a shortstop and a giant too big to play, named "Three Ball" because of his huge red nose, passed our truck. We pretended not to see the squinty little glance or notice the huge pair of overalls walking sideways and forward at the same time. Mom and I were sure they weren't gonna say anything with my dad there.

The giant looked at the rat who was looking at us, who then looked back at the giant as he ripped off the loudest fart I had ever heard. Their eyes shot into the truck cab and the rat started to squeak out a laugh, which he pretended to cover with an apology. My father already had my donut and was grabbing my mother's and opening the cab door muttering how he believed we've lost our goddamn appetite, and then fired the donuts at the head of the rat.

They stood to their full height as my father flew up to them. They were making eye contact with witnesses and acting like responsible citizens who were confused and outraged by my dad's unprovoked assault. They hadn't taken into consideration that my father had stayed up for two nights with an abscessed tooth which was yanked yesterday, had a Rainier Ale headache, and had just been arguing with my Mom.

Dad stood between them, dwarfed by the giant who was pulling a ratchet out of his back pocket. The rat muttered something to him. Dad rose up on his toes while Mom was saying to herself "Oh, no." Then he clocked the giant with a solid fist to his jack-o'-lantern head. One of his huge boots started to lift off the ground as he listed to one side. Dad hit him again and the giant fell and rolled over on his hip. The rat had his knife out, demanding to know what the fuck was my dad doing — for the benefit of the witnesses.

My mother was screaming about my father's parole, and the rat was backing up as my Uncle Pete came out of the thrift store with a hydraulic jack. The giant was trying to lift his stomach off the ground high enough to get his knees under him. Pete stood over him and the giant stayed down, pretending he was having a delayed reaction to Dad's punches.

The rat started talking about calling the law and what trash our family was, and how lucky Dad was he didn't cut him up right now. To which my father replied, "Come on." The rat swung the knife around in the air, moving in on my dad. A few spectators began to make noises. My father was talking quietly telling the rat that if he got the knife, he was gonna show him a couple things he didn't know about yet.

I was so embarrassed. All this right out in town for church people to talk about. All the thriftstore shoppers, mouths open, smelling like piss from going through the clothes racks. Holding broken toys and useless appliances in their hands, staring out the fly-spotted windows, hoping to see something real awful to talk about for a few weeks. And my dad, white with rage and staring bug-eyed, jumping like a matador while the rat swung toward him. Dad showing no sense whatever. Mom getting mad, yelling, "Go ahead you fool! If you think it's worth it!" She'd tell Dad on the ride home she was yelling at the rat. But I saw her face, I knew what she meant. Dad was losing it again.

The rat put the knife away and strutted around in a circle, making face-saving threats as my dad got in the truck. He drove us home with Uncle Pete and my mom in the cab and me riding with our dog in the truck bed. I watched them argue. Mom taking it from both sides. When we parked in front of the house and the doors swung open, Uncle Pete told my dad that Sam heard the Hoeks been jack-lighting deer over near our place.

Two nights later, I was trying to conceal from my two uncles the effort it took to keep up with their long strides. It meant walking as fast as I could, then jogging along, then walking, then skipping into a run again. It was their hunting pace; they weren't going to slow up. Pete was a little clumsy, so I'd have to make sure to give him plenty of room or he'd poke me with the end of his bow and hiss, "Stay out from under my goddamn feet."

We'd covered about half a mile toward the back road behind the farm. Behind me the silos loomed in shadow. The barn and farmhouse were dark shapes squatting on the ground. The next time I looked back, I saw nothing but tiny stars.

Sam let his brother lead. It was as though he had invisible reins attached to Pete. Pete would wear the face of a man in control of serious events. But he'd stop when it came to creek crossings or changes in the terrain. He'd wait and Sam would mutter or grunt, and Pete would make his decision, always in favor of Sam's advice, and plunge ahead. Pete would pretend to think during the pause when Sam was actually thinking. Pete'd turn slow circles and rub his neck. He would pretend to offer a suggestion or opinion, but long ago he had learned his stated views were sources of embarrassment for him. So he would get the "light bulb" look on his face and then slowly scowl and "change" his mind in silence. If Sam pondered something for more than ten minutes, Pete would pull his-idea-no-never-mind act five or six times. It made me grind my teeth. His dull eyes would squint at me. I was twelve now and had begun openly risking the result of shaking my head at him in disgust. This was acceptable within the family, if it didn't undermine Pete's position as one of the Burnett brothers in public.

Sam always had his mind set on action. He completed what was before him then moved on to the next thing. In a day's chores on his farm, you could see that Sam planned for the future. He saw the workings of each day and adjusted the rate and sequence of chores, completing more of them than any man I knew. Sam's crops were rotated to market price, his livestock thrived. His disposition was even and his judgments were fair. He had a practical patience with life.

You'd think as close as they were, all the brothers would see more of each other. But they had sort of paired up according to their ages. Sam and Pete were a year apart. While Sam had made a name for himself, Pete was widely considered a fool. Sam handled Pete as one would a ferocious dog — affectionate and firm. Right now they were both absolutely pissed off.

We were crossing our longest pasture, kicking up and slipping on cow pies here and there, soaking wet above our boots whenever we crossed off the path. Pete asked Sam why the hell did I have to come anyway.

"Because his father is in jail."

"So?"

"So he has to be here."

We walked in silence for a couple hundred yards. Pete started in on how I always brought up questions about what made people tick. His head spun on his long neck and his face dropped about two feet out of the sky, one eye cocked and squinting at me. It was malevolence designed to instruct. He did not want anyone figuring him out before he had a chance. He thought he had secrets. Jesus, I thought he was stupid. A throwback to a line that could not have survived without tolerant assistance from brothers like Sam. Pete hissed at Sam. Did he think I could keep my mouth shut? Sam shrugged.

"Ask him. Don't ask me."

They sped up unconsciously to get some distance from the irritation between them. I trotted behind Sam.

Pete pushed it, saying, "Well . . . ?" in a tone that demanded an answer.

I did not say a word.

At the same instant, Sam and Pete stopped in a fraternal choreography worked out over thirty-odd years of stalking game. Frozen mid-stride, mid-breath, mid-heartbeat for no reason other than something they automatically understood between them. They towered above me, posed like shadow conjurers. The scimitar moon staked over Sam's shoulder, reflecting the silver in the strands of his long gray hair. Pete put his finger to the side of his nose and fired a clot of hay fever in a heavy wad out of his head, missing me by about a foot. Whatever had stopped them was now permitting them to move. Sam had already disappeared.

"Well can ya?" Pete moved to grab me as I followed Sam. Sam stopped. It was time to get Pete's mind off this issue. He walked out of the dark and stood over me, his head turned to the side and looking out of one eye. He had always looked like a bird. The moon backlit his profile, his nose beaked like an Egyptian drawing I'd seen of a man with a hawk head. Pete felt he had a confederate in Sam in the demand that I answer.

Pete shifted his balance and cleared his throat. I got ready to duck. He asked again.

"Eddie, can you keep your mouth shut? I'm not talking about little jerkoff secrets now. I mean you gotta be able to. . . ." Sam interrupted him by turning his eyes on him.

I looked at Pete like I had no idea what he was talking about.

I heard the baritone growling up from the snot in Pete's throat, which usually preceded violence.

Sam sounded disgusted from the dark.

"I guess his mouth is shut."

I could hear the long grass whisking his jeans as he moved on. Pete looked at me.

"I don't want you answering nobody's questions. You ain't here."

He examined me up close for the slightest sign of sass. I looked at the ground around me. We started walking again.

I was tired of explaining the basic shit to my family and it seemed to me that now that I was twelve, if I didn't stop doing it, I'd be explaining myself to somebody for the rest of my life. I relied on the Sams of the world to see the obvious and not have to tell it to them again and a-goddamned-gain. I wanted to deal with people who had ideas of their own, not those asking for answers and explanations from somebody else. It looked like a fairly lonely ratio but I was already past giving a shit.

Pete passed me in six steps. I ran along behind him. My uncles were gliding in something like a run — low, level, silent, and real fast. We were gaining a lot of ground on the fifteen or so deer we were trailing. I thought I saw them, but I couldn't have, it was too dark. There was another sense at play, one I had no recollection of. It was just there as we ran over the pasture.

Our speed increased when we dipped into a deep grass ravine. Birds flushed. At the top of the opposite side we froze, three statues low in the field, pretending to be hallucinations, being I guess, psychologically invisible. It was part of a rhythm, a ritual of our ghostly northern clan — the hunt in the dark and all the hoodoo that goes with it. The connection with the night, the deer, my uncles, the rhythm, and the fact that I had somehow known when and how to freeze as they froze — all this burst a small dam of adrenaline inside me.

I stood there invisible with my uncles. A wave of energy passed over the field from a jittery doe. It hit my uncles; it hit me too. I felt a smile coming over my face. From the ground through our senses into our blood. We stopped and time stopped. And nobody was there but the deer. The three of us had changed into something else through the energy of standing motionless. Until that moment I thought hunting was pursuit and killing. What it is — is infiltration. Because the deer forgot about us, they moved closer and broke their own perimeter, putting us just inside the herd. We'd crossed the line that would normally have made them run, and the deer, lacking imagination, figured we couldn't be there. Like magic.

And since my dad got busted for drunk driving and they held him over the weekend because he needed to cool off, I was his representative in the spell we had on the deer. I was being initiated. Not through my uncles' intentions. Just because it happens that way. We were out in our field heading for the cutoff road between town and the county line. A road driven by drunks — like my dad last night — and state troopers. The blacktop crossed at the far end of our northern pasture. I'd been thinking the whole time we were hunting deer. But when we started to move again it didn't seem like it.

Sam was the best archer in the entire Pacific Northwest. These deer were "gimmes" as far as his aim and the power of his bow was concerned. Pete was almost as good as Sam. We stood within a herd of deer with eight-point bucks almost close enough to spit on, and neither man had nocked an arrow on his string.

It was more like we were driving the herd instead of setting it up to get shots. Sam kept up the pressure, closing space on them enough to move them, but not enough to get them to run. Just very subtle suggestions in the way Sam leaned would be enough to shift the herd. It was like a dance between us, and in the next half hour we must have moved them a half mile. By the time we had them near our fence line we stopped, and I listened to them cropping the grass and snuffling. I either smelled them or imagined it; I couldn't tell.

Three cars dotted the distance. One of them broke free of the other two and began to unwind down the road. As the light went from stars to the shimmer of starlight, the deer went from invisible shadows to outlines, and as the car growled steadily beyond, they froze. The headlights passed, the shimmer wiped away and the taillights burned smaller and smaller.

I knew the terrain well enough from walking it every

summer. Although it was black as pitch out there, fingernail moon or not, I knew the ground beneath me. I was connected to it.

I unconsciously started to move. Sam put his hand on my arm to stop me. The deer broke and then settled. Sam pointed at his eye and whispered.

"They almost see us."

Sam put me in a headlock and slowly pulled me down on the grass, breathing in my ear.

"Deer see in the dark. That's what the Hoeks is banking on. Blindin' them with their car lights, then shooting them when they's helpless."

I was freezing in the wet dew. We laid there for what seemed like a hour. The deer snorting and stamping, cropping and blowing. That and silence.

Two more cars passed by, trying to approximate the speed limit and stay in their lanes.

Sam put his mouth over my ear and whispered, "The Hoeks are gonna have a hunting accident."

I got scared right there laying on my belly, the world of men had gotten a little too heavy for me.

Sam got up to his feet, flanked the herd and moved it closer to the corner fence. Pete flanked the far side and I stayed where I was.

Two cars raced down the road and a third pair of headlights lingered behind. The first two cars accelerated and became taillights. But the third pair of lights cut out. I could still hear the engine in the distance. The sound stopped at one of our cattle crossings and then started into the field, coming our way.

Pete hissed, "Them sons of bitches is on our land."

You didn't have to see his face to know what he looked like. I would not have wanted to be a Hoek for all the deer in Watcom County.

The truck was purring toward us in the dark. I heard a

voice and the deer nearest me looked back in its direction. The truck killed its engine and rolled. I heard the heel of a boot thud on the side of a fender and a drunken, burping laugh. I saw the truck looming toward us with a figure sitting above each fender. Then the high beams flashed, illuminating several of the herd around me. Two deer facing me looked side to side with ears bent backward and took off. They went into the air in a single spring and landed eight feet away. They launched again and disappeared. Three others stared into the headlights and were frozen. I saw their chests heaving and the smoke of their breath fanning in the white light. A gun blast from the truck rocked one to its side and it dropped in the grass.

Sam was running like a ghost along the edge of the headlight's glare in the distance. Pete disappeared in a low ravine.

Sam stopped. He pulled his bow in the dark and a dart zipped toward the truck. A man on a fender yelped, and I heard the echoing of the truck hood as he banged around on it.

The men in the truck started howling. One of them was doing a crazy dance in the headlights; I could see his arm pinned against his chest. Another arrow knocked him down.

"Oh, Jesus! Oh, Jesus!"

A man went into the headlights and fired several shots in even spacing, from one end of the light to the other. I heard a pop over my head, like the air had cracked.

One deer remained in the light standing like a lawn decoration. The man on the ground was yelling and thrashing. The men in the truck were screaming. The driver was grinding gears into reverse. A man stood in the light, his shadow cast long and short as the headlights bounced. He fired off more rounds in our general direction.

Pete was yelling, "Don't, don't, don't!"

But Sam wouldn't listen.

Sam's arrow hit the man with the gun in the knees and he threw his arms in the air. One of the Hoeks jumped out of the truck and tried to pull his fallen brother to the truck. The man yelled.

"Don't move me! Don't move me!"

This in time with the "don'ts" Pete was yelling. It became a kind of duet. One of Sam's arrows went through the windshield and the driver hit the gas in reverse. The tires whined in the grass.

Why the troopers were coming I don't know, but they were. Lights spinning and sirens blaring.

Pete said, "Oh, shit."

In a second or two, Sam was over and beyond me and with Pete.

The troopers were stopped at our cattle crossing and were on their way in.

Pete had Sam around the neck and was spitting words through his clenched teeth. Sam was trying to push him away. I ran up to them as though I had a purpose, but I couldn't do anything but watch Pete work his way behind Sam, his elbow vised around his neck. Sam was trying to throw him off and Pete jerked Sam's feet off the ground the whole time saying, "Do what I tell ya. Do what I tell ya."

They didn't have handcuffs for all of us. I rode in the front seat between two troopers. Pete and Sam rode in the back seat. An ambulance was supposed to be on the way, but one of the brothers died before it got there.

Pete said he'd done the shooting and Sam had tried to stop him. Pete said he'd do it again so they might as well put him away right now.

The trooper driving said, "I believe you are gonna get your wish."

Pete got life.

His seven brothers, four sisters and their families went to see him on his birthday the first year. We've kept that tradition for the most part, but over the years, five brothers have died, and the divorces and what all, has limited the number. I've been remiss. I've seen him twice in seven years. We write, once in a while. It gets hard to keep things in common. Him in a time capsule and us outside getting the wear and tear. He reads a lot.

Sam got elected to Congress until the Republicans took over. He never missed Pete's birthday. Sam died in 1981. I think it nearly killed Pete to miss the funeral.

Last time I saw him, I went with my father. Dad hadn't seen him in a long while. I guess after a time, men aren't afraid to show what they feel. For most of the couple hours, they stood in each other's arms, laughing and talking quietly in a corner.

I sat smoking in the day room, watching the men around me trying to get comfortable with children they weren't raising and women they couldn't have. A teenager would saunter in, reluctant, hoping Dad would be cool, which they almost always were. Cool, controlled, nodding. Fingers on chins, pants pressed, collars sharp, eyes clear. Looking at their sons growing up, becoming men, leaving them behind.

With my father waiting at the door and the guards getting impatient, I finally put the question to him.

"Why'd you say it was you?"

He looked at me from another planet, one with an orbit that spun out of time, accelerating at me until the years between us caught up.

Have you ever been smiled at by someone who knows much more than you? See Pete, his eyes wrinkled at the corners, his face worn and dignified, his mouth suppressing his smile.

"Aww, Eddie. Some get caught, some don't. You know that, don'tcha?"

Before I could respond, his arms were around me. His cheek banging into mine. His old muscles still powerful.

Before I could respond, he released his grip, spun on his heel and walked to the impatient guard. His shoes were shined, his cuffs were low — an old man walking close to the earth.

Before I could respond, they closed the door behind him.

BEAR FLAG STATE

AN EXPANSE OF GIANT THIGHS spread wide, thrusting and falling, spines snaking over the Central Valley horizon. Sierra's
foothills rolling for three hundred miles in ecstasy beneath
California's fiery sky.

Shasta stands white to the north.

The Pacific blasts cliffs from Big Sur to Mexico, prehis-
toric monsters stalk beneath the Red Triangle's shimmering
surface.

The Mojave extends to the coast to the south. Sunset
in summer brings euphoria as though the day were a dream
changing below warm breezes and stars. Fertile plains lined
with mossy ditches replace lakes and marshes. The winter
blows arctic hail over valley floors, ice grips mountain peaks.

The dusk of August the tenth, seventeen ninety-two, is
hot. Heading south on El Camino Real, one hundred miles
north of San Juan Bautista, are nine mounted churchmen
recently from Spain, seventeen of Yerba Buena's garrison
leading twenty-three mules, six wranglers, and thirty-four
slaves from outposts near Shasta. The slaves are silent and
caked in dust. Each male tied at each side to a female who
are themselves tied to children. Young males are further dis-
couraged from running by having their elbows bound behind
their back. Even so, the churchmen have blindfolded two

males in sacks cinched at the neck. Two prepubescent girls tethered to an anguished priest. His lips work in silent repetition staring along the rolling ridges, becoming, to him, the inner thighs and the adjacent tendons jutting beside gaping valleys. His eyes follow the cracks undulating beneath the spines and heaving bellies defining his horizon.

Their worlds differ. Those in the dust see the plague of conquerors, replaced in the absence of their gods. Those aloft ride glory and purpose into the next century, delivering order under the stern imperatives of their own Almighty. Each hoping their Heavenly Father will choose this time to bestow his long-promised mercy.

These hours-upon-hours sway with the ripple of horses, creaking leather, and incessant whispering of this priest's pornographic mantras inhabiting his dark consciousness. The hills and the beast beneath, the bottomless eyes and unspoiled frames of these children become one thing. One huge anticipated desire for as much sin and raw perversion as he can possibly embrace in one night. Stolen away from camp where slaves are gagged and counted lost in the morning. He blinks as one girl's attempt to become invisible fails her. He turns away wondering how it is they always know.

The hours go on, the hillsides taunt obscenely before him. His eyes follow the round weight spilling from a golden giant whose curves lie still. Her leg draped over the shoulder of another, asleep. Slowly the sun casts rocking shadows on his left and in his eye's corner he sees the dark shadow of the girls, the rolling haunches of his fabulous horse and his own body high above all. His shadow turns forward. A mule squalls and bucks its burden and suddenly as though dreaming, resumes his clopping gait.

These slaves will not labor. They are hopeless servants. Two decades of torture has taught them nothing. The mature females stare blindly in the heat, their feet bled dry running at any chance to return to their spot beneath a stand of oak trees. The males sit hunched refusing to see what is before their rage-glistening eyes. The children try patience to the breaking point. Silent, sullen, seeming to owe their masters nothing, showing no effort other than ministering to those younger than themselves. Even while on their knees in the shadow of God, they remain vacant, empty of any instruction, lost with the withering that precedes disease clouding deep within the vast depth of their eyes. They are good for very little for a very short period of time. Then in a single night they are lost. As though recalled into their savage ways. They resist. Whole villages die in numbers that can only stand as evidence of God's displeasure with them. Today driven with the mules to Mission San Diego. Given their last chance in the faint hope that distance will open their eyes and return them to their knees staring as they must into God's sky above.

Gusts of wind slant yellow fields of wild mustard, catching the travelers' clothes, winding them in the raising dust, swirling everything into disorder. Swimming through gritty tears the horses snort and stamp; the trailing mule squalls and plants its feet honking a series of protests. Each mule in line responds either kicking the mule nearest, or rearing and tangling themselves in a web leaving them immobile, facing all directions at once, their necks wrapped over each other's backs. The wranglers sort them and the procession halts. The slaves face the breeze. Their impassive gaze moving along the horizon and back, their field of vision expanding with each pass until what they see is not through their eyes.

As though the beasts have discovered snakes beneath their hooves, they squeal in unison, leaping into the air spinning and stumbling. Three break clear and sprint awkwardly east. One's balance fails against its heavy load and topples on its side, rolls and stands stupidly until it begins to backtrack along the trail. The others are run down by the caballeros. Some order is restored, but the more prescient beasts must be beaten. Meanwhile riders from the garrison cross their legs over their mounts' backs and await the order to move on. The slaves are statues. Two horses scream. The male slaves glance at one another and begin praying for a puma or grizzly to descend on them, freeing those who can escape into the hills beyond. The priest whispers questions betraying his fear. The questions are ignored. All eyes search the horizon upwind. Hearts can be seen pounding beneath ribs, horses lower their bellies, their eyes wide white and wild. The hooded slaves stand resigned and motionless as though frozen in an icy wind.

The sun rides the crests to the west, blazing the rolling rims, fighting in a golden fury igniting the sky above the hills.

The beast sees dark forms in the distance and hears the pandemonium of the mules and screaming horses. It charges. Each stride shivers giant muscles under silver-tipped fur. The grizzly groans in a series that could almost sound as though it were urging itself on, if it were not so apparent that nothing represents opposition. A shot cracks. The grizzly ignores it. Three more shots ring out. The garrison forms a half-circle rotating in a wide arc, the muskets firing with the grizzly still out of range. Several riders remove their shirts and balancing under their horses' necks, blindfold their mounts. A wrangler distributes long pikes tipped in a pointing steel finger and thumb. Two horses spring into the air, their riders clinging to their backs.

The churchman yanks the tethers of the girls, losing his grip on one. She senses the slack and immediately disappears into the grass beside the trail. The tether vanishes behind her like a lizard's tail. The other captive snaps side to side against her ever shortening leash. He grabs her by her hair and lifts her cleanly into the air securing her over his mount, his reins in one hand and the other gripped in a claw on the back of her neck. The beast towers on hind legs rocking left to right surveying the pack train. A shot is followed by another and the bear spins to one side and charges again, reaching a mule, ripping its haunches and pulling it off its feet. A paw clubs the side of its head breaking its skull. The mule drops flat. Two shots thunk into the bear's hide. Enraged, it charges past a hooded slave and bowls over a horse. Its rider runs to the side of a compañero whose horse rears and throws its own rider clinging for life to the reins. He is stomped beneath his mount's hooves. The rider afoot stands behind several mounted soldiers who struggle to reload. The grizzly is hugging an old slave to his chest, biting her scalp. He tosses her aside. Now lowering its head, gouging her with rapid bites on her face and neck. A shot stings the grizzly on one side. The beast looks for an instant, curious as the ridges over his shoulder bow and swell and his neck lurches forward until it bellows a sound more horrible than those already echoing in the valley around them.

A mule regains its feet, its forelegs buckle, it falls on its face. The slaves scatter in a tangle of falling children. The garrison spurs the terrified horses in a starburst from the center of the mayhem, wheels them around and in the near distance reloads the muskets.

The priest and commander are kicking the ribs of their mounts, purchasing several yards from the grizzly turning in a slow circle and charging indiscriminately into mules and slaves. The circle widens around the beast and lariats spin in the air above him. A salvo of musket shot thuds into his back. He immediately charges the smoking barrels and the men in panic behind them. A horse falls, knocking a second rider to the ground. The rider hobbled by a broken ankle is caught in a sudden surge and slapped to the dust. The grizzly windmills his claws through the rider's stomach and chest, then leaves him in spasms. The bear lumbers toward a knot of wranglers, a lariat falls over its crimson head wet with the blood of its victims and its own wounds, oblivious to self-preservation. The grizzly runs in a tight circle around the rider. The rider's rope tangles over his shoulder and wraps around his waist. He is pulled to the ground and trails the path of the grizzly as it swats the air, charging the nearest enemy. The grizzly retraces its path and finds the rider struggling on his back, kicking the dust beneath him and screaming for God to save him. God does not save him.

The procession moves on, less six slaves, dead or escaped, three riders dead, two horses and one mule dead. The party moves down the trail for four miles under flickering torches before it builds a base camp around a fire as a chill sets in on the night. A large stake is pounded into the ground just outside of the firelight. Two wounded slaves are left as bait, bound and bleeding. The others are placed in a tighter ring of three or four at intervals which form a large circle around the horses. Between the slaves and the horses, the garrison and wranglers sit talking quietly before their small fires, their muskets in their hands. The churchmen sleep nearest the large fire; slaves are brought for warmth in the night.

August tenth, two hundred and three years later, is again hot. In less time than it has taken to dream, the rutted trail has become a highway of eight concrete lanes. The hot valley is toxic, mixing with sunlight and acrid breezes collecting over the endless malls, furniture warehouses, fast-food troughs, burger franchises, a race track, an airport, all within a brown horizon, rising, swirling, then raining silently over the valley floor.

Shasta stands white to the north. Jet trails crucifix the sky above the cold white peak, conquering and reducing geology until it is a dead language, and what is heard, but not understood, is the skyward hiss of the out-of-time passing of those strapped-in and aloft. Everything below a din of meaningless dramas, screeching, imploring, justifying, excusing and deceiving.

The low afternoon sun glares off thousands of car windows; drivers go blind. Panicked arms wave before burning eyes. Lane changes, accelerations, brakes tossing drivers at their windshields. Grim, gray faces, spruced up in latest style of goatee, Shanghai girls, the inevitable business suits, baseball caps, suburban moms, junkies, professors — vapid, empty, and alone behind their wheels. Jaws clamped tight in end-of-millennium psychosis. Each face and utterance cloned from an image provided by profiteers mindless of the penalty for robbing souls. Liars beyond not telling the truth. Oracles reaching below the belt, into the viscera and yanking the same blood and guts out for those seated and processed to see, to understand, to nod their heads in acceptance of their own fate at eighty miles an hour. They glare in Eddie's rearview mirror, their insolent wrists riding the steering wheel, their faces mouthing obscenities.

Like that Mazda cutting in front of the green Volkswagen bus.

Automatic. Precise. Mindless. One of the zealots behind the wheel, high as God, stamping to the radio bass line, fighting to gain a foot on a slow Volkswagen bus containing a family returning from a camping trip. Dad, balding and wearing his 49ers hat. His wife is in the back seat with their daughter's baby, the younger kids and his ancient, sleeping father. His mother sits beside him, a live-wire although withered by living eight decades, chattering along with slow stories of her childhood in Dublin.

The Mazda hits its brakes.

Dad panics. Tires slide. The bus noses over, hits the guard rail and bounces high, its doors ajar and twisting in the air, falling over the divider and onto coming traffic. The old woman loses her last breath on first impact. From then on she is an amazed participant in a ten-car pile-up one hundred miles north of San Juan Bautista. Her thoughts fade from the exact and blur into riddles and clues. Sifting her life's final magnificent epiphanies. Her vision dims while dying images run like ghosts through her memory. A church. Two shadows running. A graveyard. The stairs to a funeral home. A man in her bed. Her body feels inflated, light, amniotic, swimming in the dark. Her pain is real, and as it is her last pain, she finds the power to transcend it and observe it all, floating high above it. Her fingers splayed, pressed on hard transparency, cold and then shattering into a thousand cracks. Her family having to fend, this time, for themselves.

What appears to be a fastball coming over the center divider is a baby shoe careening off Eddie's windshield. The green Volkswagen bus follows, end-over-ending nine feet in the air. Inside an old woman flies weightless her fingers splayed against her window.

The baby shoe shoots over the sunroof.

Fighting the steering wheel everything is falling silent. Slow. Motion. A trumpet peals high over exploding gas tanks and collisions like mini-bombs cascade in spinning circles, metal eggshells collapse and occupants flail in flames slowing in stunning crunches hissing coolant and smoking tires.

Surviving it. Skidding and braking-then-flooring-the-pedal. Nudged and bumped, hit-but-not-hard-and-then-skidding-again with French horns heralding the state of grace it takes to still be alive here. When Eddie finds his voice, it is praying between his gritted teeth for the chance to remain, alive-here-and-for-tomorrow-to-be-here-again.

This strange internal music drowning out the clutter of television commercials, film soundtracks, thumping radio. This din normally blurs his instinct, robs him blind, leaves him sunstroked in a windstorm swirling amongst the debris of this inane culture, all the while skidding over the bones of entire tribes he comes alive, immune for a moment.

Eddie's front tire wobbles and blows, slapping until the

rim plows a trail of sparks against the concrete. He's fish-tailing, his brakes lock, his tires squeal. People around him howl.

A half mile away, Eddie knows a fifth grade teacher is standing on a school playground noticing grey clouds rising from the direction of the freeway. His windshield shatters. To his left, a hipster in a Galaxy is rocking past on two wheels. The driver's face is contorted and snow white, his mouth is wide open and he is silent, his eyes are rolling. He pulls to the far lane untouched, sliding along the bumper wall catching the cyclone fence with his rear fender, peeling grey wire diamonds off their posts until it trails him like a thrashing eel.

It all begins to slow. It stops. The Volkswagen slides past on its side spraying sparks. A terrified cartoon spins wildly past, centripetal force pushing him over his seat, his jacket climbs his neck, white cuffs rise to his elbow. He slams into an empty station wagon, its radio playing a gospel choir at full volume, rhythm exploding in clapping hands applaud-ing God's will being done. His head smashes against the dashboard, face spraying mucus and blood, his neck snap-ping back in forth in time with those ecstatic heavenly wails.

Eddie's car rights itself. He wobbles a few hundred yards and pulls into the emergency lane. A woman with a baby in a car seat pulls in behind him crying hysterically. Sirens wail from someplace. Another car pulls over, a middle-aged man stares straight ahead, paramedics will have to pry his fingers from the steering wheel. Eddie walks back through the chaos and sees a yellow dress fluttering like a butterfly and a family crying beside her.

The sun sets beyond circling lights and crackling radios. The night falls with a line of traffic stretching over the roll-ing horizon for miles, headlights blazing like torches along a king's highway.

Finally arriving at his apartment at 16th and Dolores,

Eddie can't shake the sense that the old woman has not finished yet, or has not finished with him. He turns the key of his empty apartment, finding yesterday's heartbreaking weeks of abandonment foreign, from a different world. If she loves him, she should have him. The guy is a mindless lowlife, a simpering whiner. Snaking into a friendship, then moving on her.

You'd have to kill the guy for it to complete itself, and she must not be worth it. Or it would be done already. But it lingers on.

But inexplicably Eddie is filled with the desire to live. Fueled with a rage to get back into life and find what is there for him. Like a choral climb inside his head, imbuing everything with a fresh sense of anticipation. Such a stunning change from black, mean hate. To this sense of relief, as those prayers he does not remember saying are being answered anyway. In just a matter of hours. He thinks about the old woman — she spins in the air above him again.

The world opens up. The travel section jumps at him from the coffee table. Laughable to rehash the split, the tears, her beauty, weighing the chance she might come back.

Face it, the best sex was behind you anyhow, all that remained was habit. Eddie, she lied to you anyway. Your appreciation of her beauty was, after all, narcissistic, some tribal resemblance, some link to auburn hair, blue-eyed Irish fantasy. Your kind. Blood lines or something. Weird how simple it is when its power is removed.

In an hour, music reappears in Eddie's apartment. Three hours later, the floor is slick with album sleeves — he's drunk, stoned. It's time for a walk.

Outside. The clear air carries distant sounds. Echoing parts of conversations, cars clearing intersections, dogs on tinkling leashes. A drunken shout. Breaking glass. Eddie forgot his jacket and the fog is streaming over Twin Peaks. A mist descending. Past the mission cemetery, all the McNamara headstones. Duggans. Kennedys. O'Briens. Eddie lays on his couch. The glass. Her old face behind the glass. Shattering. Asleep. Her fluttering dress in the highway. The gurney, the disconsolate son, the confused grandchildren.

Just sixty years ago someone else was holding absolute possession of her body, and certain that much of her mind, and parts of her soul were also his to keep in what was becoming an eternity. Aroused beyond what he thought possible, he gave himself away. He saw her face more beautiful, and then almost horrible, in her release of love.

What he was thinking was wrong, what he felt was misleading, what he hoped for was futile. She wasn't on the bed with him, not really before him, laying loose and lost within the close, hot room. It was her sweat and her ragged breathing, her muttered sputters. The nails in his back were hers. But she was not there. Her senses were within her mind; her eyes saw nothing open or closed. She was gone and didn't know how she had done it. He never guessed the intensity he felt within her was not sourced in her body, but in her complete absence. She was betraying him. She violated him further, taking him into a chamber he would see just once, an ancient treachery coming over her like an echo, unwanted, undeniable. Coming over him like a sunset on a distant horizon. A sight, which at that moment struck him as indescribably beautiful, although strangely familiar.

In the next moment he fell into a panic, sensing exactly what the problem was, and unable to contain his accusation. She wiping tears off her face; her lips pulled tight over her teeth. Her tentative denial driving him crazy.

She turned her face to the wall as he raved in the hallway. She saw thousands of women choosing black, pleading with the Virgin for relief, finding a faint recognition and communion in her downward gaze.

Dawn at 16th and Dolores. A wagon rattles along the corner, horses tired and rocking voluptuously, hips swaying, halters creaking. Four longshoremen jostle easily in the wagon bed, smoking and complaining. Two automobiles compete for the right of way. The intersection clears into a right angle of fate timed with a closing alley bar and the end of a late-night card game. The two men recognize the identity of each other. They stride the gray walkway with an increasing pace, each in the path of the other, as though hurrying to pray beyond the marble stairs of the towering Mission San Francisco de Assisi, turning harsh in the reddish light above them.

One of the turning points in violence is in fear's pause, providing second thought's first grab at irresolution, provoking the leap into action by the foolishly brave. A hand reaches into a jacket and removes a fishing knife. A man stoops and snatches a beer bottle, cracking it on a stone curb.

The first swipe with the knife misses. The fist juts under his swing and glass rakes deep along his wrist and over the forearm, torn veins gushing and splashing. The bleeding man steps back, amazed at the damage. His bellow echoes off the plaster walls above him. The bottle gashes him again, tearing a red belt around his waist. He snatches the knife clattering along the ground and moves into the man who's standing with his head tilted as though he were drawing a conclusion. The knife drives into his thigh and would have run up into the groin if they hadn't slipped, the blade glinting downward leaving a line to knee. The pant leg changes color. If they didn't know one of them would be dead at first, they knew it now.

They circle each other, shuffling and scraping. Eyes fixed with cold purpose and forlorn sadness at the result of it all gone hopelessly out of hand. They spit in muttered taunts. They levitate above a half-dressed crowd standing in shafts of sunlight, unable to take their eyes off this passion making death entirely tangible before them. The spectators protest, then reconcile. Eyes dart from one to the other wondering who will stop it, until they realize they do not want it stopped. The figures flail in the muck until one dies and one lives. The mute crowd turns away, their thrilled faces glancing back, their shame driving them home. A voice calls in protest, a choir responds in kind. The crowd vanishes.

A man lying face up twitches for twenty minutes as shock and blood loss lift his ghost. The other stands for a moment over him, then walks four blocks to find an empty horse stall at his brother's livery and collapses. His arm is amputated ten days later at the shoulder. Convicted of murder a month after that. No chance for parole.

She moved out of town to a place on the outskirts of Shasta, married a milkman. Had four kids. Never had a love again that came close to either man. Never wrote the prisoner. Visited the grave every year, until she turned eighty-two and died in a ten-car inferno. Never lost her Irish accent.

SOUTH

CRICKETS OUTSIDE. DEW ON THE GRASS. Dogs asleep. Dawn coming.

Walking down the stairs into the foundry of his dreams. Figures shimmer in the heat, staring at him — old men, black and sweating, heroic Rivera renderings. WPA posters come to life. Huge Soviet women with thick-soled boots, bare-breasted, laboring, surrounded with flames, pausing momentarily, leaning on the handles of their shovels, watching Eddie dreaming of them.

A woman is doused. She steams and draws an artifact from the fire, passing it to a crippled man who fixes it on an anvil with a series of deft and practiced maneuvers in a dance. His tongs ring like bells as the women's hammers clang, waking him in full adrenaline spasms.

The radio alarm gives news of thunderstorms and murder. Eddie's middle age moves part by part. The bedsprings creak. His feet hit the floor; he stands up unsure of his balance. Dizzy and nauseous, he totters to the bathroom. His face in the mirror looks like an astronaut breaking through gravity's pull.

He splashes his face — eyes tired and empty.

The radio drones on. Washington is moving to Salem. Maniacs are devouring children. Playmates are beating each other to death. Mothers are tossing their newborns off bridges. Racism and misogyny are holding hands in the back of the hall.

Someone's body is whomping against the wall. He waits until he is sure no one has yelled for help.

The newspaper hits the front porch. Chronicles of the worst the city can offer, huddled in blankets in doorways, breathing in the sidewalks littered with condoms, tubercular oysters, piss, blood, grease and shit. Old men flapping in their jackets to keep from freezing to death. Enraged youth menace the street looking for the chance to prove that they really don't give a fuck about anything, no more than anything cares about them, which is, let's face it, not at all.

Eddie grimaces in the mirror and begins to examine his teeth. A clap of thunder rolls over the house.

Pausing, rubbing the warm terrycloth under his balls, he stands there in vapor, naked and beginning to sweat. Stunned by a memory beginning to take shape, he waits.

A throbbing BMW filled with junior high warriors shakes the bathroom walls — blunts, a chorus of psychotic lyrics, fingers on the trigger, eyes cold for anyone outside their set.

Maybe the Vikings were right. Maybe you want to die in battle because you know every succeeding battle is worse. If we're heading toward Armageddon anyway, why not get it over with?

Eddie had his chance. The roar of automatic fire drowned in the whomping blades above him. Hugging his weapon, burping rounds at anything moving. Buffaloes collapsing where they stand, peasant kids splattering, grandmas face down, shreds of vegetation spinning in the air. 'Cause he is getting his ass back to the world.

Getting dressed, changing the radio's channel, hearing the old tunes again. All of them so unbelievably sad. He believed in magic. He was ready for life.

Looking through his drawer for socks that match, he recalls the bitter November in 1969. Mascots blowing over the border into California all night long, landing on high schools, over taco stands, affixing themselves as logos on business cards — Matadors . . . Aztecs . . . Toros.

A long time ago. Nineteen years old, crossing into Mexico with his girlfriend Diane and her family. Heading down to the Tecate mountains to meet three other families for a weekend of desert camping, drinking, and card playing. Bouncing over dirt roads on a black moonless night. Mom and Dad in the front seat, his hand on the inside of Diane's leg, her little brother sleeping on Eddie's shoulder. Dad pulls over to let Mom drive because he started drinking before they left San Diego.

He has a funny feeling about this. It started back on the paved road before they hit the switchbacks climbing the mountains behind Tijuana. The old man squealing tires on each turn, past a yellow sign that reads *Peligroso*. He answered her little brother's question.

"It means dangerous."

The words squashed flat in the low roof of the station wagon, disappearing with the engine noise. The air smells sweet with gin, tonic and hair spray. He cracks the window. Cold air rushes in.

They set up camp. Gathering wood for the fire falls to Eddie.

High desert holds time still. Crumbled granite crunches under each step further into the dark. Ghosts appear and transform him, sprinkling coats of dust from sage and manzanita. He's becoming indigenous. He hears them breathing. The branches shake above him. Their ankle bells stamp in the dark.

They're praying in other words, timed with the thud of the desert's pulse, exorcising his civilization, putting him in harmony with the moonless night and its cold November wind.

Stumbling the armload back to camp, trying to make out the whispers around him. The desert observing the invaders, watching the bumbling strangers bustling in the shadows. He can hear their voices shaking with fear. The wind picks up and turns him back toward camp.

There should be three more families meeting them out here. It's too dangerous to be isolated this deep in fugitive bandit territory. There's no sign of anyone. No bleary toasts, no hearty camper greetings, no snapping cards. One family in the middle of the mountains, just asking for it.

Diane's father is gently forcing another gin and tonic on his wife, domestic style.

"Here, honey."

She is fighting for the focus of her husband through his Bombay and Schweppes blur. He has an office girl under his desk. She has two kids and a drunk whom she never takes her eyes from — a high school sweetheart, the one and only love of her life. Her self-definition as wife and mother, the only goals of her life, coming down around her shoulders with lying phone messages, missed meals and sexless nights. Eddie hears her pleading, "John, look at me," in everything she does. A blanket for him, another drink, hushing the kids, laughing at his jokes, taking his mumbling bullshit seriously.

Eddie drops the firewood and escapes toward the brush. Diane, in the later stages of Juliet, raw and combustible, intercepts him.

It's in her expression. She's scared. She holds him in her arms in a grip that is not affectionate, more than sexual. It's a need and it comes from fear. She tries to disguise it with a long kiss. When it doesn't work, she disappears.

The trail boss is drunk. Sloppy, tongue out of synch,

"Thaaaa, thaa, thaaa." Body weaving. He's becoming aware that his family is alone. He needs another drink. Eddie thinks he hears something. His face turns up to the sky. It is cold, clear, moonless. Stars. A canopy strewn above. He revolves; the silver dots spin.

He stops, having unconsciously determined the hour of the day in Vietnam, wondering what is happening over there. Wondering what he would do. He is fixed dead center in the draft board's crosshairs. Appealing . . . being denied . . . appealing again . . . being denied again. First appealing as a conscientious objector. Interviewed by seven adults seated at a gleaming wooden table. The women tight-lipped, layered in makeup, beehive hair with pencils sticking out. The men in JC Penney suits and run-over shoes. Every face white and lined with suffering.

Appeal denied in the mail. Report for induction the next week. Appeal the appeal. Same seven criminals hardened in the last few weeks by statistics of casualties, enraged by Life Magazine's page after page of soldiers killed in one week's issue. Schoolboys in helmets, pointing their fingers.

"Son, no one wants war . . . least of all us."

Stated clearly that he will not carry a weapon, will not shoot anyone. Will be a medic. The seven jumped in their chairs. Saying he understands that under Geneva's rules, aid can be given to the men, women and children of the farming class in Vietnam, which the government seems to see as the enemy.

The second appeal is now a shouting match. Eddie hot, pounding the table. The chairs flying back as the men take to their feet. The women shocked. Security summoned.

"Bullshit. You'll be inducted. You will serve in the U.S. Army and you will do whatever they demand of you."

"I'll punch the first guy who gives me an order and keep punching. . . ."

"Your way to prison."

Quiet.

"Listen here, son. When you fuck with the Army, you ain't with a virgin."

She says this coughing as she lights up another cigarette, which by the time she says "virgin," is lit and bouncing between her lips.

"Put you in a Negro barracks and you'll be the best soldier in Fort Ord. Or you'll be the most pathetic little doggie you ever saw."

"Fuck you."

Appeal denied.

Stumbling over a root and staggering to keep his balance with his armload of branches, Eddie thinks of his friends in boot camp and shudders.

A new vision in the dark — the smell of shining silver coyote, the snap of a branch with the percussive pop under his boot. Land mines, schoolmates, shrapnel. Another world, where there is war. Where there are people, there are wars. Not here, not now. Arguing with himself in the dark. The prelude to prayer.

Moving into the light of camp. Dropping the firewood. Going to the station wagon, waving off the voices saying, "Finally." Turning off the headlights, starting the car. Answering "Nowhere" when Dad slurs an inquiry about where the hell ya been. Watching his face, his eyes beyond focus. Leaving the engine running. Back to the pile of firewood, the little boy placing hardwood from home over the brush. As you douse the pile with lighter fluid, you apologize to those elements who watch you out there. Whoosh. Warmth coming soon, sparks flying already, flickering light over shadows. Animation of imagined giants and specters standing on the edge of firelight and fifty miles of desert. Deadly silence.

"Don't waste gas."

He's falling into a chair he has dragged too close to the fire. "Sorry."

You turn off the engine. Hoping the generator recharged the battery enough to start the wagon again.

Coming back to the fire, watching faces staring into flames. Diane sharing her parka with her brother, rocking back and forth in a crouch before it. Her mother turning to rub her round ass over the flames. Hands cupping bottom for an instant, curving up and over, down and cupping again, more pressure. Unconscious shift widening her stance. *Peligroso.*

A truck gears down in the black valley, about the point where the asphalt road turns to dirt. Diane's head turns down toward the valley. Her mother steps back from the fire.

"Must be the Reynolds coming."

Relief in her voice. The release of tension drops the drunk deeper into his chair. Something tells Eddie the muffler is too loud.

Knotting his forehead in a series of fleshy question marks, his eyes bugged in disbelief. One eyebrow climbing, he signals Diane to follow him. She does. She tries to speak. His finger presses her lips. They listen in silence. The muffler is too loud.

"Diane, go back to camp. That's not the Reynolds down there, it's someone else. I think . . . We . . . Diane, listen to me."

His arms unwrap hers from around his chest, his tone becomes firm, absolutely condescending. A movie cowboy telling the little lady to get in the wagon. There seems to be no other way to communicate but through these ridiculously inadequate means. This is no time to struggle with the new vocabulary they've tried to teach each other.

"Diane, I said go back to camp. I'll be there in a minute."

She gives Eddie a look that chips a part of what they hope for away. She takes his patronizing culture with her back to camp, strides stamping, pounding out her fear of not quite knowing why she is so offended.

Every breeze, the cold of the night, the scratch of the

brush, the crunch under his boots, the dryness of his lips — all combine to alarm him. Fear engulfs Eddie whole. An isolated family in the Tecate mountains, a drunken father, a dependent wife, two children snared in the convention of family hierarchy, and an outsider boyfriend as a wild card. And something looming. Something real bad. His spine jumps as though he's fallen in ice. His heart pounds, wondering if the fear that is coming is really that far out of his up-to-now known experience. *If this is the first wave, then shit, this is more than I can handle. I'll fall apart.* The ground opens under his feet. He feels like he is doing a very slow back flip. His head is jabbering; the voice inside is screaming.

"*Hide. They'll never find you. But they'll find Diane and the rest of them.*"

Recon. That's what you've heard it called. See them before they see you. Who? How many? Other campers coincidentally out here in the high desert mountains late on a November night? Not likely. Say the word. Go ahead. Bandidos.

War coming here? Violence is a living, breathing being stalking the world, bearing down on those in the path and tearing them to pieces. Eddie's best friend is on the other side of the world, coming in from the jungle. His letter is in Eddie's pocket. Five Hueys in, two Hueys out the first day in Vietnam. Three helicopters of teenagers in uniform blown to splatters and flames before they had time enough to . . . do what? Says there are things you do that you know you'll never forgive. Feels like everything he does is part of a ritual. One that keeps playing out in different places with different languages all over the world. A black mass casting magic on everything. And it must, because it creeps in through the skin as far away as these lonely mountains in Mexico.

Eddie swings from bush to bush, grabbing branches, slowing his descent. Fear rising in unpredictable waves, engulfing him, stealing his breath. The distance from the known, the familiar and the recognizable is immense. A sense of the convergence with faceless powers turning the corner, planning to take his life. The sense of what it is to be, and what it is we have by just being alive. Win or die. The last, most horrible and intimate human encounter. Dying at the hands of another. The final disgrace.

The muffler is silent. Eddie hears more in the next seconds than he has heard in his life. The wind, branches snagging his jacket, rustling in the distance, and voices — males speaking Spanish . . . coming this way. He turns and runs uphill silently.

Is this what makes you whole? Is this how you reach your entirety? Are you alive now?

Layers of fatigue bring new layers of pain, ushering in new levels of himself in the ascent to camp. Balance requires additional strength; noise will bring disaster. Control the breathing, gasps that whisper. Stop at the sight of the campfire. Breathe deeply. Do not make them panic. They're still moving in pretend comfort, still acting what they each hope passes for normal.

Diane's mother's face is shocked. Eddie demands that she keep her control. One look combined with a silent flick of Eddie's fingers is all it takes. Her eyes lock on him for the next move. He heads for the station wagon, his eyes searching for the shotgun. She moves toward the door, opens it as he crosses the camp. Diane's brother is asking an innocent question about scorpions and winter and sleeping bags.

"Not in winter, under rocks."

He reaches the open door. Her fingers shake as she points to the blanket she has yanked aside, the cloth case. It weighs nothing as the zipper is yanked down and all eyes in camp look up. The barrel slides into view. Eddie's hand pats down the case looking.

"Julie, where are the shells?"

Never used her name before.

"Glove compartment. What is it?"

"Nothing I hope. A truck stopped down the hill. Men are coming this way."

Her mouth opens and closes, her eyes see something grim. "John, I. . . ."

Her voice is hard, demanding. She looks over at the man in the chair balancing a weaving glass toward his lips, eyes half shut.

"John, we have to start packing. . . ." Her eyes look to Diane, who has frozen, hearing the sound in her voice and watching Eddie load the shotgun.

Diane is immediately by her brother's side. He's aware that his child's body is unprepared for what may be coming — what is coming. Eddie's body grows rigid in determination, his shoulders square, his feet are no longer touching the ground. He clears his throat.

"John. . . ."

His name.

"John. . . ." His voice is changed. "We better get out of here." Eddie slides another shell into the chamber.

"John, please."

Julie's voice hits an upper register near panic. She cuts herself off and freezes her face into place. Her heart drops down down down, spiraling down in one more utterance.

"Dammit John!"

Diane and her brother are moving toward the car. John is beginning to sense something and gathers his balance for the effort to get to his feet. The moment stops.

"Buenas noches."

Eddie is addressing the ghosts at the edge of the camp light.

A man walks into the flickering light. His rifle glints in the red flame. Dusty boots, baggy pants. Down jacket. Cowboy hat. Eyes deep in burned brown face.

"Buenas noches."

His words signal the steps into light of two companions — one probably a brother, with missing fingers on one hand, the other much smaller, with a belt buckle catching light. They're drunk.

Eddie steps away from the family. The shotgun in his hands points exactly to the middle of the distance between him and the man who spoke. The man smiles a mirthless grin. His eyes have scanned everything. He sees nothing to stop him. His companions fan out into a semicircle taking control of half of the camp. Three rifles. Three men. One shotgun. One boy. One man drunk in a chair, jumping to his feet, catching his balance and walking toward Eddie, his hand out for the gun.

They'll probably open fire when he hands it to him.

"Eddie, give me the gun."

"Qué quieres?"

Eddie stares at the man who's watching Diane and running his eyes over Julie. The companions move three easy steps closer. John's voice is snarling.

"Give me the gun."

Eddie pumps the action. The sound is answered by the cocking of the rifles.

"Qué pasa?" demands the voice across the fire.

"Nada, pero no quiero. . . ."

In the exchange of these words is the last chance to give the gun to John before he tries to grab it.

John has the gun. Eddie is disarmed. The men are nearly laughing in his face. There is nothing to do but to try to act as though this situation is no cause for alarm. An attempt at normalcy. Disarm the situation, make the world around him consistent with his own helplessness under the guns.

Eddie walks to the beer cooler.

"Quién quiere una cerveza?"

There is a light chuckle from the man furthest to his

right. He steps forward. During his strides, his rifle points at Eddie's balls. As he reaches him, it slowly lowers to the space between his feet. He knows Eddie felt the threat. Eddie hands him a beer.

"*Gracias.*" Big smile.

Diane and her brother are beside the station wagon. The man cracking the beer watches her with something going on in his head. She will suck his dick. The boy will suck his dick. The boy will take it up the ass. She will suck her brother's dick. The mother will scream and cry. Nobody will hear her. Their drunken father will go out of his mind. His smile rests on Eddie's face. His eyebrow raises wondering what Eddie will do. He turns away, ahead of Eddie. He's been there before. He can almost see the twisted bodies. He sees strangers finding them days later.

The circle has closed; the men can almost touch each other. The companions never remain completely still. The first man reaches out for the shotgun, gesturing with his own rifle that he would like to trade them.

John hesitates. The thought races through his mind that he can parlay this into some sort of male ritual. His companion walks to the cooler and takes two beers, stuffs one into a jacket pocket. He sucks the other one down in three long gulps. John is offended. He wants to assert himself. He weighs his pride against his fear; the scales tip. He loses what is left of his confidence. He notices a powerful need for a drink press in on his throat.

David's voice is barely out before Diane has slapped her hand over his mouth.

"Dad, don't give him the gun."

John comes to his senses. He begins to think about shooting his way out. The barrel moves half an inch toward the man who stands grinning, his own rifle held away from him, his hand on the barrel half a foot from the trigger. John is giving his thoughts away. The man scowls hard.

John shakes. His face reddens to a lobster, veins pound over his forehead.

"*Quieres mas cerveza?*"

No response. Eddie's voice gives away nothing. His own tone encourages him. He hasn't gotten on his knees in this strange new world yet.

"*No? Entonces. . . .*"

He hunches over the cooler, grabs the side handles and begins to walk it to the station wagon.

The four men don't move. The man who offered the gun exchange squats down on his haunches.

"*Amigo. Una más, por favor.*"

Eddie puts down the cooler next to the station wagon. He lifts the cooler into the back. Eddie's eyes meet Diane's; she blinks in desperation. Eddie tries to smile, but his lips only grimace.

Eddie walks, two beers in hand, across the campfire, directly to the man rising from his squat and hands him a beer. Eddie raises his beer to the three of them.

"*Salud.*"

He laughs and returns the gesture. Eddie looks him in the eye and says, "*Buenas noches, y adiós.*"

Turning his back, grabbing a camp chair and folding it as he reaches the station wagon.

"*Sí, adiós,*" says the man and he begins to move backward out of the campfire light. His companions leave with him.

In the dark, one of the men begins whistling. The three of them walk loudly, two speaking with animation and laughter in sentences no one can make out. The sounds fade.

Eddie gives Diane and David orders. The sound of it is strange; the energy behind it is both affectionate and absolutely final.

"Lay down on the floor in the back seat. Don't move. Don't look up. Don't do anything no matter what you hear."

Eddie senses that he may never say another thing to them. Eddie leaves before they can think of it.

The truck starts up. The muffler begins to grumble down the hill.

"We have to pack. We have to get out of here."

Julie can talk.

"They're between us and the highway," she realizes out loud. "I don't care. We have to get out of here."

Adrenaline amplifies the gin in John and he fires four shots into the night sky. Exactly the wrong thing to do. Panic on display.

He pulls shells out of the box and tries to cram them into the cylinder.

"John. . . . Stop it! Stop it! Stop it!"

She's hysterical.

He's dropping shells on the ground and managing to fire off four more rounds into the surrounding brush.

A shot from down the mountain side. Three echoes and the truck's gears winding higher.

"Julie, where's the keys?"

She pounds her pockets. Eddie runs to the driver's door, jerks it open. No keys in the ignition. She's screaming.

"Where's the goddamn keys?"

He's muttering. The shotgun's jammed.

The truck stops.

"OK, Julie. . . . " A hard sentence comes out of Eddie's mouth. "They're coming back."

His voice sounds deadened and flat. John is reduced to near convulsions, his hands shaking, the gun falling. He picks it up. Dirt fills the jammed chamber.

Two more shots echo from below, louder and closer. Eddie runs to the back of the station wagon, yanks out the cooler, runs to the fire and douses it in a hiss of smoke. He kicks the embers of the wet pile.

John is defeated. The gun is hopelessly jammed and

he's too drunk to solve it. He slumps, his shoulders drop, his head is down. He's thinking about himself, what he's done, where he is, what he is. He can't move. He's about to cry.

Julie is moving in silence. She frisks her husband, going through his pockets. No keys.

Eddie is suddenly warm. He sways inside, his soul getting a glimpse of everything. Nothing can reach him. A weight so dense he can't be moved. The message the desert whispered to him in what seems like a lifetime ago is the closest thing to love he's ever felt.

"I'll already be dead before I see anything happen to them."

He grabs the camp shovel, its blade folded down, the pick sticking out at a right angle. He tightens the blade down, twisting the hand screw on the short handle. He walks out into the brush, listening for their steps. He crouches beside their path.

He waits, hearing their footsteps crashing through brush below. Eddie decides to use the edge of the shovel blade. The pick might get stuck in the bones of their faces.

WHEN RELATIONSHIPS GO BAD

EDDIE'S MIND HAS BECOME A prisoner. The battle for his soul was lost before his age had two digits. The remainder of his life becomes an anguished search. In the dark. In strange terrain.

It is understandable that he would eventually lock himself up, hiding from these cities filled with cannibals, like vultures, up to their necks in the chest cavities of the fallen dead, their spasms twitching to music they try to call their own. Obscene gyrations and thrusts in doorways and on street corners. Everyone thinking they're on time, bopping to the rhythm, nodding with the bass, mouthing the words, thinking that's enough to own it, to have made it, to be it. On hands and knees, the vultures grin down on your face and shake hands before turning you over.

Eddie seems safe inside himself. A red stain rings the walls of his prison cell. His fingers bleed as high as he can reach. I have been made to understand that he will forever be denied parole. So he wrestles around in there with his fear one minute and the guilt for dirty fighting the next. I don't see any way out. They see right through him. You probably have a better story than his. They'll probably believe you. You get along better with the others anyway.

I still get time in the yard. They let me out on cold days.

I shiver in the wind like an ice carving. Eyes are grey and sightless; cannibals walk past me without comment. I just stand here . . . waiting. Feeling myself going numb, until the season changes and a smell comes from me that fills the air with this year's progression toward complete rot. Then feeling returns, and each nerve ending screams. The impulse is to go north to the ice, to freeze and be numb again.

But they smile, encircling my bent shoulders in their arms, pushing the plate in my direction, testing the bathwater, boiling the tea, making the bed, setting the alarm. Locking the door quietly, telling me they'll come back. In warm sleep, the body gains strength and wakes. I hear the key in the door. Their faces peer at me, patient and infinitely understanding like nuns above reproach. Vicious in their tolerance, and spiteful in their understanding. Thinking I don't recognize this love as something feeding itself on what there is to hate in me.

I walk outside. Hands in my pockets, head down, walking and thinking, walking and wondering. I witness an underdog. I hear insults following him down the street. I wonder about Eddie. How he's doing. Is he still making it worse for himself?

In a park, I watch in the pale dusk, children abandon each other. That night I make it to the edge of town where the bars and clubs hold the wicked and the chaste, mingling in an unholy and inevitable attraction. I hear the snide, witty condemnation that seems unarmed, and watch it blow a hole right through the innocent person not quite up to understanding the words snaking out of the hipster's broken mouth. Parked cars shine with predawn dew, and in their windows my eyes look a lot more tired. Another loser begs for a quarter to make the bus.

This is a battlefield without honor. It evaporated from the trenches, the camps, under the blaze of Christendom's ground zero.

You don't get a quarter. Please don't make a fool of yourself seeking mercy. Here we kill children as a matter of course.

I keep walking. A dog lifts its tired head and lets it fall back in the dust again, as if it knows there isn't much use in aspiration. The hollow sound of my footsteps blows away with the trash. He jumps and howls in an afterthought behind me.

Then one of you helps the cranky lady off the bus, and a lonely kid hears his name called to him across a barren street. An ancient black gentleman in suit and tie tips his hat, turns the corner and passes me. I hear horns climbing, a warm percussion surrounds me, something genuine happens for an instant in the slightest nod of our heads timed with something we can't understand.

I find it worth living in these simple human gestures, carrying the assurances of shared centuries, the potential for dignity, the promise of something more than the waste around us. The nod of one stranger to another. These singular moments of communion in every church in the world, formalized in the minds of philosophers from every echoing palace throughout time, and failing in every eon.

Wars are fought to retain the nod of one man to another. We call it by other names. We demand allegiance to it — prayer — torture in its name. It has to be disguised, distorted, and defined to fit the need of the commandant. Made into a flag, or symbol, or sentiment fed back to us, to fatten us for the sidewalk. Giving us names and identities so that we can recognize each other. All systems operate to replicate your shadow, to give you company. This single demand of those who rule or who have ever ruled to do this, to duplicate what once was you, is the proof that it takes strangers to dignify the world, to make it safe.

As I near my cell, the reverberation hits the deep keys. I stumble and apologize into my jacket cuff. The door swings open and I reclaim my life, giving the commandant my regrets but I won't be serving chocolate tonight to those educated friends yawning on the living room couch. All of them comfortable, pretending the halls were built for them, that the towers above them aren't dwarfing them, and the dogs outside aren't waiting for a lot more than the scraps no one can really afford to toss in their direction.

A woman is sharpening her feelings for me, grinding her glinting angry woman's broken hearted blade, mouthing incantations. The blade snaps between rib and cartilage. I stagger in circles.

A grass fire burns down the prison farm. The well runs dry. The livestock go mad in the heat and run off. Parasites eventually drive them to blindness. They run in the ashes, tongues swollen, kicking crazily in the air.

We try to be good. We adopt what we associate as good. Grass fires burn down our communities. The wells run dry. We go mad in the heat, killing and running through the night. We go blind. We fight in the ashes. Tongues swollen from repeated lies, we whip ourselves bloody. We move to Salem and the trials begin.

Nobody notices. It's not on the news. All communication becomes complete fiction designed to intimidate. It works like a charm. The Christians win it all and it turns to shit in front of them. Their children begin to revolt. Infections decimate millions, the rest turn to brutal methods of what they see as self-defense. They snap at each other across the dining room table. Spit sputtering in invectives in the disagreement of the moment's entertainment.

It gets quiet for a few hundred years. Small groups of tribesmen begin to communicate, resulting in blood feuds. The night falls.

YOU'LL RUIN THAT BOY

My parents left the trailer park behind. For weeks we'd heard about a place called California. A place where a lot more was possible. Oranges. Beaches. Summer all year long. California for us meant moving into a housing tract populated by ex-military families.

Fathers were guards at K-Mart, Fuller Brush salesmen, owner-operators of big rigs, fishermen in the tuna fleet, gardeners, awning salesmen, supers at Lockheed. Or like my father, they were still sailing in fleets around the world, afraid to come home.

In school I made friends with other boys who missed their fathers. Boys who knew they'd see them six or nine months later when the fleet came back to port. We rotated between houses where a man was home, trying to see what they looked like, what they might expect of us.

The Monroes from Texas lived a couple houses down the street. Lyle Monroe became one of those fathers. Lyle always did what he wanted to most of the time. He drank when he wanted. He slept when he felt like it. Got into more women than he had a right to. He was scary, which we as boys interpreted as some organic link to the vindictive, jealous Father in the clouds who for generations had been sending the men in our families to hell. A man of physical strength and nasty disposition who especially despised education and the things that came with it, he broke horses and worked as a prison guard.

He stood over me. His eyes searching my face for the fear I was hiding from him.

"You'll ruin that boy."

I had no idea what he was talking about. What could I do that would ruin his boy? Robert Monroe was beyond ruining. But there are times to keep your mouth shut, and in a canyon alone with Lyle when he'd been drinking was one of them. I was surprised he didn't already know that his boys Robert and Grant were indestructible. The only ruination in their future was whatever they brought down on someone else. But Lyle was in a telling mood, not a hearing one. He stood up straight, almost to his toes. He shook his head and clenched and unclenched his fists. He turned his back to me.

The sweat in his shirt patched between his wide shoulders. He was the kind of man no one could reach, a dangerous mystery to everyone, including his family. His brothers were similar. Lyle was the eldest, each one meaner than the last. The youngest, Boomer, came through town twice a year and slept for the night in the garage. Lyle warned us away, telling us that if we went in there, Boomer would rape us for sure. We peeked under the garage door, watching him laying on the floor masturbating in a drunken stupor. Lyle would always give him two days, then run him off. The two of them in the front yard, bashing on one another's head until Boomer staggered off, screaming threats.

I thought that Lyle was going to walk away, that his comment about my effects on his oldest boy was a passing bit of alcoholic insight, lost and forgotten. He was likely to just start walking, or he might whirl around and slap my face. It had happened before. I waited.

His hands hung like hooks, knuckles thick and callused. He could have been a tall man but he was compressed with a psychic weight that pressed down on his shoulders like Blake's God. He turned slowly; his eyes narrowed with the impulse to hit me. I stood looking up trying to determine the correct response to appease him. That morning, I had knocked his son's front teeth out.

I had my reasons and any of them were sure to make it all worse. I had already been naked in bed with his daughter. And I lusted for his wife.

I didn't really know what having his wife would mean beyond a fascination with her loose curves, her generous lips, the greasy black hair, the deep cleavage of her breasts, the darkened alley between her legs. Her smile and her warm voice. Her quiet ways and her secret rumbling laugh. Her loneliness. There was really nothing I could say.

She ran through my dreams unencumbered with the weight of the guilt she inspired in the daylight hours. Her dark voice speaking a language I could not fathom, but engendered such a need to follow that my waking hours were filled with memories of the sight, smell and sound of her. It was something beyond love and there was no way to tell Lyle that I couldn't help it. It was impossible to explain how it led to the fights I had with his son.

He walked back toward home without saying another word, as though he was stating what was preordained, and there was no point in trying to change it.

I was trying to change it though. Between fits of violence, I would try magic. Just a week before, I had one I was pretty sure was going to work. I prepared it gradually over most of the spring, plotting the celestial chart, timing my requests with the phases of the moon. Making sure I asked each of her children on the day of the month corresponding with their birthday. It took an effort to line her five children, oldest to youngest, under the full moon in the back yard. The eldest daughter stood bored and bound by her promise after hours of pleading. Grant and Little Lyle had to be bribed, Robert threatened, and the youngest daughter was in love with me. I put my hands on their heads each in order of their birth saying nothing. Their eyes closed, the boys snickered and stood still. It was as though they'd been hypnotized. I hurried down the line, lingering on each skull as long as I dared. I cupped their faces and my fingers shook. The thought of each smooth orb passing between her legs and into my hands somehow intended to lessen the vast distance between her and me. The eldest daughter's face compressed with a hunch about this ritual. I trusted that it was beyond her imagination. She would not let the thought take shape. It was right there in front of her.

"Eddie, you are so damn weird."

The ritual ended. In the days that passed, nothing happened.

But the pressure built until I caved in Little Lyle's ribs. I bulldogged Grant's neck in my arms and flung him to the ground. I attacked Robert and knocked the air out of his chest. An older boy came to his defense and I hit him with a power I didn't ask for, didn't want, and loved more than anything in the world. I had access to something wrong and undeniable, something bad that no one seemed to have a defense against. The kid went across the street and started screaming that I was crazy. I faked a slap at Robert's ear and drove my other fist at his chest. Robert ducked; I caught him in his face. He dropped holding his mouth and his fingers turned red. He sputtered what a "thon-of-a-bith" I was. I got him to his feet and tried to get him into the canyon before he could get home to show Wanda the damage. He followed me for a few steps, then his tongue felt the hole where his teeth used to be. He freaked. I watched him walking home, each step like he was stamping out a fire in his path, his hair electric in anger.

I was ruining him. I transformed my best friend into a player in my rituals. My friendship with him was based on the beauty of his mother. I had nightmares at night and my heart pounded when I woke up. There was no excuse for me. It was all so obvious. I couldn't understand why everyone pretended not to see it. I knew everyone needed to keep a sense of order. Mamma Bear, Daddy Bear and Baby Bear. I knew that everyone needed to play their role or they would go crazy. But I couldn't find a place for myself so I just lived. And I wanted Mamma Bear. I could feel it like an electrical charge buzzing and snapping between all of us. She must have known. I could see it in her walk, in her eyes.

There were two levels of living. One on the surface with smiles and hellos. We all went about our daily activities as if it weren't there. But there were always little giveaways to another darker hidden level. I could see it in the animosity Lyle and his wife shared — the tightening of jaws, abrupt ends to conversations, eyes lingering on turned backs, dishes clattering with anger. I could sense it all around me.

Her sons watched us whenever we were in the same room. She stared at me for longer than she should have. She stared with curiosity. Her body spoke. I'd hold my breath as she untied the apron's knot behind her back and turned to hang it on a hook next to the door. I could feel my arms around her thin waist so clearly that she must have felt them too. Her fingers would tangle through her black hair, her forearm wiping her brow.

She whistled low looking at me and said, "Boy, it's a hot one today."

I jabbered something in response and she half-smiled, her eyes growing soft and sympathetic. Offended and angry inside, I'd leave.

I'd lay low for a few days, sleeping and trying to rest. Then I'd come back down the street and weave stories to her children. I'd tell them their secrets, infiltrate their minds and alleviate their fears with insights that I hoped would balance the violence I rained upon them. I celebrated their names, offered them views to the infinite potential hidden in us all. I won back their hearts and captured their imaginations. All the while I could feel it coming.

Then after a day or two, the emphasis would shift back to her. I'd go into her house with eyes hunting, sitting in the room pretending to nap, watching her sitting in the rocker singing softly to herself. Waiting for her tongue to part her lips. Waiting for the moment to say the funny thing that made her laugh. Waiting to say the words that meant two things. Watching her eyes look into me. Searching for the second meaning, to see if it was there. Speaking dirty things to her in my mind without saying a word.

But it always built into something that triggered me. I'd wake one morning with my eyes blazing and molars grinding. I'd get dressed and climb out my bedroom window. Making my way to her house through the canyons bordering our houses, I'd try to go along the ditch, climbing from tree to brush to tree without touching the ground. I ran over the stones on the creek bottom, went through a storm drain leading to a path behind her fence. I'd climb it and drop into her back yard. The boys would be sitting around the patio behind the garage listening to the radio. I'd have to get control of myself if a grownup was there. But if there wasn't, they'd take one look at me and run. But I was a cat and they were mice. And then I'd beat them and rampage through the neighbors' yards, breaking windows, screaming and destroying whatever was near me, defiling anything of sentimental value, spitting and fighting everybody until they put me in my room alone to masturbate again and again.

A day or two later, I'd review the wreckage. Hearing doors close as I neared houses. Enduring anguished lectures and cowering under threats — a repentant son, a satiated angel. Inside, knowing I was an animal who ruined anyone who came too close.

I could affect them all, but I could not get to her. I inspired her anger. I made her face contort with revulsion and something else that seemed like curiosity and a desire to fathom what this force was that drove me to these strange, violent lengths.

Basic conduct must have originated in the need for tribes to survive, but this was not instilled in me. I could not be overwhelmed or made to submit to any convention. I could not accept it; the face of the want was so great that I already recognized it as my own fall. I did not expect to plead to anything that had an ear toward forgiveness. Forgiveness had nothing to do with me.

There would be a price and I would pay it the moment it presented itself. But it never did. It just existed like a thing that just was, and had nothing connected to it. And over time, it faded.

Her sons paid it. They found their own needs to trust beyond instinct, to defy the truly dangerous, to risk finding something they could not understand, to go where they did not belong, to be drawn to all of those things. Before they were thirty, they were murdered in San Berdoo behind a garage by a new friend for failing to see what should have been plain to them. They had seen it before.

WHOPPER

THE TRUTH IS ROBERT MONROE was a liar. He was lying when I was six. He was still lying when I was ten. He needed lies in his life. He needed falsehood. He said the truth was too boring.

One morning Robert started in on a long story and this guy home from a CYA detention camp out in Poway groaned, "What a whopper," and spat through his teeth, hitting Robert on the shoulder of his T-shirt.

Robert looked at the ground in front of him for a week. Then he started telling about the time his father got his fingers slammed in the truck door, which we knew was true because we were there when it happened. That story led right into one about the day his epileptic uncle pulled a V8 out of an Oldsmobile with his bare hands. The way his eyes went red as he stood up with the whole works balanced on the inside of his forearms. How he shook, and the pressure blew his boots off.

Someone finally just started calling him Whopper. The shock on his face said he knew for sure he'd been tagged. For the rest of that Saturday, every time someone called him Whopper, everyone would crack up, rolling on a lawn under a jacaranda tree, flowers crushed under our brown backs, hysterical in the delight of such an outrageous disgrace of one of our own. Whopper kept trying to threaten us into dropping his new name but it was no use.

Didn't stop him from lying though. He'd quit for a while, then he'd get away with a little lie. Then he'd try a larger one to see if he could still pull it off. We'd bust him. He'd even cry when we didn't believe him. It got so he'd really bug you.

In July, he tried to pad his batting average and we caught him. We shouted the lie at him through the fence when he got to bat, watched him strike out. We mentioned it at the concession stand in front of his sisters. Brought it up about ten times during the long walk home after the game. He took it pretty bad. He'd want to fight, but being in the wrong, his heart wasn't really in it. We laughed at him instead.

That turned out to be his last lie. We didn't notice at the time really, but by the time we got back to school, Whopper hadn't whopped since baseball season.

First day at school, at the bike racks. A cloud of dust and a deep circle of boys. Fight's gonna start. I'm walking over with Whopper beside me. About twelve sixth-grade boys are in a circle, yelling in horror. And in the center is Jimmy Johnson, the toughest sixth grader who ever lived.

Jimmy Johnson was already building a reputation that was to peak two years later in the eighth grade, when he got impatient only being the toughest kid in junior high. He wanted the high school. He made sure the word got to the toughest kid there, a Golden Gloves boxer named Matranga. Then Jimmy went right up to the guy in the middle of school and said, "Let's go somewhere where the teachers can't protect you."

That afternoon at a hamburger stand, in front of about three hundred kids, Jimmy Johnson kicked the shit out of Matranga. Thirty seconds. It was strange to see the will of someone evaporate like it did in Matranga. Jimmy showed him a whole different level of violence. It went beyond trying to hurt someone or sensing victory or anything like that.

It was without honor or logic. It was Jimmy doing what he was born to do. And when Matranga's car keys popped out of his jacket pocket, Jimmy snatched them off the ground and threw them on the burger stand roof. Jimmy yelled to his buddy Benny. Benny tossed him a can of lighter fluid. He sprays down the guy's hair and lights him up. Whoosh! Matranga ran around like a horror movie until a couple of friends threw him down and smothered the flames. By then, Jimmy and Benny were gone.

At the bike racks, Whopper and I approach the circle and peer through the shoulders. Jimmy Johnson is down on his hands and knees, cutting the legs off of a thrashing ten-inch alligator lizard. The lizard has red stubs at its tail and at one leg. Jimmy puts the leg in front of the lizard's mouth hoping he'll eat it, which he doesn't. Jimmy is getting ready to cut off another leg when Whopper says:

"You have to stop doing that."

Whopper is in the fourth grade, a third Jimmy's size and skinny. Jimmy Johnson's got nothing to prove. I'm standing next to Whopper, praying Jimmy hasn't heard him.

"Or what?"

As soon as Whopper begins to talk he sounds miles away.

"I'll try to kick your ass."

All the boys go "Whoooaaa" at Whopper and start laughing at him. Jimmy ignores him. Whopper says, "I mean it, Jimmy."

When Jimmy presses the knife on the large joint of a hind leg, Whopper pushes past a couple of kids and shoves Jimmy over. Jimmy struggles to keep his balance, but finally falls on his back holding the lizard in the air so that it doesn't hit the ground and get crushed in his hand. He's protecting it. The lizard twists its head, snaps the air, three legs twitching and a red stump left for a tail, like the burning end of a cigar. Jimmy's getting his awkward body realigned, pressing one hand on the ground, pulling his legs under his hips, using one knee and then the other to finally stand. He seems to be waiting to hear the boys snickering behind his back. Something seems to be crying deep inside.

For the first time I notice that he's wearing big, stupid-looking hard-soled shoes, the fashion of geezers at the beach. His head is plastered with a lot of vaseline melting in the sun, his scalp visible through his very thin hair. I try to see it all at once, but I lose it beyond a vague sympathy for the lonely awkward life of Jimmy Johnson. But he is focusing on Whopper with an expression saying, *"I'll fuck you up in a minute."*

Then he puts the lizard back on the ground and slices off two legs. He stares at it, hunting for the connection beween the lizard's fate and his part in it as its vengeful god.

Jimmy stands up. The circle widens, like it wants to get a little distance, but at the same time it moves and shrugs and jumps and ooohs and ahhhhs and groans like it's alive. Jimmy starts punching Whopper's arms and shoulders, letting him know how hard he hits. But Whopper doesn't try to run. So Jimmy moves in, going for his head. Knots and bumps turning purple on Whopper's face, nasty gaps forming over his cheeks and eyes. And Whopper keeps swinging anyway, making Jimmy more and more pissed.

What should I do? Jump in? Get the crap kicked out of me in front of everyone? Just because Whopper feels the same thing as I do about torturing a lizard, but has the guts to do something about it? What I'm seeing being done to him, I don't want done to me.

I think fascination is not necessarily a good thing. I mean, we didn't want to watch. But everyone did anyway. And we would have looked if Whopper was the lizard and Jimmy was chopping him up with an axe. It's one of those unclassified sins. You will watch. But there was something clean in it anyway, as certain uses of our spirit can sanitize anything no matter how foul, because Whopper wouldn't quit. Like he was taking it from nothing but an ass kicking and making it into something else. We waited for him to quit. We couldn't see any point not to. Except Whopper had discovered something that was beyond anything he'd ever felt. It was pure purpose. Whopper was the only one with the balls to go in. I'm not making myself clear. I mean that Whopper had found something — new territory, a place that he ruled, his place. He was between Jimmy's knees and on the ground, but he'd get to his feet just to get pounded like no one we've ever seen get pounded.

Guys are yelling at Jimmy to quit, and Jimmy is yelling back.

"Not until he does!"

Whopper keeps swinging, once or twice landing something feeble on Jimmy's face. But the little pop bouncing off Jimmy's head had so much . . . I don't know . . . class. Finally, Jimmy goes nuts. Blood is flying in the air, girls are crying, but Whopper only gets more determined. I mean you can see the thread of concentration. It seems kind of calm. He was definitely following something and it was changing him into someone else. Hammered at the bike racks on Jimmy's anvil like they are in it together. Like Whopper needed Jimmy to show us his heart. I can't believe what I'm seeing. My feet are buried in concrete. I just stand there. Time already stopped.

Some little kids peek in the circle and start screaming and a teacher is running over. We all scatter for different parts of the canyons. Some girls wait around to give the teacher names.

I walk home with Whopper, following him down the canyon trail, listening to him cry and catch his breath. What am I supposed to say? He must hate every one of us who didn't back him up. I would if I was him. I'd especially hate me. He always calls me his best friend. I'm even a year older. I feel two things real strong. The first is that I am proud to be walking with him. The second is that I am ashamed of myself. But at that point, the distance between us was so far that I knew he couldn't blame me. I could see that he didn't. I mean, he was pissed, but who wouldn't be? I wanted to tell Whopper everything I just told you but I can't get the words at the time and he wouldn't listen anyway. So I just say:

"Man, that was the bravest thing I ever saw."

"Stupidest."

He answers in a way that had a sort of joke behind it, one word, calling it stupid, not saying it bitter but more like I said, a joke.

I couldn't believe it. I left it alone.

He told me for a while he hoped somebody would stop it. But when he saw no one would, he figured what the fuck.

Then he says, "Where were you?"

So I lie to him. I tell him I thought he didn't want the fight stopped. Then I go further and tell him I was thinking about helping him, but a couple of Jimmy's friends were looking at me, waiting. I knew it right away. I wished I'd never said it.

"Don't lie, Eddie. . . . Don't lie to me."

He looks like he's gonna bust me in the face. He was pretty hot and he had a lot he wanted to tell me, but it's plain I wouldn't understand. Nobody would. Maybe my Uncle Adrian. But none of us Whopper's age. The rest of us will just have to wonder if we'll ever have balls.

I am as amazed at this ascension as if he had sprouted wings and lifted right up off the ground. And everything he did told me he was free now. He couldn't change it if he wanted to. I always saw him in the air from then on. I mean like, in the air. I noticed how he always sat in the highest place. Like on the kitchen counter, or the tree in the front yard. He began talking about parachutes and astronauts. This is gonna sound funny but he seemed kind of wise, informed or something. I mean right there, he knew more than either of our fathers or any of our older brothers. I knew it wouldn't last to tomorrow but I knew for sure that right then he could tell me about things even our mothers didn't know about men. He was in on the secret.

Whopper stands for a minute, starts to walk, mumbles and sits down. He looks at me through the bruised mush around his eyes. I check out his cuts and stuff. An eyebrow has a slit that is still bleeding. He hangs his head to see how much of a puddle he can make. He tries to write his name with the drops in the dirt. He has put a tooth through his lower lip. His cheeks are blue and black, skinned and filled with dirt. His hands are raw. He's a mess.

He stares at the skin hanging off his knuckles — bright red orange scrapes you can almost see through. He chews off a large piece in the middle of his hand.

I look back up the trail, the fence on the top of the mesa is filled with kids and teachers. They're all staring down the hill. One teacher is calling out Whopper's real name, but since we're behind a stand of manzanita, we can't be seen.

I can tell Whopper's beginning to see what he's done. It's beginning to dawn on him that it's all over. He has made it. The isolation he felt in the fight was really the isolation of his own courage.

I tell him about the fight. Some of it he didn't remember and it strikes him as funny. He laughs a couple of times. He says, "Really?" when I describe how brave and tough he was. I even tell him about how he looked changed and the anvil and all. He smiles like he thinks I'm crazy.

We walk home the long way, wondering what his mother is gonna say. I ask him if he is ever going to talk about it. It seems to me to be the only way to get something out of this for himself. He can't really just go back to being who he was. He doesn't answer.

"Because it would be so righteous if you didn't."

Whopper says, "Why?"

I don't say anything. I just hoped he'd figure it out. I can see him hiding the smile on his busted lips the color of plums. He stumbles down on the edge of a deer trail overlooking a huge patch of anise. The stuff grows all over San Diego, thickets of bamboo-like stalks with big splayed flowers — tall, sometimes eight feet. The seeds taste like licorice.

He mumbles, "Yeah, I'll act like it didn't even happen."

He practices the shrug he's gonna use when people ask him about it. Every boy and girl in school will think he is God. Still, none of us would have done what he'd done to make it that way.

It worked. At school his name became ironic, like the names they give huge guys, calling them Tiny or Half-Pint. Overnight, Whopper was a name of honor.

Except at his house, because his little brother wasn't buying it. Whopper and his little brother had problems. They hated each other and I guess I was a part of it. We did things to him we shouldn't have. He was only a year younger than Whopper but we treated him real bad. He brought it on himself because he demanded so much attention. So we used to beat him up all the time. Like one year on his birthday, we tried to set records for making him cry. We got him eleven or twelve times on his tenth birthday. And he was real hard to make cry, because he had a lot of pride and he was tough as hell. In a way, he was even tougher than Whopper. Everything we did was as far as it could go. We were masters of ridicule, and knew how to cover what hurt our feelings, and say things that would really hurt his. We didn't want it to be that way but the meanness had a life of its own. Nobody could stop it.

Then Whopper decided he needed to bridge the gulf of trust between him and his little brother. The time had come to put hate behind them and form a team of brothers, a gang. All for one and all that. It sounded like a good idea since we were getting into too much shit with the old man over all the "roughhouse crap," as he called it.

Whopper stopped fucking with his little brother, told him how sorry he was, that he was his brother and, as such, they had to trust each other. And what they needed was a ritual to restore that trust.

His brother told him, "Yeah? Well fuck you."

This went on for days. Whopper telling him that it was the most important thing in the world for him to reestablish the trust that brothers need to become men. A couple of times Whopper nearly cried. He meant it, I could see that. It was always on Whopper's mind; they just had to pass this test of trust together or they'd never become men.

Finally Whopper proposed the "ritual of trust" as he said it a million times all day long whenever he had the chance. Whopper wanted his brother to stand on the edge of the roof, with his eyes closed and his arms spread like an eagle, with Whopper standing behind him. After that they could trust each other and be true brothers . . . after the ritual of trust.

It took Whopper all summer to get him to listen. Around Halloween he got him to come up on the roof with him for just one minute, no blindfold, and Whopper on the far side of the roof. But his brother wouldn't go back up there, saying that was enough ritual of fucking trust for him. It took working on him day and night during Christmas vacation to get him to finally do it. His little brother was beginning to believe. I would have, too. Whopper had been the perfect big brother since the fight at the bike racks.

It was the day before Christmas. There was Whopper, walking with his blindfolded brother. Whopper talking in a low quavering voice, speaking of the ecstasy of blind brotherly trust, right into the ear of his brother. He led him to the edge and told him he had to let go of his hand so that he could stand behind him. His little brother stood unafraid, free of the mistrust and hurt of the past. Ritual of trust. Solemn occasion of brothers turning into men.

They looked like angels up there, their faces in the blue

sky. The winter sun glowing golden and pale behind them. I was amazed again at what Whopper had become. I knew I could rise too. I could become a man who could atone for my wrongs. I could stand up for the right things, all of that. A smile broke under the blindfold. Whopper's face went cold and he pushed his brother off the roof. His little brother didn't believe it. He thought it was a cosmic trick. Or maybe he went into shock or was just dumbfounded, because he held his position like a diver. He did a head plant from a ten foot roof onto a cement stair. Everything slowed down. The blindfold jammed down to his little brother's shoulders, his neck disappeared, and he looked like he stood on his head for a long time before he crumpled. I swear, the noise is what made the neighbors look out of their doors. The sound wasn't like anything else I'd heard, a melon or something. I got scared, like we'd finally done it this time. Whopper was ecstatic. His arms spread like an eagle, his head cocked to one side, looking over the edge at his unconscious brother.

"Sucker."

It was plain Whopper thought he had done something important. He didn't feel the need to celebrate it with me. I don't think Whopper thought there was anyone else there. It was his thing. His brother was a part of it but it was his. I got my voice and said:

"Shit Whopper, ya killed him."

The little brother wheezed a deep breath and his eyes fluttered like mad.

"He'll be OK. Don't sweat."

As weird as it sounds, Whopper looked kind again, more like an angel than ever.

"It's the best thing I could have done for him."

I started walking and it was like the street was asleep. People were looking out of their doors. The cop across the street was frozen on his lawn with his hands on his hips and his mouth open. Nobody moved, except Whopper, who was doing a little slow spin dance with his arms spread out and his face to the sky above.

I took the long way home through the canyon bottom, winding along the edges of trickling storm ditches, slipping along mossy stones, old underwear and wads of stringy paper. I can still see Whopper on the roof, turning in that circle.

After he got out of the hospital, the little brother wore a white turban on his head until after Lincoln's Birthday. Talked like he'd been drinking for the rest of the year. Their mother never trusted Whopper again. She hardly spoke to him for a long time. Their big sister left that year for Texas. And then the years just passed like clouds and all of us lost touch.

Jimmy Johnson got killed in his second tour in Vietnam as gunner on a helicopter. Whopper got murdered in a bad drug deal. He brought his little brother along — they killed him too.

HEY KID, YER A BANGER

THERE'S A BEAUTIFUL BLACK TILE doorway leading into the Sixth Avenue Gymnasium and Boxing Club in old town San Diego. Bookmakers, sportswriters, slumming socialites, sharks, punch-drunks, pimps, trainers, and fighters have been crossing its threshold since 1912. Sixty years ago, fighters coming up and going down fought just across the border in Rosarito Beach. The Hollywood elite spent summers below the border, gambling and lavishing purses heavier than anything a guy could squeeze out of the cutthroat promoters in the USA.

A bent old figure rose from the drinking fountain, wiping his lips with the back of his hand. His age suggested a crisp discolored leaf, or days when horses still rattled their carts down Sixth Avenue, when one war was won and the next three were yet to be fought.

The old man turned painfully and tottered around the outside of the ring, reeling over his collapsed hip.

Eddie looked down at his own skinny white legs swinging beneath him toward the heavy bag. He shuffled to his left, released a flurry of punches into the bag's midsection and backed up. He took a lot of pride in his speed. He figured in a few more months he'd develop a punch to go with it, and then after a little more time with the old man, maybe he'd get in the ring and see what he could do. He sensed a change in the room. His hands dropped to his sides.

A young woman stood two steps in from the front door. In the bleachers, conspiratorial heads bent closer together, eyes fixed on her. She was tiny, a perfection of hips and curves, all the more appealing in miniature because of the power that emanated from her like a contradiction. Fighters began to hit harder, dance faster. In the gallery, forced laughter rang from one corner to another. Whispers grew into audible comments. If her body understood the craving around her, she seemed oblivious to it.

Her gaze searched the corner where Eddie stood. She took a place by herself in the bleachers. Eddie turned to the heavy bag, but dropped his hands again. Embarrassed, he pretended to need an answer from the old man. He crossed the room. She ignored him, fanning herself with a folded sports section. She crossed her legs and her skirt rode to the middle of her thigh.

The old man cleared his throat.

"Yeah, kid, whatja want?"

"Oh, uh, I was wondering if. . . . "

". . . Maybe that girl in the stands is looking for a fighter?"

Eddie's face grew hot.

"No . . . I uh, . . ."

"She's got a fighter."

"No . . . I wasn't. . . . "

Eddie lowered his voice.

". . . thinking about the girl. . . ."

"Bullshit, kid. I can see right through you. Is that what you are? Bullshit?"

"Hey, c'mon."

"I'm putting you in with Ray in twenty minutes."

Eddie's mouth opened and shut. He was not ready for Ray. He wasn't ready for anyone, especially Ray.

"That's what yer here for kid, am I right?"

Fear jumped jagged through his bones and spun in his stomach. He couldn't reply. His heart thundered.

"Isn't it? Kid?"

The old man yawned wide and turned to end the discussion, calling over his shoulder, "Twenty minutes, kid."

Eddie made it to the heavy bag.

"Ray Starkey, you're in with Eddie Burnett in twenty minutes."

The old man's voice boomed. The bleachers responded with a flurry of activity.

Ray Starkey's voice echoed as he came out of the locker room.

"I had five rounds yesterday, Pops."

"Yer getting five more today. Twenty minutes."

"OK, Pops. Whatever you say."

Eddie fought the urge to unwrap his hands, to take a little humiliation and leave. He tried to think up an excuse that would sound right when he'd have to explain. The room closed in.

He lost his heart. He began unwrapping his hands. He heard mumbling from the bleachers. He heard steps coming up behind him. The old man unwound the remaining twists, smoothed the wrinkled cotton and rewrapped.

"C'mon kid, just do what I taught ya."

As Eddie began to plan a way to lose like a man, the thought hit him.

"I'm a coward. I'm too afraid to walk out of here, and too afraid to fight."

The old man pulled the tape tight, breaking Eddie's trance.

"I just want you to get a feel for it, see what it's like. Starkey ain't gonna kill ya, kid. You'll be alright."

Eddie could hear Starkey walking down the bleachers. He heard him begin to hit the bag. The thuds shuddered through the room.

"Just use your speed to stay out of his way. I just want him to get a little tired. Just don't trade any punches with him for Christsake." Eddie's corner faced the bleachers.

Bell.

Everything was brighter, higher, quicker. Eddie and Ray started innocently. But after the first two exchanges, they went into another world. They stepped in. They stepped up. They slugged it out.

"Hey hey, kid."

Eddie's footwork was reduced from flying strides in workouts to a shift of one inch, enough to find room to return a shot under the elbows, into the ribs, on the side of the head on the way out, all the while holding ground and absorbing the thuds and jolts of pain. The intimacy horrified Eddie.

Bell.

"Hey, kid. What the hell ya doing in there?"

Eddie waited in the corner for the second round. No stool. Headgear isn't right, gloves too clumsy to adjust it, too tight, too loose, something. When Ray connected, he might as well not have the thing on. He knew he didn't get to Ray half as much as Ray got to him. He wanted to quit. That was impossible now. He wanted to puke. That might be possible.

Bell.

Ray rushed him and pounded him backwards. Six unanswered punches landing first on his face and then falling to his neck and arms as Eddie lost ground and headed back to the ropes.

"Easy, Ray. Easy."

Eddie exploded into Ray, desperate to give him some back. A few men in the bleachers started yelling. Eddie connected, missed wild, and connected again deep into Ray's ribs.

Someone yelled, "Upstairs!"

Eddie shot a hard jab into Ray's nose and blood blew over Ray's mouth. The gym groaned. Ray went into another gear.

"Ray! Ray! Hey!"

A tide of bloodlust washed from the outside into the ring. Eddie saw the ropes beside him. His elbows drew into his body. His face dug into his gloves. A hammer was denting the bones of his forearms, banging in a slow, controlled rhythm. Ray was measuring him. Ray was setting him up. Eddie was his heavy bag.

"Kid, get outta there!"

He felt Ray move to his left. Something hurt Eddie to the point of a kind of horror. From just above his left hip, a flash exploded into the middle of his chest. His breath exploded out his mouth. His left foot left the canvas, his body rose, his mouthpiece fell. His mouth empty. He had to get out. He could not take — Another flash exploded near to the impact of the first, but his feet swept the floor and turned. Something whistled past his ear. His stomach caved in over a hot busting blast that took what little air he had. He got his shoulders square to Ray and slid along the ropes. Ray took deep breaths, waiting. He let Eddie move to the center of the ring.

Eddie realized Ray thought Eddie beneath him. Someone to punish, someone to put away and to smirk, "Nice fight," after the pats on his back were over. Eddie pulled Ray toward him, feigning collapse of nerve. Ray's pursuing shots were weak taps. He believed Eddie would retreat to the corner again. But Eddie stopped two feet from the corner and caught Ray walking into him with a right. The thumb caught him over the lips. His knuckles spun the headgear and Ray's head followed. Ray lost his balance. Eddie stood over him. A feeling similar to God standing Eddie on his feet. Ray was nearly down and Eddie knew he could hit him a lot harder if he could last long enough to see his chance. It was something joyful. A promise of what he needed from somewhere within that he never knew existed.

Eddie swung on instinct, the wrong hand. A left landed

under Ray's neck. Ray regained his balance. Then Eddie threw a punch that couldn't really have happened. Ray took it on the hinge of his jaw. He dropped like a doll.

Bell.

The men in the bleachers looked at each other then shook their heads. They were still solid on Ray. Men leaned on hips digging wallets, jackets opened and money changed hands.

Voice yelling, "Ray all the way!"

"Oh! Fuck you! You want Eddie?"

"I'll give you two to one! You like that kid?"

"Twenty bucks? Come on!"

"Ray'll kill him."

A second passed. Same voice, "Anybody. Three to one, Ray nails him in the next two rounds!"

Eddie sick and dizzy, looked at the straw hat above the seated bystanders. The man wearing it defying them to take his bet. A small crowd of heads met over the bag of a man in the stands. The straw hat reached down and everyone started to laugh. He threw a towel in Eddie's corner. It bounced off the top rope and landed down on the floor.

Eddie nearly laughed himself. Everything stopped cold. Everything changed. Eddie knew it was a different world now. Those outside saw him but didn't want to believe it. Wanted him to fade on himself, knowing it was the only chance they had to remain above him. Eddie stared at the towel knowing that all that was behind him.

The room was loud and then it settled to silence. Ray was getting checked. Eddie wanted it over. The conversation went on. The bell should have rung. An argument. What was going on? The bell should have rung. Ray was nodding his head. Ray argued. Ray wanted more.

Bell.

Ray charged, but his heart wasn't in it. He had talked his way in. Or someone had talked him in. Eddie was part of that too. The bets were all laid against him. Everyone sat in hopeful consensus. They were calling it a lucky shot.

Eddie had a mean surprise. From the top of his shoulder down through his wrist, electricity jumped through the flesh of his cocked right arm. He tapped his left into Ray's face. Ray wanted more rib. He crouched smaller hoping to set up an uppercut. Eddie could have laughed.

Eddie shuffled twice to the left and there was Ray's huge slow head trying to turn to face him as Eddie's left hook spun his wet hair in a wild circle sending a shower down the front of Eddie's legs. Eddie planted his feet and drove a right between Ray's elbows losing half of its power. Ray nearly fell. His eyes widened and he backed up. Eddie realized the intimacy of this fighting brought with it telepathic communication. He saw Ray so clearly he could hear what he was thinking. He addressed Ray and his face responded as though he were saying the words:

Com'ere motherfucker I got this . . .

Another left exploded on Ray's face. Ray dropped his left glove, his eye dimmed.

. . . for ya.

Eddie popped up on his toes and flashed down with a right, then popped a left under his shoulder to stand him up. Then threw again with everything behind it, something crunched behind Ray's headgear and he dropped, unstrung. Eddie made his way to the corner looking over his shoulder. Ray was flat on his back, one knee twitching. Eddie stared for less than half a second. In it, Eddie saw the woman in the doorway, her legs spread, his tongue soaking her.

The old man was saying something. Five words, began with, "Hey, kid. . . ."

But the rest didn't matter. Eddie knew he could kill and it turned out to be closest to the awe of church. He wanted to get down on his knees before something and beg for an end to what evil remained in his heart. He had the knowledge of the pulpit, he wore black without being ordained. He could comfort, he could punish. He'd come close to the left hand, and he hated what it had made of him. His life had come down to one monstrous moment of self-love.

He had been there, and the guilt was branded in the beginning of any thoughts of himself. Any voice giving his life a meaning would be invalid. A declaration of love would be a tragic mistake. A long trail leading toward sudden euphoria and plunges into misery. He'd forever worship at an altar of his own making, in celebration of who he was and what that meant. The guilt was here to stay. Every time his fist closed, his hand would be empty.

BLUE

I BACK INTO A DARK ROOM, surrounded in a hot enclosure of fog. Her eyes are feline; the soles of her shoes embedded with little hard-earned diamonds of broken glass from broken streets, reminders that you can leave but something comes with you.

Her mouth is on mine. She brings tears to my eyes when she bites here for a second, letting up to give a second's relief, the pain reverberating and then gone. Like a message about the events of what is before us, what lingers, what passes. She's always immediate, like storms, prides, packs, tribes. She is insistent, demanding. Why does this make me think of forgiveness, of solitude, of a state of grace?

Androids watch us from another room. Shafts of light give their features razor angles, lending any expression an amplification. A smile is the baring of teeth. Repose is a judgmental stare, a long look, a century to come. Past caring. Travelers beyond our time. They turn in unison. One throws open a window and begins to sing a dirge over the cracked and bleeding streets.

She wants to get me off, to put me someplace safe, someplace I have been in collected seconds over my past decades —a place I belong. She pushes me further into the room, into the deeper shadow. Her laced boot, with a galaxy glinting in her soul, kicks the door closed. Her hand gripped tight and me thinking,

"*I've never let anyone jerk me off.*"

Never had a hand on me, and her grip remains the gravest and most hopeful coming death and sacred send-off. I look at my hand stretched out before me catching the light. I see through the skin. Cables pull at muscle. Blood rushes in, presses out, rushes in. I put my hand over my eyes.

I'll never come. Her mouth breathes hot, and in her chest, a groan rises like lava up the vent of a volcano, bringing the message and another burning bite. I wonder if this is coming . . . if this is coming . . . if this is coming, while her hips rock and her grip tightens. My cheek is between her teeth and her warm spit splatters on my face timed with groans that can only mean, to my amazement, that getting me off will get this sweet girl off.

And I can't think anymore, something takes over. Is this coming . . . is this coming . . . is this coming, and I give it up. I go blind. I leave all things behind, and Baby Girl who can cut you in, or cut you out, opens her soft eyes and I'm not making sense saying:

"Red tide. Sticky when you get out. Most people don't like it. Glows in the dark."

And she asks, "Glows in the dark? Really? Never heard of it." The Androids lean against the door, their weight creaking the floorboards.

And I say, "Yeah, glows in the dark. Really beautiful."

I'm glistening under a streetlamp, shining like a smeared star. Blue like the lonely moon.

WEAK

I was in withdrawals. The sound of sixty thousand people celebrating a catch that you weren't sure you could pull off is a rush that is hard to duplicate. Waiting under the lights for a kickoff to drop out of the sky in the clear cold night, the adrenaline coursing through your legs as you run on instinct, making a cut here and dodging a flying assassin there, is an experience that every young man ought to have. The beauty of it is that so few do.

Walking into the stadium before a game, high on a handful of bennies, headphones raging "Exile on Main Street." Anticipating a night where anything is possible. Abject failure and injury or the pinnacle of accomplishment. The come-from-behind victory. Circus catches and the party afterwards. The women getting you a beer, the guys hanging around laughing and coming down with a few joints. Driving out to the beach with Diane, feeling the aches begin as the adrenaline wears off. Listening to the radio, hearing the news broadcast announcing the touchdowns you scored and the smile you just couldn't hide. An ego thing that you have no choice but to give in to because it is just too cool. And you want more. You want it to go on forever. Keeping it going at the big relay meets in the spring. Running down someone with a lead like they are standing still and the crowd on the fence screaming their heads off.

You can't stop. It's a life so full of camaraderie, challenge and adrenal/ego rushes that it's hopeless to consider quitting. You just keep going until they say you can't play anymore or you just aren't fast enough.

The echoes of roaring stadiums still haunted me. But it was gone. I fed the memory like an addict. I couldn't let it go. But I wasn't playing anymore, and the next step up was the pros or the Olympics. I was a husband and a father, splitting time between trying to be a man and wanting to be a boy again. I was living in the past, certain that I could still pull it off if I had taken the chance, if I'd believed in myself just a little more. Getting high enough to fantasize victory at one more Olympic trial, or walking into pro camp and fighting my way in. Getting it worked out in my mind, rolling another joint.

I was living in Los Angeles. Rubbing elbows with hipsters fresh from the Rolling Thunder Revue. Hanging out with movie stars, hard-time fallers, ascenders, heroes, saints, whores, gypsies. All of them dying piece by piece. All of them tough enough to laugh it off.

I was just hanging out, carrying what I thought was my own weight. Included in the tribe of dervish angels. Invited to the party, in on the shit in the back room. Watching the big dice roll and the bloody knuckle closing the nostril over some of the most beautiful smiles in the world. Around sundown on a porch overlooking the private beaches of Malibu, celebrating a friend's Academy Award. Watching the pelicans coasting and sliding the troughs of breakers, the sun dropping like Icarus into the blue horizon. Cocktails clinking, faces all over the place competing for the funniest line, the coolest vibe, looking for the best sex. Everybody hallucinating on fame, wealth, power and every drug you can name. The sweet, sticky taste of marijuana still on my teeth, another joint between my fingers.

Getting all the mileage I could from my athletic past. Not knowing that it is part of the mystery and bullshit of Angelenos to make each other larger than life. I believed it, never guessing that no one paid any attention to what anyone said. It was just a huge mutual adoration society. The echoes of the past making it all seem so much like the reality of the stadium. I'd done the impossible with my body; there was no need to suspect that I hadn't earned the acceptance and backslapping exclusivity of Hollywood too. I knew I had a right to anything Movieland had to offer, that the doorman at the gates to Olympus would recognize me and usher me right through.

There was a big league pitcher hanging out with the hipster underground. Everybody knew his name. Everybody talked about his eccentric tendency to drop a couple hits of acid, go out to the mound and retire the side for a few innings until a laughing fit brought the manager out to point the direction to the dugout. On this afternoon, he was standing next to me listening intently. He wanted to know my story. Wanted to know what had become of me, what had happened, why I had dropped out of sight.

I explained. I told him about the war and how I couldn't stand to compete in front of those masses of Americans wanting me to run down their racist white hope dreams for them. How they wanted me in the big stadium, the biggest game. The Games. Representing apple pie, Mom, and the goose step. How I couldn't keep time with the mindless lemmings jackbooting through suburbia. I pretended an acceptable level of modesty, smiled when he suggested I'd have undoubtedly made it to Montreal. After that, the pros would be almost automatic. I mentioned that the scouts for Dallas, Oakland, and Green Bay had all shown interest. He mentioned the names of my old teammates who were working in the pros now. How I could have done it. Yeah, it was in the bag. I sighed with a kind of weighted resignation. But the war, and the stands full of Nixon backers, and the higher moral ground was so elevated that the events on the field just didn't really justify coming back down. I was just so . . . illuminated up there beyond the clouds that shade those mortals beneath us who just couldn't understand the pressures and the hopes pinned on us by the fans. I had a responsibility to reject and to live beyond the definitions of competition. I was in it for the art and not for the winning or losing. That competition is a metaphor for warfare, and with Vietnam raging, I felt used. I wanted to create great races. I was into transcendence, not out to see who was the better man.

I rolled another joint. I had more to say. The pitcher smoked it with me and I went on. He asked me more questions and I went deeper into my logic. I found new levels of brilliant insight into why I was better than the production of my abilities, beyond the crass expression of my god-given talent. I finished.

He looked at me and said, "That's so weak." And he walked away.

SLIDE

I'M SO SPACED IN THE early morning sun that the question is not where am I, but where will I puke next.

Right here.

My stomach contracts in a single spasm. It's mostly spit. I see a lawn sprinkler and follow the green snake to the spigot, turn it on and return to the splashing puddle in the dirt. The cold water uses my stomach as a trampoline and flies up and out of my mouth. I breathe a little air, then what's left in my stomach blasts out of my nose. Alright, I'll wait.

I circle around like a dog and pass out, curled on my side in the hot sun. I hear voices, tiny and deep from within a cave somewhere in Africa. But when I open my eyes, there are tips of roughout boots in front of my nose. The voices are discussing what to do about me. They're what pass as friends. Big guys who try, and succeed, at making people shit themselves. Last image I can think of is a shotgun in some fuckup's mouth as he gets the time and date straight for his last chance.

We're supposed to be planning the details of setting up a black funk soulster superstar who has a tendency to go off behind cocaine. The object, of course, is to get the funkster's coke and money without getting caught, which would mean getting killed. I had a plan to use two sure things: greed and ego. Get him to overextend himself and then get him irrational when he tries to cover his embarrassment. But before I could work out the cast of characters, I got drunk.

So far, the plan calls for me to deliver a pound and hang around in the front room, waiting for someone to get back from somewhere with a lot of money, and then stall until my friends come in and take us all off. The pretext is women and some problem with airline tickets.

Then my job is not to freak out while all these psychos strut around and try to fuck with me. It's a delicate balance between knowing how much to take and where to draw the line. My bit is stupidity. I am the butt of jokes, conversations going on around me that I shouldn't be hearing, gleaning this, figuring that, then doing something off the wall. It's worked in Mexicali, Juarez, El Centro, San Ysidro, El Cajon and Santee. Now we're gonna give it a try in Malibu.

I'm getting to my feet, listening to my friends argue about my condition. Standing up blinds me for a second. The top of my head comes to their chests. They must weigh two hundred and fifty pounds apiece.

"I'm ready."

I expect the laughs. Here they are. Laughing, then silence. One guy is about to utter a challenge. I can tell because he's from the South, and he telegraphs his hostility by curling his lip — Elvis damage. I interrupt him.

"I'm more effective when I'm underestimated."

He's about to say something devastating to my interests. I edit the movie playing in my head, which stars him in an amazing scene of beating me to a humiliated pulp. The estimates of his weight are ignored behind the central thing in my mind, which is hit him real hard and real fast. Then as he recoils, swarm him. When those thoughts get strong enough, the imagined action follows. Guys are pulling me off and I am praying my target is unconscious. Hit him twice and no one saw the punches. Believe me, if you have the choice between size and speed, take speed. He's doing a little half turn. His upper body is out before his knees know it. He's buckling backward with his knees still trying to hold him up. Finally his heels flick out in the dirt and his back thuds. I start to walk toward the car saying, "Let's stop for breakfast." We cram ourselves into a Valiant and drive off. Beautiful Malibu flying past the open windows, a joint fired and passed around. Going up to Trancas to rip off a superstar. This is the life. Except the radio . . . that seventies music — weird, imitative, overproduced stuff. Right now, the eagles are flying or something, and then someone is running down the road trying to loosen something with women on his mind.

Driving through empty Malibu, up carless Pacific Coast Highway on a hot spring Wednesday makes you feel like you're getting away with something. There's the ease of residential opulence; the only faces you see are locals, and most of the locals are stars, near-stars, were-stars, know-stars, want-to-be stars, think-they-are stars, sexual-partners-to stars, suppliers-of-vice-to stars, parasitic-servants-to stars. And on the road blasting past, you almost think you're rich and famous. Actually you think you're too cool to be famous. Especially if you have Phoenix Program washouts riding with you who manage to kill a couple people a year.

Killers suck the air out of the room, but you have to look close to notice. Intense implies some kind of action or energy. What these guys have is a complete absence of energy, which they try to cover up with an act. Like the funny wheezy guy in Pacific Beach, the sharp-dressing Romeo hair-combing guy from San Ysidro, the four-eyed schoolteacher who always reads the dictionary to improve his vocabulary, and dumbshit losers carrying piano wire, plumber's wrenches and hammers like the ones I'm riding with. Their guns are inside the spare tire in the trunk.

The guy driving changes channels looking for Willie on

the country station. These guys will damn near cry if they hear Willie singing "Somewhere Over The Rainbow." That's almost as scary as the weird scratching habits and teeth-sucking sounds they're always making.

The highway is dead. Everything is going on behind the walls that line a five-mile stretch of PCH. You can grab a glimpse of beach between a restaurant and a gas station. Other than that, it's a rolling line of walls to the west. Behind each one, somebody famous getting sucked by somebody who wants to be. OK, that's jaded, cynical. Every other wall.

Eventually the Spanish tile is left behind. Pass the hidden gates of the Colony, home to huge money and temporary power. The whole place is paranoid. Neighbors never speak except in hails called across the street. Everybody busy with the effects of the latest hit, or big deal, or heavy meeting, or this or that. Usually just pantomimed cool.

"Yeah, bitchin. Thank you, thank you. We are all stars together here. Isn't it just wonderful in the cool terrace and tile hallways in this I'm-scared-to-death-to-get-older-smaller-less-powerful-land? Yes, yes, no autographs here. We are all stars."

All said in waving hands, cool shade tilts, and casual hundred-thousand-dollar-car-door openings. The scared-to-death part reserved for shrinks, or as confessionals to appear human enough to get somebody's pants down. Out here on the narrow Colony streets, it's strictly the celebrity benediction, neither one believing the other. Some remnant of the papal wrist-swinging acknowledgment of access to the high and fucking mighty.

Breakfast is on me. The waitress is in worse shape than we are. She's cranky and nauseated with a healing rope burn on her wrist, nose ring, blond hair, cigarette dangling, eyes patrician and smug, body dreamed up by a fuckbook artist before the age of surgery. See-through cotton dress. Her girlfriend arrives, sits on the inside of her ankle, leans over the counter. Twists the counter stool, left beaver shot, right, left beaver shot, right. Blinding me like a lighthouse beam. Hard to concentrate. Anticipation for the next twist, attempting to keep from being busted. As if she doesn't know. As if she fucking cares. I'll take half a dozen scrambled eggs. Steroids need that extra protein. I rattle three little blue pills out of a plastic brown bottle — Dianabol — discovered by farmboys who wanted to make the team out in Texas and found out the meat their daddies put on a steer could be the meat they put on themselves for the Cotton Bowl. People will tell you steroids create a feeling of invincibility. I'll tell you, a couple months on a steroid cycle, and if a cop car gets too close, you'll rip its door off. Makes you horny, too.

Up on my feet heading for the lighthouse. Big smile. No response. Under-my-breath request for a couple of lines. Girl never looks at me. I take the little envelope that materializes out of her hip pocket. My Frye boots galump toward the bathroom. Her voice sounds like Jodie Foster accepting the Deepest Voice in America Award.

"Sixty bucks."

I'm still thudding my heels toward the men's room, slow and steady like a gunfighter. Sometimes I act like that if a woman blows me off and makes me disgusted at myself. I should just tell her I want attention.

"Hey, I said sixty bucks."

She's used to being paid attention to. This is a contest of wills. I'm in the men's room. She's in the men's room. I lock the stall door behind me. She's coming over the top of the stall. She's pissed, yelling this amazing shit at me. I say, "Go ahead," to all her threats, throwing in, "I hope you do," to a couple of her suggestions. Envelope is open; she's pulling my hair above the toilet tank. One of my friends is laughing a beery, bluster-boy haw haw. She's getting tired and isn't yelling. She's hissing, "son-of-a-bitch-mother-fucker" at me. Fingernails in my scalp. Alright already.

"Hey hey hey. . . . Here, take it. I was just kidding."

She pushes me around the stall.

"Asshole."

Yeah, sorry, I know. She fills a spoon, puts it under my nose. Boom. Malibu dentist's daughter I guess.

By the time we get to Trancas, the funkman has departed. He's living elsewhere. His parties have come to the attention of the police. His guests' drunk driving has become a problem for tourists. The general scene is turning sour. I'm getting this from a guy who feels important for a second, having all this information about a famous hipster-superstar. I gotta put up with it. It's pretty warm today; all the windows are open and this guy is wearing one of those huge knit hats that flop down around one shoulder. He's wearing tight, tight, tight pants. It's plain to see it hurts him to move, but he must think it's worth it. His shirt has huge wet rings under each arm. Little drops are running rivulets down his shiny black neck. He walks back and forth across the deep shag rug, sniffing deep with a knuckle pressing first one then another nostril closed.

"Where is he? We're late already with this and my man said he was pissed."

He ignores me.

"OK, well, when he asks about it I'll just. . . . What's your name?"

He sneers at me.

"OK, I don't need to know your name. I'll just say you said that he should fuck himself."

He starts telling me about my white ass.

"Let's just drop the racial shit, OK?"

He's not listening.

"OK, OK . . . right before you get to the part about the last

four hundred years and all, why don't you just call Adolph?"
He asks me who the fuck is Adolph.

"Adolph is the man who takes care of your boss."

He yawns and tells me the studio is in Oxnard. He bought a house. It's better for him out there — no white folks hanging around. God, the guy doesn't quit. I ask him if it's near Pt. Mugu. He says it is. I ask if it's around the Angels' place and he says it's across the fucking street. I tell him thanks and if he talks to his meal ticket, which he will, to tell him we're on our way.

"What do you mean, meal ticket?"

"Just tell him."

Oxnard is where the pigs, like all pigs, will look the other way after their taste. We get up there past Pt. Dume, around the corner of a huge rock along the highway, and we meet a few friends at a little bar for a couple of beers. We try to see if our program is together, but it's hopeless. We can't remember anything, so we decide to play it by ear. A couple of guys stay at the bar and we call the Angels. We ask one of them to go across the street to see if anyone's home. He comes back saying there is. That, it turns out, was probably our mistake. Angels are so fast. I mean, you give them a half second to fuck something up for you and next thing you know you're saying, "Ow, ow, ow."

We drive over and watch three big dogs' heads pogoing over a redwood fence. After a minute or two of standing around timing our spit and the dogs' heads, we hear a whistle and the dogs are rounded up. A man asks us what we want, and we try to sound like gangsters in an old movie but we start laughing. The fence gate opens. An old black man looks at us. He's got to be the funkman's father. He lets us in, closes the gate. He's a little drunk . . . and he's holding a gun.

"You funny guys?"

"You drunk?"

"Yeah, you funny?"

"Where's your son?"

"Which son? I got eight."

"Oh, c'mon. . . . "

"You crazy?"

"Yeah, sometimes."

"Sometimes" hits the old man's funny bone. He doubles over. I get embarrassed. I feel my face getting red. I knew right there that something was real wrong.

The patchy lawn is dotted with white and brown piles — every square inch. The place stinks. The door to the house is wide open. Doris Day is singing "Que Será Será" over a zillion-dollar sound system. An Amazon crosses the doorway. Three-inch platforms put her about eight feet tall. After she leaves, a voice comes from inside, whiny, and at the same time trying to be demanding. It's a man's voice squeaking like a neurotic queen. It's the kind of voice that has no power but instead wears you down — a "with-it" smart-ass assuming a superior position over somebody.

My eyes adjust to the darker room. A little white guy is sitting on the sofa. Blousy shirt, sunglasses. Guy talks fast — East Coast — makes a point of using it. Trying to conjure up mean-ass streets to someone over the telephone. I hate that shit. I begin to realize he's doing a version of what he thinks is Mick Jagger. A lot of these guys are doing that androgynous bad boy bit these days. He knows he has my attention and carelessly lets a little English lower-class nasal snarl rise at the end of his sentences. Fake people busting themselves everywhere.

He's a mogul of some kind, using the funkman's name. It begins to dawn on me that he is directing this stream of abuse to the funkman. He's screaming now about money, then a couple insults. Whoa, personal insults. Definitely impressive.

I walk out the door because I'm too stupid to be impressed. He'll have to try something else. The Amazon clomps up behind me. Eight feet easy. She's talking to the guys and wearing a loose halter top. When's she gonna bend over? Five . . . six . . . seven. Bend. Big jolt when the cleavage shakes loose for a good glimpse. Up . . . big smile. Phoenix Program licks his lips. The other guy drags a few thinning strands of what was once a pompadour through his fingers and does something like a smile or smirk with his mouth. I stuff my hands in my pockets and turn to see if the guy is off the phone. His hands are waving in the air, bouncing up and down on the sofa with each accented threat. There's no telling which continent he grew up on now. He's a cheesy Londoner one phrase and a cheesy Brooklynite the next. He gets quiet and listens. I better fall for his big-shot routine.

The Amazon is telling Elvis damage where the funkman is. Blue mountains outside of Kingston or recording at Muscle Shoals. Someplace, you know how it is, never can tell. He is making a point of looking directly into her halter top. She emphasizes that funkman is elsewhere one too many times. Elvis is going to lose his balance rocking forward on his toes.

I'm back inside. The international big-shot is off the phone and now he's assuming I'll be interested in his problems with superstars. How it's so hard to make them do things when they already have more of everything than they know what to do with. Basic business, a deal is a deal and you gotta be where you say you're gonna be. Yeah . . . right, I understand.

I cut him off before he starts the standard rhapsody beginning with "Well, he's a genius," and blah blah blah. I stand still and ask can I use the phone.

"Sure, go ahead."

He glowers down at the coffee table. A gigantic ashtray is heaped with butts. He lights up. I leave a number out of my home phone. I start talking.

"He's not here." Wait. . . .

"He's in Kingston. . . . I guess so."

I ask the mogul his name.

"A guy here named Phil has just been talking to him. . . . I don't know."

I check to see if Phil is biting. I direct a question to him.

"Phil, do you know when he's coming back?"

Phil shrugs with disgust.

"No telling. . . . What should I do? Bring it back or what?"

Phil sits up on the edge of the couch. I turn to pretend to try and get a little privacy. He stands up and walks to the fireplace and gets a little box from the mantel. He's nonchalant as all hell about it. The phone is gonna make an off-the-hook tone any second.

"Well . . . shit, I don't really know. You want to talk to Phil?"

Phil turns, walking with his hand out for the phone.

"OK . . . then listen. I'll just see what he wants me to do. The money? Yeah, I know."

I hang up. Phil looks a little miffed.

"Phil, Adolph says you can take the load if you want to pay for it all now or get a taste on account to get you through until he gets back from Kingston. What you want to do?"

Phil's dreams are coming true. He says, "I'll take it all now."

He can barely contain himself. I say OK and Phil goes upstairs, saying anxiously, "I'll be right down."

This is a bad situation. Phil doesn't know me. He's ready to pay out a ton of money? Sure. He's ready to set us up before we set him up is what he's ready to do. The Amazon selling funkman's whereabouts tells me he's probably upstairs. This house isn't permanent; he'd never live near the Angels. He's got something going with them, some kind of split. Pretty soon the place is gonna fill up with people. They'll try to fuck up my team.

I walk out to the porch. I look at the guys.

"Let's go."

Just a little direct to Elvis, just a little "gotta go now" in my voice. Over his head. He's watching a carload of women unloading by the gate.

The Amazon is playing with the attack dogs in their cage. "Big boy. Tough boy. So vicious." The guys take it as a hinted invitation. Upstairs, a couple of Angels we know stick their heads out of windows and howl cheerful greetings to us. How the fuck we been? Jokes about watermelons to the black women walking toward the house.

If I press the guys to leave, I'm fucked. I start yelling to the guys upstairs about who's buying the beer. Not them. I collect about ten dollars from people at the front door. I swing my leg over a Schwinn and thunk thunk thunk off the porch steps on a beer run. I leave the guys there.

Out the gate, heading west to find a car to steal or a ride to hitch, whichever comes first. My friends are going to be dosed with big, cringing, paranoiac versions of every nightmare they ever dreamed. What the payback is about must have happened before I got here or maybe this is something initiated by them. The end result is the same. They'll get buried alive in the desert and no one will ever hear from them again. Tied up and thrown in a deep hole, covered over. They'll scream their heads off. They won't gag them. They'll let them talk, let them cry, let them beg, let them scream. I hear he does the digging himself. Has to do with who the baddest man in the valley is, and I guess in this case, it's the guy with the shovel. He's gonna get a ton of blow, kill two guys, and has the other one pedaling like a bastard for home. A good solider would sneak the coke out of the trunk of the car. Too close a call, and I don't have the keys.

There's a party up Decker Canyon. I know this guy. I can't call him a friend, nobody can. He's just finished a movie and is hanging out spending his millions, on what you can guess.

He's the most photogenic young god in Hollywood.

Redford won't work with him. He carries the bad-boy mystique to a point approaching realism, beyond what anyone in Hollywood has done in years. And that's saying something with all the freaks, degenerates, and homicidal maniacs that have been burning their images in the world's brains for the last fifty years or so.

Bruce Lee has been up there for about a week, hanging around and impressing the girls. Conceited little fucker. Don't tell him I said so. Anyway, you've heard about the parties and what all goes on there. He throws the lowest, most barbaric of parties, in lavish style, making it glamorous. And to go with that, he's got a lot of big-wave riders around. Big waves, not to be found in California. The kind in Hawaii, over coral that no one in their right mind challenges. Except them. And they know it. Four or five of them up at the star's house. Idols and legends all high and happy. Pulling dozens of the most amazing eighteen-year-olds you've ever seen. Sprinkled with these fearless women and musicians, or songwriters and actresses, or camera operators who are in their thirties and irresistible if they decide to focus a second or two on you. Everybody fucking 'til the cows come home.

Everything bigger than life and so comfortable with the servants cleaning the slop in seconds. The pool drained of puke, filled and reheated by Mexicans in uniform. Great parties, even if those fucking guys from the Eagles are always hanging around.

But the immediate problem is getting out of Oxnard. Nobody is gonna go too far out of their way, but if they happen to run across me, or if they pin me on their way to funkman's place, or if . . . Jesus, this is the real concern, if they see me on their way to the desert. . . . Well fuck it. . . . That isn't likely to happen for at least a couple of hours. Meanwhile, I'm thinking all this to avoid thinking about pedaling the Schwinn to the parking lot, which is a lot further than

I thought and I'm getting real hot and tired. And I need the motivation before I say "Fuck it" and stop off someplace and get nailed on account of being this lazy fuck, which is what I am. I can't tell you how many guys are sitting around in the slam because they took too much time doing this and that, or stopping off to get a little, or you know, just procrastinating instead of doing the right thing. The right thing is to get out of here.

Too late. Camaro grumbling toward me . . . or is it. . . . No . . . probably not. . . . Yep. It is.

The Camaro pulls to a stop, blocking my path. Nothing but fields around. I can outrun them if I have to.

"Fuckface." He's talking to me.

Doors on either side of the car swung open; three guys pile out. What is all this hostility about? They got on bathing suits, big baggy things about down to the knees, flower prints, big bellies on two and the other — Mr. Washboard. They must be ready to do something; they got the strut going. Why do guys strut? Jesus, like they got a hard-on down the pant leg, or just a dick so huge it has to be dragged behind them or I don't know what.

I'm sitting astride the Schwinn trying to look as confused as I can for the benefit of the tough guy walking real fast, one foot hitching and then sliding and then hitching and sliding. And because they're moving fast, they gotta hop along sideways in order to keep the strut. Looks so stupid. But they're serious, I can tell. One of them is looking over his shoulder for traffic. Highway Patrol always uses this cut-off.

I lay the Schwinn down on its side. A butterfly darts in and out of the spokes. Every time something violent happens or is gonna happen, I see a butterfly flitting around. I remember being in a football game once and right down the line of scrimmage goes this little white butterfly. Made the whole scene seem stupid. Another time, I got jumped by about a million black dudes. They got out of their car, left the doors open, and with the radio blaring "My Girl," they tap-danced on me and my friend's heads. A moment filled with irony, because at the time, that was my favorite song. That bass line and vocal became the soundtrack to our ass-kicking. I thought it was so weird at the time. No butterflies, but a butterfly type of irony. Anyway, here they are. Back to you in a minute.

"Nice. Calling me fuckface."

His fist passes over my head. His balance is overcommitted and he's over the Schwinn. Good, shove him onto it. He gets tangled in the chain and sprocket, tries to keep his clumsy balance but fails. He's down.

"Hey, what is all this about?"

Better not wait for an answer. One guy has long hair. Why do tough guys wear their hair long? I'm swinging him around by it and the other guy can't get in. My knee hits his face, not too solid, just enough to double up his adrenaline. He's grabbing for a handhold on the top of my pants. He's got me. Thumb hard in his eye. He lets go and grabs his face. I plant two shots on the back of his ear. Bingo. His body stiffens and he drops on his face. The third guy trying to get me down has just torn a long trail of skin off my back with his fingernails.

Fat fuck has just gotten to his feet. He's bouncing up and down with his fists prepared like a goddamn pugilist, all darty in-and-out and all showy. Pussy. I'll get him later. Mr. Washboard has a piece of wood from some farmer's fence. I see a guy coming from the Camaro with a tire iron. I am out of here.

Mr. Washboard breaks the wood over my head. Dry rot, nothing to it. But it's the thought that counts, right?

There are times when the universe works against you. When guys much like yourself are doing a job on you and you know that the sun and moon have had some kind of convergence and the planets are set up for a spinning red light and the wail of your ambulance.

But you never can tell, so you lead with a right that has your body behind it from the tips of your toes through your hips that were low to begin with and everything is lined up perfectly so that you're gonna break your fist or break a face. And then the guy contributes to the beauty of the moment. They call it "walking into a punch."

Mr. Washboard actually runs into this one. I never felt a thing, like connecting perfectly on a baseball and knowing immediately that it's out of the fucking park. So you can drop the bat and do that long look of admiration that the other team hates and watch the ball disappear. To top it off, I had a perfect view. I felt my fist caving into his nose, heard the sound like a chicken leg breaking. Down he went.

What you gotta do when you're gonna get hit like that is give them the top of your head. It'll hurt you but it will also disintegrate the guy's fist and probably break his wrist too. Mr. Washboard must have been doing sit-ups when he should have learned about taking a punch.

Still have to consider the tire iron. Fat fuck is not jumping around anymore; he's admiring my shot on Mr. Washboard, who is twitching on the ground with what looks like serious central nervous system damage. I feel so fulfilled. Time has just kind of stopped here for a while.

I know there is an ethic against running away from a fight. And although I'm hot and bloodied from the battle and all, and I want to stay because of something stupid I have learned, I am also calculating. I deduce that the tire iron, plus the fat boxer, and maybe another guy getting off the ground are more than enough to kill my ass.

I'm already booking fifty yards across the bright yellow field. Mustard plants are snapping at my legs as I drive past, pollen from their heads exploding on me. Just jetting toward another road a half mile away, hoping to avoid a ditch here or a trench there. These guys will never catch me on foot. I hear the Camaro screeching off somewhere. I hope they don't have a way to head me off.

Just then the terrible things I do to my body begin to catch up with me. I'm gonna faint. No doubt about it. I stagger down to my hands and knees and try like hell to stay conscious. Nope, I'm gonna take a little nappy right here. The last thing I remember is rolling over on my side in a giant field of tall mustard plants. Everything settling down dark and quiet, the hum of a thousand of bees all around me.

I heard later that the Camaro guys drove around for about an hour and the last place they thought I'd be was sleeping in the field. Maybe there is a God. Think so?

Anyway, around Christmas the next year, one of the guys in the car bought me a few pitchers of beer and told me the tale. Fat fuck boxer guy was married to a woman I had been in bed with a week or so earlier. What he didn't know and should have, was that she brought me home with one of her girlfriends. I was finished in about a half hour or so, but the girls went on all night. I couldn't get any sleep at all until I moved to the couch and I still couldn't sleep with all the racket. I think I made their scene hetero or something. When she had to confess her infidelity, she left out the part about the girlfriend. To the fat guy with his hurt feelings, I looked like some rival.

In the late afternoon, the temperature in the field changed abruptly. The wind shifted bringing in the fog, which revived me. Headache. Worse than that. . . . Intestinal volcano.

I hitched down to the coffee shop. Invited the waitress to the party. She gave me a ride. Slept it off. The night pretty uneventful.

Next day at about three in the afternoon we're having breakfast, sitting in some kind of breakfast nook, sunlight filtering in through the windows. Antique carved table with every kind of fruit, roll, exotic breakfast thing you can think of. There's the movie star I told you about, the big-time surfer I told you about, and the movie star's wife. She is trying hard to hold her family together.

They have a five-month-old daughter. Mine is about a month and a half younger. His wife is pretty cool, but in what you might call denial. She thinks things are in some way alright; she thinks they have a family. It's pretty sad. The sadness carries over to me. I have a wife. I have a baby girl and I'm out doing all this shit all the time. Stuff they'll never know about, because once I get it together, I'll rescue them and we'll live the good life and I'll have this colorful past to season myself with. I'll be like a retired pirate, or like Turner in that Nicholas Roeg movie, so that I won't be some kind of weakling that kissed ass and got to be this big success at whatever it was I was fantasizing about at the time.

But right there at breakfast, things changed. I was still thinking I'd be a star somehow, since I was sitting there with one, and he wasn't any real big deal, and he liked me and probably would use me in his next action movie because I was the real deal and blab blab blab. . . . So I rolled a few joints and listened to the stories about the movie these guys had just finished. Location in Mexico. About surfing and the dynamics of all the personalities, and the challenge. and the American values of men against nature and against the nature of themselves, and overcoming themselves to find a higher meaning for life as the sun sets on the giant waves that they surf to change their lives and learn about the beauty of the world and the stuff that Hollywood wants you to believe.

Meanwhile, behind the scenes they're doing all the drugs a pickup truck can deliver to the set and fucking anything that moves. These guys do get girls — women, wives, duchesses, singers, writers, brilliant talents and hard-living, hard-loving babes. This is their reality; this is how they live. The wives look the other way, not to forgive, but to blind themselves to it. Like I said, denial. Which was where I was at, since I was never gonna be any goddamn star. I was a sort of joke to myself, but I didn't want to think that anyone else could see it. You should learn it now; if you can see it in yourself, then so can everybody else. There are no secrets, only delusions.

So they started comparing the girls to dogs. The ones they had, you know, they'd think up a poodle here and a Doberman there. All bringing laughs. The surfer guy commented about the Chihuahua that my movie star friend had, cause she was so little.

He looked at me, winking the sinsemilla out of his eye and tapping the ash, passed me the joint. His face was real handsome for that moment, and it had a bitchin'-looking killer sneer on it. It was easy to see why he was a movie star. He did a cool quick take over his shoulder to see if his wife could hear. The baby was patting the table in his lap and he looked at me real deep and knowing and said:

"More like a Mexican hairless."

Hmmm. I felt my shoulders shrug, not getting it at the moment. But then I got it. He liked them young.

I felt like making everything right again. Going back to a place that wasn't full of shit, cleaning it all up. But I knew I couldn't without destroying myself along the way. I'd have to stay this way a little longer, being in the habit of it, having what you'd call my identity a part of it.

I got up from the table and walked back home.

I lay on top of my roof, under a huge sycamore tree, with my baby girl sleeping on my chest. Wondering if I could get back what was left of my soul.

REACH

Eddie was walking until he found train tracks. He was drunk and feeling disillusioned. His youth was long gone, nothing could replace it. He'd pretty much screwed up his relationship with his daughter and wife. He turned out to be one of those men who secretly resents the ones he loves. They were in the way of his self-destruction, of living a way that had a few thrills to it. He hadn't turned out to be one of those men who uses the ones he loves as a means for self-ruin. He loved them more than that. It was himself he was beginning to hate.

Eddie had a hypothesis that he was trying to prove. He'd waited until the women were gathered in the kitchen, since he didn't drink anymore, to spin the top off his tequila bottle. He hit it, and passed it to the guy next to him saying, "If they ask, tell 'em I'll be right back."

The guy rehearsed. "Said he'd be right back."

Walking down the driveway, he sang under his breath.

"I've grown so used to you somehow. Well I'm nobody's Sugar Daddy now. . . . "

His wife was cheating on him. He was cheating on her. His daughter knew it. He was determined to make it out to the tracks. In ten minutes, his boots crunched over the gravel in the train yard. Along the way he'd reached back to some of the music of long gone days, when he sat next to his uncle in his old three-quarter-ton International pickup. Those were cowboy songs mostly, but his Uncle Adrian would stomp along with one of Sam Phillips' boys too. Adrian would tilt his chin down on his chest and take deep breaths, singing with Johnny Cash. He'd beat the steering wheel with Jerry Lee, and if the drive was at night, you could see him taking private moments with Patsy Cline.

Being drunk, it was easy to call up all those memories. In his blur, he could see them from another angle, which always made him feel like he was getting something done. The uneasy feeling that makes a person do things like leave a dinner party and wander down the hill was only getting worse.

His wife, like any good liar, knew a lie a mile away. Constantly changing stories, going over old evidence, taking depositions, asking trick questions, and generally living each moment together in dread and resentment. They were locked in a struggle that knew no peace and gave no quarter. It was all about pain now. He knew she'd figure he had a woman on the phone or was meeting one someplace. He knew she'd never believe he was walking around the railroad tracks. He looked forward to being able to tell her a reason that was based on the truth. The self-righteousness would feel good for a change. It didn't matter if she believed him or not.

He was on a mission to the train yard, hoping he'd hear the seminal sound of American rock and roll. A moment of ecstasy was waiting in the dark when those railroad cars rattled and clacked past. A beat fathering the bass line used by all those pointy-shoed, longhaired, duck-butted squawlers who played out their lives in halls, clubs, barns, hayrides, tents, and on frying stages out in the clearing at county fairs. All those songs Uncle Adrian knew by heart. Those songs he said were little lessons in life. Warnings on what to expect from the human condition.

Words sung over the mathematics of music, making life

a series of hints and equations. The addition of this loss, subtracted from that gain, the sum never making sense, the answer always wrong. Like standing next to these tracks. Waiting for the train to tell him if the culture that surrounded him really came from trains. If rock and roll, besides fucking in the shanty, also had something to do with leaving.

Eyes closed, he approached the coming train, his boot tips butted up against the wooden tie. He smiled. There it was, the clackety bounce pulling him along the steel black path, promising him something better. Urging him to change everything, himself, the place he laid his head, the food he spooned in his mouth, the dog in the back yard, the shoes under the bed. Change it all, take himself somewhere else and see if he didn't like it better.

The train passed, leaving him with the memories of a hundred songs. Hearing his uncle's voice. Remembering one time when the whole clan went down to Mexico.

He was eleven, trying to laugh along with the wry wit and irony that his uncle's songs seemed to contain. But when you're eleven, you don't see the humor in things like lost love and crazy consequences. You see your mother crying and your father slamming the door. You get up late at night and one of them is in the front room sitting in the dark waiting for the other one to come home. And they don't. The house stays empty forever. Your love for them is beyond words; it runs the border of the unfathomable. You don't have a grasp of time or a lick of the good sense a man or woman needs to take care of themselves in that bedroom, in those hushed phone calls, in those chance meetings, in those second glances, in those strange smiles that Momma wouldn't like. It hurts. All that expectation, all that desire, and nowhere to go. Just something whispering that the whole world is in your young heart. But you stand there empty-handed, listening to someone fighting off tears, telling you to go back to bed.

Sixty miles south of the Mexican border, down the coastline are a series of volcanic cliffs. Black protrusions jutting out into the Pacific. At one place, two fingers point out one hundred yards and the swells surge into the palm, exploding against its jagged edges. Geysers of salt rain and torn seaweed launch with a horrifying gulp and roar, beyond and above the expectation of any boy standing under the chilling mist, shivering as the echo rolls past him back out to sea.

Uncle Adrian watches him scrambling over the tide pools, running barefoot over the volcanic mass, his feet nicked and bleeding. The rangy man stands wondering why his nephew has nothing consistent in his behavior. He raves and screams, stumbling along the ridges in one moment, then sits staring at the sky for hours. He has tried to settle the boy down, tried to find a way to communicate. Everyone has taken their turn, and the response is shrugged shoulders and raised eyebrows. From day one, he's been a weird kid. No one in the family can relate to him. He walks over to hear what the boy is saying, but it's a song he is singing to himself.

The swells begin to come in thick walls. A huge wave blasts into spray above them, coming in like silent rushing trains, carrying secrets. The boy watching, wanting something, From somewhere.

The uncle takes it on himself. He reaches back to another coast, in another world, and thinks about what he needed most and when he needed it.

Geysers pocked the shore's surface, whizzing shrapnel exploding the air around him. GI's vomit on each other as the landing craft's hull makes its walloping journey through artillery shells, to a beach. Spitting them out, to race through this metal rain. Strange popping sounds dropping farmboys like himself into the shallows. Running over men floating face down. Hitting the sand, weaving into a nightmare that stops them open-mouthed in wonder.

Huddled together, faces white with fear, certain of

absolutely nothing at all, wanting only to get out alive. One by one, he watched the boys beside him fall, until he dropped and watched his fingers tremble before his eyes. So he crawled and waited. A soldier beside him had assumed the posture of one of the dead. Lying on his back with his face twisted, staring at Adrian. Managing to get his attention with the desperation in his eyes. The soldier's eyes looked upward toward the beach, then they stared at Adrian again. Then he understood the strategy. Wait until the next wave hits the beach and move forward when the machine guns strafe the troops behind them to pieces. He waited.

Large guns opened up, their explosions hitting the beach behind him. The machine guns clattered before him, their aim over his head. The screaming behind him was incessant. He crawled. The soldier flew up as though an invisible hand had grabbed the front of his helmet and pulled him toward his feet. The boy dropped, the sand yellow and red above his neck. Adrian crawled under a cement bunker, heard panic in the voices inside. Tossed in a thudding explosion and then another. He made his way to the back hatch. A torso twitched in the doorway. He waited by the body, watching his sergeant lead up eight men. They stayed protected by the concrete while the war wailed past them. They waited all night, and the others told him what he had done.

He thought again of the soldier who made him wait there in the sand. What would he be doing now? Adrian was on the other side of the world vacationing with his brother's family, wondering how to reach a nephew he felt was becoming more distant with every passing hour. The soldier forever in a cemetery in Italy.

Earlier that morning he stood leaning into his camper shell, rank with the smell of salt-caked, drying starfish. He reached for the burlap sack and found Eddie's collection, stiffened in asymmetrical twists, some gripping the rough brown edges of the bag, some on one another. Sad remembrances . . . misplaced, forgotten, dead. Adrian wondering, *"Where do we learn about life?"*

The boy sits, watching enormous silence roll below, rush past and explode above him. On the slick black surface, near kelp and seaweed, clings a huge red starfish. It appears for a second and then is submerged as the next wave rolls over. The boy stands peering down, anxious for the next glimpse of that beautiful and now impossibly treasured starfish.

His uncle appears over his shoulder.

"You want to get it?"

The boy freezes. The air pounds with the latest and largest swell; the geyser lingers above them. The boy shouts in the rain, above the roar.

"Yeah."

And then in the silence of the next wall looming toward them.

"But it's too far away."

"I'll lower you down between the waves."

The boy can't stay in the gaze of that challenge. His eyes look down into the chasm. It's a challenge coming from a kind man. A challenge alone can be answered either way. Kindness combined with challenge has to be accepted.

Adrian looks at the boy and imagines the surging wall yanking Eddie from his grasp, taking him for a long sub-surface journey beneath the enormous surf into the black rocks. He sees himself leaping into the darkening sea, flailing against the mountains rising, tossing him with the boy's frail blue broken body. He weighed this against the boy's burlap sack.

"If you miss. . . ."

"I won't miss."

"OK, then."

The boy squats down next to the man. He looks beyond the ledge and sees the dark mound rising toward him. He listens intently as his uncle explains that after the wave breaks, and the backwash surges past, he will have his ankles in his hands and drop him down into the emptying hole.

"Let's count."

After six, right between seven, the sea rushes back in, and by eight it explodes against the wall.

"I'll be dropping you on one. You'll be down there on two. . . ." Another larger swell rises and nearly overflows the edge. "By five, I'll be pulling you up."

The air explodes, an avalanche of solid water douses them, filling the small pocked holes with white water and foam.

"We really gonna do this?"

"Yeah."

"OK, then."

"Next one, see the starfish?"

The boy looks down to see the red giant.

"Yeah."

He isn't heard as a wave blasts high on the rocks and sends the next shower down on them. It suddenly seems so much darker. The backwash bounces beneath them. The boy scrambles into position. His uncle's vise-like grip hurts. The boy rolls over the side and drops for a second that stops his heart. The boy lands hard against the cold kelp lining the inside of the wash. The starfish glistens a foot beyond his grasp. The boy stretches, hearing his uncle's count of two. Out of the corner of his eye, he sees the surging tide rising above him, a black rolling wall racing in, rumbling at his intrusion.

The boy touches the starfish, his hand on the rough contour of its back. The animal is much bigger than he thought, larger than both his hands together which now pull against its grip on the rock wall. His uncle bellows four. The starfish starts to release. The boy feels his light weight raising and the wall of murky water looming above him. The heels of his hands fight for ledges to push upward, aiding the speed of his ascent. Fingernails tear into his back under his bathing suit as he feels himself yanked onto the rock edge, his one trailing arm submerged up to his shoulder under the surface as it rushes past.

"I can get it."

"OK, then."

They turn together to face the next wave. The backwash swirls past. His ankles are again in the vise-hands of the uncle. The boy drops, bracing his fall with an outstretched arm. He bounces from the kelp wall, his eyes focused on the starfish, and he twists his return to land beside it. The fingers of both hands slipped under the edge of two legs and pry the starfish loose. He hears his uncle counting three and the sound of fear in his voice. He shoots a glance at the oncoming wall. The starfish hangs in the boy's outstretched hands.

"I got it!!"

He realizes he can not help the climb back up and hold the starfish at the same time. He feels his body begin to rise slower than it had the first time. The wall of water bearing down.

The boy blows his breath out and takes a huge lungful of air. He feels the hand dig viciously into his back, desperately pulling. His ribs catch the edge of the rocks and a sharp line of skin tears over his bony chest. An arm surrounds him and pulls him from the edge, rolling him over onto the sharp tide-pool edges. The entire space swells with a foot of water. The crash against the rocks sends backwash rolling over them, the uncle clutching the boy, the boy clutching the starfish. The water recedes. They get to their feet.

Eddie holds the red starfish the size of a hubcap in his hands. His uncle looks down at it and whistles. "That's a beauty," he says. The boy spins it over an oncoming wave, watching it fade from the surface and disappear.

Adrian turns and walks back toward the International. Eddie follows him at a distance, and then runs until he catches up. They walk hand in hand until they see a narrow path leading them to a cliff. Adrian sweeps his arm from the ground to the cliff edge above.

"Lead the way."

Eddie runs along the cliff wall, dodging cactus, tufts of grass, his feet dislodging volcanic debris, sending stones bouncing over the side and falling into the surf. When he reaches the top, he looks down at his uncle slowly rocking his long strides up the incline. Eddie stands as close as he dares to the cliff edge and closes his eyes. He thinks he feels himself falling forward. He feels his balance adjust and doubt thrills him. He smiles to himself.

"I'm not gonna fall."

He opens his eyes and looks down, yelling, "C'mon Uncle Adrian!"

The old truck always takes a few tries before starting. Adrian lights a cigarette and stretches his arm along the top of the front seat. He squints through smoke and coughs.

"Eddie, you were born in June, huh?"

Eddie nods. "The eleventh."

Adrian repeats the date. "June the eleventh. And you're eleven, ain't ya?"

Eddie nods.

Adrian pauses and stares through the windshield in concentration, exhaling little clouds.

"Well, see there? Hank Williams made his debut on the Grand Ol' Opry on the day you were born."

Adrian tries the ignition again. The engine turns over and dies.

"First time he sang 'Lovesick Blues.' Goes like this. . . ."

Adrian takes a deep breath, twists the ignition. The truck rumbles and he sings as though he was standing at the back in a tent at the county fair.

"Ah got a feeling called the bluuuees, oh Lord since my baby said goodbye, I don't what I'll doooo. . . ."

He thumps the steering wheel in time.

"All I do is sit and cryyy, oh Lord, I got so used to her somehow. . . ." He licks his lips, looks out the side window and puts the truck in gear.

"Or something like that."

CLEANLINESS IS NEXT TO . . .

MY FATHER'S DESTROYER WAS DUE to return to San Diego from a nine-month Cold War cruise. Postcards, letters meaning very little, sent home. Mother always counting the days, then crying herself to sleep when he left again, and me wondering why. They never treated each other like anything but distant uncomfortable relatives after his first few days home. Awful awkward silences during television commercials. I'd do annoying things to break the tension and was usually spoken to harshly by both of them. Making them agree on something. I missed him. I missed something he was supposed to provide, and the fact that I didn't know what that was made the longing greater.

We waited on the dock. The sun was shining bright and my mother was drinking coffee from a dock canteen, sharing a powdered donut with me provided by the USO cart making its way up and down the dock. We saw the USS Isherwood pass the line of silent ships at mooring. My heart jumped and we waved at the sailors in formation standing on the deck of the ship in the distance. Minutes crawled as the ship made its way to the pier and shaded us in its shadow. Piping whistles, thrown lanyards, horns, and the ship's band playing the Navy Hymn. I saw my father walking above us along the cable barriers on the edge of the deck. I could recognize his walk anywhere. My mother intoning, "There he is." We waved as his back dressed in blues and his Chief's hat disappeared into a hatch.

The plank was lowered and the crowd of dependents moved up the plank and onto the ship's deck to hug and kiss their men, sobbing smiles, introducing babies. Solemn handshakes from boys to fathers. Down the gray ladders, down the gray halls and into the Chief's quarters. Finally released, my father was permitted to leave ship and return with us to our house for a few months until the next cruise would take him around the world.

My father at the wheel of the Oldsmobile and my mother turned toward him in the front seat speaking about details of life beyond the scope of a third grade boy just happy to smell the diesel on his clothes. The smell of manhood.

Then the hours changed to days and the monotony got to my father, bringing back the tension, which eventually drifted downward toward me. My father tried to reestablish his fatherhood by using discipline. I wanted to be taken in his lap and held, lifted into the air, taken on walks. Invited into the garage to smell the wood burn on his table saw, watch the spinning blade whirl near his thick skillful fingers. Instead, I played down the street and left him alone with his depression and his boredom. Conversations about trespasses I'd committed in the days of his absence led to lectures and punishments. Reduced television privileges. Boring busywork after school. Disappointed looks directed at a sailor of nine who was not making the grade.

My mother and father sat stunned in catatonic silence watching the fourth steady hour of regular television programming. I wandered from the cupboard holding a handful of Oreos and an orange. I laid down on the floor under the blue television light and was thereby noticed by my father.

"Go take a bath."

Just that. Deadpan.

I kept my eye on the screen and said "No."

Silence. The mindless dialogue droned on the set.

"I'm not going to tell you again. Take a bath."

My mother made an unintelligible noise of protest, a groan or something. My father wasted no time.

"Go get a belt."

I stuffed another Oreo in my mouth and walked past the stares coming from the couch. I turned on the light in their bedroom and opened his dresser drawer. Pulled out a plastic braided belt I'd made for him when he was overseas. I walked out into the front room and held it out to him.

My legs were bare. He went for them. He swung hard enough to count but not really committed to damage or to venting his anger. The sound wasn't too impressive, but it hurt like hell. He waited. He hit me again. I gained some kind of strength from it and I knew I'd be OK. He shook his head like a television character about to shrug off some homily. But he didn't say anything. He hit me instead. I thought how stupid he was not to know that my leg was getting numb. He was really getting upset.

"Get your ass into the bathtub or. . . ."

He hit me in the other leg, let it glide past me and back-handed me on the other. He did it again. The pain was constant and harder to stand. I got a little scared that I wouldn't be able to hold on. But his eyes were tearing up, and he was losing heart. He hit me again. My mother said that I was bleeding. I was crying on the outside, but not on the inside. His shoulders sagged. His hand dropped to his side. His eyes were full of tears. My voice sounded so calm it startled me.

"I already took a bath."

MY DAD CURED ME OF GUNS

CHRISTMAS AT THE MEXICAN-AMERICAN BORDER usually brings a heat wave. The temperature peaks around one o'clock at 90 degrees. The sunlight is bright and the air is crisp; it's absolutely beautiful, shining and clear. The air shimmers. The winter sun doesn't burn; it blesses.

Waking up in the early morning, Eddie examines what is wrapped for him under the tree. Being eleven, he is in the limbo years of his youth. Between the playground and his first car, the no-girls-allowed-club and his first crush. His place in the future is a source of anxiety. Who is he? Who will he become? Is there a way to affect the outcome? His assessment of who he is today is embarrassing. He is tired of childhood. Next spring, he wants a spot on the baseball team; to find out if he can hit the curve, take one for the team, hang in there, play the field, get low on the ball, steal second and prove that he has what it takes to become a teenager. Right now, any thirteen-year-old could easily bulldoze his life.

One present has a note written in his father's formal hand. Lifting the package, its weight and density triggers his curiosity. The other presents under the tree lift easily. They rattle; they lack dignity. Presents probably containing toys and games that will prove his parents still regard him today as the child he was last month.

Eddie's father and mother have taken their place on the couch. Eddie opens the front door and sunlight streams through and leaves the faintest trace of tiny squares on the floor. A sunlight so bright, sharp, and clear that it seems like music. His father clears his throat. Eddie turns, watching his mother stretch and yawn behind one hand.

"Let's open them presents."

Eddie stands looking at these familiar strangers. Two middle-aged figures slumped beside each other like Martians, a canyon of alienation between them. The distance between the man in his boxers and the woman in her robe so vast that she begins to hug herself as though she were cold. Eddie walks to the Christmas tree.

"I been wondering what could it be that was in here."

His father fixes him with a mocking challenge.

"Well, then you better open it and see."

His father takes his mother's hand. She shifts uneasily.

The present is even heavier than he remembered. Something in it makes him open it slowly. He's eleven; he doesn't just rip the paper anymore.

"Read the card, Eddie." Her voice is admonishing.

"I did. Says 'To Eddie, Christmas 1960.'"

The cardboard box is open at one end and the blond stock, blue-grey barrel and bolt of a Remington .22 Savage slides slowly onto the carpet. Astonished, Eddie looks at his father. His large arms are folded against his chest; his mother's abandoned hand trails absently through his long black hair and down his neck to rest on his shoulder. He takes on something more manly than Eddie has seen in him before. A look as though he were letting him into the clubhouse. A reassuring smile that could be saying:

"Had you worried there for a while. Didn't know where ya stood didja? Welcome to the first stair to the man's world, kid. Ya made it."

She seems pleased and tries to participate in the admiration of the weapon, but her comments are drowned in the solemn instructions of gun safety as the weapon is assembled.

Eddie is over-attentive and over-respectful, feeling phony, but the strange occasion carries such weight and is so reverent that the delirium of this new passage forgives his corny effort at maturity. He can almost hear the theme from *Bonanza* playing in the front room, Pa intoning in serious sermon the principles of men. His father standing with feet wide as a cop's, assembling the rifle, breaking it down.

"Now you do it, Son."

Eddie frozen, the gun offered in his father's outstretched hand. Eddie thinking, *"He's never called me Son."*

He takes the bolt, sets it on the table, places the barrel beside it, takes the stock and fits the barrel to it. His hands shake. He waits for his father's humiliating comment. But he remains silent while Eddie fits the bolt to the barrel.

His father gets up for a refill. Eddie's mother hands him another present. A black mohair sweater with athletic stripes at the biceps. Perfect. She opens the photo album. His father returns with the coffee and opens the series of blades and bits for his power tools — neither gift a surprise, both of them acting as though it were. The room opening into a chasm of lonely phoniness that years of practice has made excusable.

Christmas 1960 passes through the crucial phase. No one has broken the suspension of disbelief. Cheeks are kissed, thank yous are muttered, embarrassments are left unexposed. Eddie's father heads for the bathroom. His mother begins pressing the wrapping paper into neat folds to be put away to wrap presents next year. Eddie heads out the screen door.

The sun amplifies the greens, golds, and blues outside. Everything shines. Eddie walks barefoot in the cool grass, the sun warm on his back. The street is silent. Birds swoop to the wires hanging over the house, change their minds and settle in the jacaranda tree across the street. A neighborhood girl flies past, her chin over her handlebars, her legs motionless, having pedaled as fast as her Schwinn's gear will torque. Her hair streaming behind her, face ecstatic. Eddie whistles through his teeth and her hand waves behind her, the spokes of her bike glistening.

Eddie walks into the front room. His mother is on the phone checking in with relatives, feigning interest in each other's gifts and in the dinner plans for later.

Eddie stands there watching. His mother taps ashes into last year's present, nodding on the phone, already bored with her call.

Eddie can never locate reality. It keeps slipping into these deceptions between all of the people he lives with. No one tells the truth. Television means more than any of his close relatives. Conversation means nothing; affection is forced and painful. No spirit, no soul, no pride anywhere. And where is the appropriate place to deposit this anger? On the woman on the couch, pretending she cares about the next twenty-four hours? Is she so stupid she can't see that she is slaving for a son and husband who can't see her? What can his father do but go to sea, take orders, come home, and wait to ship out again? What does this make Eddie? Eddie does not want to answer that question yet. He does what he always does — watches them and stalls for time.

Eddie knows this Christmas was intended as a rite of passage. He walks into his bedroom. It has changed. The rocket ship wallpaper is childish. The toys are embarrassing. He has a gun.

The water's running in the bathroom sink. His father leans into the mirror examining his neck and tapping the whiskers from his razor. His words are distorted as he cuts the stubble on the side of his mouth. He asks if Eddie would like to take the gun out into the canyon.

"Yes, sir."

Eddie never calls him sir.

They're walking along a dirt road that's twenty minutes by truck from the house. His father pulls a box of shells from his jacket. Eddie carries the rifle in the crook of his arm, balancing it like a television mountain man. He lowers his voice when he speaks, struggling to deepen it within his rib cage. They walk along, talking in mature, slow tones, struggling for subjects worthy of manly discourse. Not much to say. They fall into the gulf of father-son relationship. They slip a .22 Long into the bolt. Eddie is taught to squeeze the trigger at beer cans. In a few minutes, they spin under the impact of newfound ballistic acumen. Eddie examines the holes tearing through the metal. He struggles to find some noble imagery. Frontiersmen bring home food for the young. A Bud can is the sternum of a bear, pawing the air in his last seconds of agony. Eddie's friends behind him, reloading after their panicked shots have missed; him saving them from the giant clubbing claws.

Eddie's father sights and shoots. Reloads, shoots, reloads, shoots. His smile is bitter as the last shot slams into the dirt. Eddie cannot find a disarming comment to ease his father's embarrassment.

Slipping another bullet into the bolt, his father is muttering.

"Rusty cans don't mean shit."

Eddie follows his father beneath brush and tangled sycamore. His father's tattooed hand parts a green sunlight-speckled branch. A blue jay nods, bright-eyed, head tilting, wings ruffled and shaking back into place. The barrel levels and Eddie's father's jaw sets, his eye widens, his breath stops. He squeezes the trigger.

"Merry Christmas, bird."

POST PERFORMANCE

A TRAIN ROBBER AND A FOURTEEN-YEAR-OLD GIRL are left following an unsuccessful attempt at stopping a train. The horses wheeled, the guns fired, bullets whizzed, a few of them splattered through men intent on defending or stealing money. It ended five minutes ago. The girl and the thief remain in the aftermath.

She sees his torn, dusty jeans, dried sweat, dirt encrusted, hollow-eyed exhaustion. He is high on adrenaline and the euphoria of escaping death. His bleeding cracked lips are smiling. There is no skin on his right forearm, shoulder and hip. There's a blue knot on the side of his head; bramble has torn an ear. His canteen is three-quarters empty. They are thirty-seven miles from bath, food, lace curtains, and a wide bed where his woman turns over on her hip sleeping deeply, dreaming about shady canyons with fire running along their ridges. He looks at the girl. The first words out of his mouth are an excuse, or an explanation. In either case, she will miss the point.

"So, when they sold the farm out from under us . . . and didn't compensate us, other than to remind us of our poverty . . . I got pissed."

He shrugs, offering her the last of the canteen, which she appreciates since she is thirsty as hell, and has had more than her share already. He looks away, saying wordlessly that he expects her to finish it.

"And you know, it feels real good to be an outlaw. To stand exactly in the square of slings and arrows, and directly in the path of outrageous fortune."

He laughs at himself. Remembering Lilly Langtree.

She is stunned hearing Shakespeare quoted out here in the dust storm that is picking up around them. When she left St. Louis, she thought it would be an adventure and here it is standing in front of her — a coarse man limping off an injured hip, flourishing his words by throwing his arms in the air.

He waves his hand in the direction of his lost land and the empty railroad tracks, an hour ago the stage of life and death.

He pulls some of the worn shirt off the raw skin of his shoulder. Tears fill his eyes and he winces, which surprises her since she thought he'd make a show of being brave. He squints down at her.

"Next time, I won't bother to wear a kerchief over my face. . . ."

She doubts that he'll have to.

He clomps around in his boots; one heel is broken off. He pitches to the side with each stride. He pulls off his boots. He walks over to a ditch where most of the shooting came from, and comes back wearing someone else's. She hasn't moved a muscle. Sweat is running down her face, her hat has nearly blown off in the wind. He mops her face with his kerchief and hands it to her. She tucks it between her breasts. He is oblivious.

"It's a damn sad day when you have to shoot your own horse. Well, it's a long walk, so I guess we'd better get started."

They begin to walk at right angles from the railroad tracks.

"You don't talk much, do you?"

The girl just shakes her head.

RITA

SUMMER OF 1964 WAS A HEAT WAVE blowing over flaming cities, police dogs, draft induction centers, universities, prisons, self-immolating monks, civil rights workers deep in the
slave states, and San Diego asleep on the Mexican border.
Eddie Burnett's relatives are visiting from Chicago. Over
the past months, his mother, father, uncle, aunt, and three
cousins have driven up the coast to Seattle and seen the
Space Needle. Gone to Disneyland, driven to Marineland,
hit Knott's Berry Farm on one of the smoggiest days in Los
Angeles history, and spent the last month hanging around
the house.

Because of his father's flatulence, and the weird squawk-
ing whine that his mother has developed, each undoubtedly
a form of passive aggression designed to avoid proximity
with the relatives, the inter-family trips have come to a halt.
The summer vacation was planned to last until August, and
last it will, even if the meals are eaten separately, or in re-
sentful silence.

Eddie's aunt and uncle are early risers. They read the
paper first, pissing off his mother who likes to get it fresh
off the lawn and read it without egg and coffee stains. The
aunt takes long showers, using most of the hot water. The
deaf uncle follows her, singing at the top of his lungs. Show

tunes waking the rest of the family who fight for the remaining hot water.

Around ten o'clock Eddie's mother grinds her toast into a paste by chewing it hundreds of times, annoying all hell out of the cousins, who are slurping cereal and making jokes at Eddie's expense. They like to make him spell words, and laugh hysterically when he fails to get them right. Eddie opens a can of fruit cocktail and swallows it in four non-stop gulps. He disappears out the screen door, leaving his cousins to hang around the house while the bickering adults shift from one room to the other, whispering shit about each other.

But the next day is Eddie's fourteenth birthday, and to celebrate everybody is going to the zoo. By seven o'clock both families are clogging the door to the bathroom, bumping into each other in the kitchen, and yelling at the kids. The race to be ready first begins with Eddie's aunt pointing out that, judging from the amount of fruit salad Eddie's father had last night, it might be best to take separate cars. Eddie's mother takes her sister to the side and whines that this teasing about a little fart now and then has gotten out of hand. Eddie's uncle has the T.V. cranked up to maximum, listening to the morning news, announcing at the top of his lungs that there won't be any rain today. Eddie mumbles that he doubts that it will since it's already 102 degrees, and there ain't a cloud in the goddamn sky. The biggest cousin tells Eddie to watch his wise-guy mouth and Eddie suggests that he fuck himself. This of course, gets the feathers flying, ending with a broken chair and both women running to separate rooms to cry over it.

Eddie's inability to follow simple instructions costs his racing parents too much time in the contest to be ready to leave first. Eddie's family's efforts are regarded with disgusted snorts from his aunt's family, who stand beside their car and wait patiently for the less competent Burnetts to finally get ready.

Eddie's aunt barks, "Eddie, front and center!"

This she expects will elicit the same response it does in her own sons, or maybe it's meant to demonstrate the hopeless state of discipline in her sister's boy. In any case, Eddie does not make it front or center. He makes it out the door and down the street, yelling honk when you're ready to leave.

By noon on one of the hottest days in San Diego history, Eddie and his father are sitting on a bench under the trees that shade the largest collection of primates in the world. Seventy cages of varying species, all of them clearly out of their minds, imprisoned in hot-boxes, and fed up with another season of peanut-tossing tourists. Ambulances are wailing in and out of the parking lot treating twenty sunstroke victims an hour. Thousands of sunburns are already lobster-red heading toward purple. The heat is driving everyone into delirium. An old man standing near Eddie's father has eyes that sit back in his head like a cadaver's. His face is red wax. His tiny wife's old ankles are swollen over her shoes; her mouth is open and she is panting. Eddie whispers they should give up their seats to the elderly couple before they collapse. As they stand, two high school girls pretend to be oblivious and sit down. The old couple shuffles off in the direction of Deer Canyon. Eddie and his father join the mindless amble of exhausted and suffering vacationers milling past a row of monkey cages.

Monkey eyes follow Eddie. There is not a single primate looking anywhere except directly into Eddie's eyes. Each face frozen in disbelief. Time stops. No one breathes, no hearts beat, there are no birds in flight, no one speaks, the heat is gone. The entire zoo hovers in a vacuum. The bars are optical illusions. We are caged in our mindless condescension. They are crucified. They understand everything we are doing to them. Eddie becomes terrified.

A single wild cry unleashes a chorus of slanders and shrieks. Gibbons scramble up the cage screen, stabbing their arms out of the wire mesh at Eddie. The shrieking does not decrease as he passes. Wires shake in fists, eyes roll white, leaping figures fly from floor to ceiling, banging full speed into the fences between Eddie and these homicidal creatures.

Seventy monkey cages are in full riot. Suspicious attendants begin to arrive. People are muttering, pointing out Eddie who must have somehow tormented these chimpanzees rolling drunk with rage on their deck, arms flailing, gibbons' unhinged jaws snapping spike teeth, spider monkeys gnashing and whizzing above him. The shrieks engulf and shame him. He decides to find a place to retreat. He looks back toward his father who is laughing, convulsing on a bench holding his stomach yelling, "Hey, Eddie, where ya going? Where ya going? Eddie?"

Eddie heads down to Deer Canyon, which is an inferno without shade. The asphalt road mushes under his feet. There is no breeze. A tour group trudges up the hill, each tented under a canopy of newspaper. An attendant with a walkie-talkie is leading the old couple toward a curb. Eddie plunges down into the canyon. People coming up are gasping things at him.

"Don't go down there."

"Too hot, go back."

Eddie picks up a discarded newspaper, places his head in the fold and disappears down the hillside.

For the next two hours, Eddie stays near a drinking fountain watching a cape buffalo frothing in a cloud of flies. When the setting sun leaves the canyon shaded near closing time, Eddie, with nothing else to do, reads the paper. A church was bombed in Birmingham. A bible class of kids his own age were blown up. Four little girls died. After the third loudspeaker announces the final call before closing, Eddie sneaks up to the baboon cage.

He holds his eyes down. Sliding over the rail, he crouches against the screen. A guy with a broom ten cages down is sweeping slowly. A huge graying male leads an ancient female's approach. She sits turning her back. The male watches the guy sweeping. The old matriarch turns her head.

He waits, expecting a sign, looking for some kind of answer. Her bloodshot eye slides slowly over his face. Knuckles whack the concrete floor. Callused lips pull up, revealing black gums and the top quarter of huge yellow teeth. A nostril cave blows wet hot gusts on Eddie's cheek. Her face recomposes without a trace of anything from this millennium.

The snoring and the musings of apes asleep buzzes low in the late afternoon heat. She stretches and lumbers away. The male follows her, looking backward over his shoulder on every other stride.

"What the hell are you doing? Goddamn it, we been waiting an hour."

Eddie is marched out of the zoo, across the parking lot and thrown into the Oldsmobile. They leave the park and drive home.

Eddie looks through the back seat window. Time stops again.

A church. A neon sign glows *Jesus Is Love*. A fireball blows down the church's front door. The explosion lifting him out of the back seat, his head thuds on the car roof. His father asks him what the hell is going on. Then everything returns as it was.

Eddie mumbles.

"Don't mumble."

"Where's Birmingham?"

"What?"

"Nothing."

"Birmingham is in England. Don't they teach ya nothing in school?"

"Dad, everything is really a war isn't it?"

"What?"

"Everything is a war.

"Ah, yeah, I guess so."

"I mean everybody is against everybody else, right?"

"Uh huh."

Eddie's mother says, "That's not true, honey."

Eddie's father waits at a long stoplight.

"You shoulda seen those monkeys screaming at Eddie."

"What?"

"When we were down at the monkey cage. Shoulda seen 'em. Right, Eddie?"

"Yeah."

"What do you guys want for dinner?"

"I dunno."

"I dunno. Hey, Dad, ya know they bombed a church in Birmingham."

"They did?"

"Yeah."

"Hmmm. Too bad."

Two thousand miles away, Rita sat over the wing watching the green land below, the intermittent flashes as the setting sun bounced off the web of the Mississippi's tributaries. Nothing registered. Fatigue and fear had disembodied her. The plane dropped, the airfield below rose, the tires bumped, the plane taxied toward a little tower with a small cafe beside it. She watched the blurring circle beside her.

A low cyclone fence in front of the cafe bore the weight of three baggy-suited photographers, each with a jacket in the crook of an elbow — sunglasses, white cotton shirts, loosened ties, and expressions on their tanned faces that seemed to know plenty. Tight thin-lipped mouths that said little. They were blurred in the rippling heat like three emissaries from hell, moving toward the shade under the wing of the airplane.

The doors opened. The windows steamed over; Rita's

clothes stuck to her skin. The other passengers waved news-papers under their chins. Her suitcase weighed a ton and bounced off her knee as she descended the stairs. A knot of reporters and onlookers waited.

Microphones obscured her vision as she tried to walk. She searched the crowd, hoping someone would shout over the mob of reporters, policemen, and gawkers.

"He's alive! Turned up five hours ago!"

There was no voice. Just the mumbling of the reporters and Klansmen like gravel rolling under water. She strode on saying nothing to the increasingly demanding questions. A loud snarl.

"Why are you here?"

She searched the men towering over her until she located the eyes laughing at her. He continued.

"The best place for you is right back where you came from . . . and the best place for your husband is right where he is."

Eyes shifted from Rita to the voice shuffling through the crowd as it parted for him. The eyes slowly revolved back to her and waited for a response.

"I am here to find out who killed my husband. The best place for anyone to be who knows anything about the whereabouts of my husband, or anything pertaining his dis-appearance, is on the phone with the Attorney General of the United States. I have been promised an FBI investigation beginning tomorrow morning."

Six reporters turned and ran for the telephone hanging on the wall inside the airport. The FBI . . . here. Any fool could see a Commie troublemaker happened to fall into the wrong hands.

"And if you people don't like it, you can go ahead and kill me just like you killed my husband."

Nothing moved, until the soles of shoes scratched uneasily around her. A half-circle of men stared at her, occasionally spitting through their teeth, hands in pockets. Three in the center slowly shook their heads from side to side. One smiled broadly.

"The heat must be getting to you, Miss. Nobody wants to see anybody killed."

They turned in unison and walked toward the parking lot.

As Rita passed, a young man's voice rose in volume and screeched out of his chest.

"Excuse me, Miss . . . er . . . Mrs. . . . ah . . . Can I say something?" Rita kept walking.

"Does it have to do with my husband?"

"Well, ah . . . yeah. It does."

Rita faced him.

"Would it help him to get yourself killed? What good would that do?"

She turned toward him. He began to sight his camera on her, his hand twisted around the lens, and then he lowered it.

She examined his face. It was self-conscious, ashamed. From head to toe, a tall, rumpled, chinless wonder, lost, scared, and ignorant. His face reminding her of her mother telling her to stay home; her father, resigned, turning slowly from the front porch to the screen door.

She did not really hear the young man explaining that she was only falling right into the Klan's hands, that she didn't understand how it was down here.

Her words fell out so weary and sad.

"I don't think you understand."

She walked past the staring faces and found a booth in a tiny coffee shop.

The photographer stood in the doorway changing cameras, hoping for a shot before she left for her probable appointment in some ditch by the side of the road.

He noticed his hands shaking and realized he was afraid she'd see him and address him, confront him and tell him more things about himself that he wouldn't understand. He began to hate her.

Rita crossed her arms, turned her head and stared straight at him as he found her in his camera. He lowered it, raised his eyes and saw her smile faintly, the slightest softening in her face, and the smallest movement of her mouth.

She turned her hipster-sunglassed gaze toward the telephone on the wall. One hand rose slowly, her thumb rubbed her bottom lip, then it folded into a small relaxed fist, and froze. The camera clicked. Rita stared into eternity.

5-28-92

THAT LOUD CLEAN SNAP MEANS a sharp blade. One that leaves you staggering and aching from lack of blood before you can judge the depth of the slice.

But a serrated edge tears a rip that lets you assess the depth, the speed and the damage, via an unforgiving pain. The ragged edge sawing past skin that yearned for more kinds of living than minutes provide, pulling through muscle made weak in the refusal to take less than the treasures laid at my feet. Stopping me in my tracks, asleep at the wheel, under the influence of fits of euphoria producing nothing but insight, turning to hindsight, mocking me as time moved on.

That was the sin that made those angels groan. Made them turn their faces and sing in tongues that I couldn't understand but had that simple refrain, about living only once and the time is running out. Just barely long enough to fit in one more promise.

The edge tears more than it cuts. The surface just broken, then torn gashing to the bone. Past skin slick with kisses, wet with the labor life requires, rivulets of saline rolling down the cheek now opening in a red instant. The vicious need we have to work each other over to something we think we want, but don't know what to do with when it faces us.

Our shadows fade in the light; our tired eyes grow weak. We jinx ourselves muttering, "What's the use?" We stare, recognizing a curse when we utter one. Because we need it all. And that bus left a long time ago and it's only the echo of its gears grinding around the turn we hear, making us believe we can catch up. So we wait there alone in the dark. Crickets sounding invitations to a warm night, breeze blowing in a way we think we remember, stars above us like a map we can't read, newspapers sliding around us like snakes in the air. Waiting.

Transforming in the dark, she is a dervish dancing and singing that she loves me, or what I was, or what I once imagined myself to be. Becoming a blur, whirling and pulling a bent steak knife, hissing, "Here. I'll give you something to remember me by."

TRIP THE LIGHT FANTASTIC

DON'T ASK ME HOW LONG this'll take. I don't have a fucking idea. If I did then I'd be done with it already because the reason it isn't done is because it's gonna be fucked and I can't stand the idea of getting started, and then you know, having to go on and on and on with all the shit that goes with it. Anyway, I gotta wait here for a minute more, the fuck will be coming back to his car any second. Meanwhile, I gotta wait here and try to look inconspicuous. The car radio blaring, the light's on and the key's in the ignition. Is he asking me to just jump in and drive? I see his brown, shiny shoe stepping out the door, his expensive and tasteless slacks snap in the breeze. He isn't even looking where he's going. So I bump into him and he's a solid fuck; he doesn't budge. I say excuse me to throw him off, and he gives me a funny look and before he can tell me it's alright, he sees the knife in my hand and he looks at me again. I nod and hold out my hand saying something to him that I can't remember even though it just came out of my mouth. I'm scared, that's why. And I hate to be scared. The guy is slow so I tell him to give me his money before I. . . . But I just did cut him, right down his arm and I'm now punching the blade under his ribs. He's backing up and the look in his eyes tells me he's another asshole who won't go down. Fuck, I hate this. I hope he doesn't die. I hate this.

FOR THE RECORD

THE LINCOLN BRIGADE WERE VOLUNTEERS from the United States who fought in the Spanish Civil War against the fascist forces led by General Francisco Franco just prior to World War II. Picasso's piece "Guernica" condemns the first use of air warfare on civilian populations by Hitler's Luftwaffe in that same war.

The Spanish Civil War was a slaughter in which another chip of mankind's collective soul was lost. A war where Germany tested its twentieth-century weapons on cities without air raid sirens, without any means of defense, with nothing but an innocence that was left burning in rubble. The world stood back in horror, pounding pedestals, screaming protests in newspaper headlines, and waiting to see how far the Third Reich was willing to go. In the most real sense the first battles against Hitler's extermination camps were fought by men like my friend Bill Bailey. Communists, labor organizers, and blue-collar heroes from New York's docks who were used to standing up immediately when they faced heartlessness and violence rained on innocent women and children. They formed a brigade without adequate ammunition and weapons, far outnumbered, fought in a country where they did not speak the language, understand the culture, or know the terrain. They fought and they lost.

Bill Bailey is respected for his participation in that war, and in later years for his courage on the stand during the McCarthy era of political repression in the 1950s. By the time I met him he was in his seventies. His hands were the size of baseball gloves. He was tall and stooped slightly with age, his face craggy and his eyes looking sad as though he could see right through you and what he saw made him isolated, distant, alone. His manner was warm, grandfatherly. He seemed to be always on the verge of saying good-bye.

On a December in the 1980s, Bill and I sat on a bench overlooking the slate-gray San Francisco Bay. The morning overcast and cold, container ships plowing under the Golden Gate, seagulls suspended in updrafts, rush hour traffic stopped, a bakery smelling sweet to the point of nausea. The Contragate scandal was threatening to explode; we were talking about Ollie North, his connections to Reagan. I was hoping the administration would fall. But Bill shook his head saying that the government would never let an assassination be followed by a resignation be followed by impeachment inside of twenty years.

"The instability would bring the entire government down."

I was younger then. I thought at the time that a corrupt government's fall would be worth the instability. Expose the whole thing. Embrace Thomas Paine's *Common Sense*. Bill's look stopped my end-to-end sentences.

"Anarchy would be a ugly thing. It's always comes down to people. Not the people governing, but the people being governed. Right now they're too comfortable. They'd never handle it. It's easier for most of us to be exploited than it is for us to look out for each other."

I adjusted, agreeing with him. I raised the question about the CIA killing, torturing, and repressing people in our name. Bill looked out at the container ship heading for Oakland. Beneath his face I could see something hurting. He swallowed. He stood and we started walking.

I told him I thought the war raging between Iran and Iraq was the result of the United States' efforts to destablize the area and keep oil prices down. During Christmas a battle had killed thousands of kids pitted against each other by both sides. There was no sign of surrender, just climbing casualty lists. Riverbanks piled with the bodies of wave after wave of suicide charges. Their God had assured them a spot in heaven if they'd die today. I didn't realize who I was talking to, or what it was I was evoking in his memory. I didn't care. I had theories, I needed facts. I wanted someone to make sense of it for me. Bill nodded his head with my breathless tirade.

Ten minutes later I was still at it, telling him in Honduras, American troops were poised and ready for invasion into Panama. Death squads yanked families apart, people disappeared. Central America was a war zone fought without lines, without explanation, without the slightest compassion.

I went on. The nature of fascism. The fact of it in our own governmental policies. Bill was engaged in part of the conversation when we recalled President Eisenhower's farewell to the nation in 1960, when the President admitted the existence of and warned us about the dangers of what he called "the Military Industrial Complex." I went on to the television media discovering its power in the election of that year — Kennedy defeating Nixon by virtue of his onscreen charisma. How the country became brainwashed, and economics tied directly to the Pentagon had set the foundation for what was now our fascist state. He tried to tell me all these issues had a validity, that in his mind the facts supported my anger. But something kept coming through — his emphasis was on the spirit. I thought at the time it was the result of his age and his proximity to the end of his life. That somehow the years had run the urgency out of him. That he was trying to make peace with something.

"We can identify all of these things with our minds. But what it comes down to is what we feel in our hearts . . ."

His old hand covered his chest like a child saluting the flag.

". . . how we treat each other, what we will stand for and what we won't. But people are mistrustful of what they feel these days, so we're sorta lost."

But I knew despite all of my information, what he was saying was lost. We walked on and I wondered how a person could say so much with so few words. I wanted everything I could learn from him; I was in such a hurry.

I asked him about his involvement in the war in Spain. What motivated him to risk his life for a losing cause.

"What da ya mean? Ya mean at the beginning? Ah, it was a lot of things. But I remember seeing a newsreel of a Nazi beating an old woman, and I thought, she could be my mudda."

Simple as that. Left his girl, left his job, sailed across the Atlantic, fought with strangers against strangers because a thug was filmed beating an old woman.

On our return from our walk along the bay, we stopped again at the bench we had been sitting on. I tried to explain what I thought, what I felt in my heart. I got nowhere. The words were inadequate. Bill's gigantic face creased into a smile, his huge hand covered my shoulder and shook me gently.

"Don't despair, don't despair."

Don't despair? I could almost hear him from half a century past telling his overrun comrades, "Don't despair."

1993

Just read what the commanding officer of the United States contingent of the forces in Somalia said explaining the actions of the "Peace Keeping Mission." He admitted they killed over one hundred civilians, mostly women and children, shooting them with 50mm cannons from helicopters. Said they were combatants. Women and children. Our enemies are women and children. Should I despair yet? Guess I'll call Bill.

1995
When I leave, the warm bed creaks. Carmen usually sleeps late, having worked until one or two and needing another couple hours to finally settle down to sleep. She breathes where am I going? I tell her, "Coffee and the paper."

This winter it's usually raining when I make my way out to 16th Street. The car's morning headlights wink over the Mission District's streets. The slanting shower splashing sidewalks, windows, awnings, umbrellas. The asphalt is slick, black and hissing with passing cars' tires.

I get the paper with the same bad news from the same girl behind the counter, get the same smile, exchange an extra sentence between us trying to make the transaction human, and then I cross the street. The dealers stare and lope around the corner like dogs. Skinny, scabby junkies bum change and crack wise with each other. Someone is always raving. The cops fly past to tape off the latest crime scene. Ambulances converge on some fixed point in the near distance.

They make a double espresso and drop it in a cup of coffee when they see me come in the door. There's a seat at a window table, I settle in. As I read, the coffee grows acidic as I grasp, again, the meaning of what I am reading. All these killings, technological advances, and hype for sports and entertainment. All these personalities we are supposed to care about, the latest disaster, the coming ecological disaster. The insinuations that some countries are doomed and some aren't, the reduction of health, education and welfare. Kids killing kids makes the news, but not unless they are under eleven. Everybody pointing their fingers at everybody. Everything selling out from sea to shining sea. Movies extolling the same stupid macho garbage. Music incorporated to the point of a bad joke. Art unfunded. The mass worship of the consensus opinion. The empire in a tailspin.

An older gentleman is a fixture at the coffee shop. He looks like a Southern general. White goatee. Hair around his collar. Tall, weathered from years of sun and windburn in Minnesota. He's a translator. Worked for Army Intelligence during the early Cold War years in Germany during the occupation. He writes on a thick pad for hours, occasionally taking a smoke on the sidewalk.

We've become friends. One morning he walked to my table and identified the absurdity I was reading, which the newspaper passed off as governmental policy, as I laughed to myself. We commented to each other regarding the harshness of contemporary society, hard chic defined as the style of psychic self-defense adopted by many of the young people within the city. We wonder at what is happening to us. We dodge the topic of our fear. We omit our complicity in our community's distancing of each of us from the other. We tackle easier problems — racism, sexism, the problems of the generations' misunderstanding of the view of the other, the advancement of biotechnology and the potential for disaster within its runaway acceptance and rush for product. This brave new world. This new world order. The conglomerates, the war industry. We wonder what we will tolerate from our military, what we will tolerate from the government, the Republican agenda, the Christian Right's takeover of education, the privatization of prisons and what that could mean. And we try to find our place in it. And we fail. Which is what it really comes down to. Our failure.

His father was a union activist on the railroads of the Minnesota-Canadian border. He and his father had fallen out when he was young. Never really regained the closeness they needed. Almost made it, almost understood his relationship to his father, but his father died. The rest of the family froze him out. More respectable people I guess. More in line I guess. Playing it safer I guess. Christians I guess. Good Christians I guess. We were getting nowhere, so I mentioned Bill Bailey. Of course he knows who he is. Heard his name many times. Saw the television special on him. Read his book, *Kid From Hoboken*, even. Never met him. Would like to someday. His goatee spreading over his face.

I did the normal routine the day I had to catch the plane to Florida to read from this book and be the guest of several literature and writing classes at a small university there. Thirty thousand feet over Arizona, I was reading the paper and chuckling to myself. I turned for some reason to the obituaries and there was William Bailey. A long piece revealing the modesty of the man. It was there in three long columns. He had done more, said more, seen more, and put more at stake than those of us who met him later in his life would have dreamed. He had claimed to have been in the rear for most of those losing battles in Spain, when it appeared he was never out of the action. He had admitted taking part in a demonstration in which the Nazi swastika was ripped from the flagpole and dropped into the New York harbor while the *Bremen*'s crew and a handful of protesters fought on the deck. He hadn't said it was he who had cut it off and thrown it into the water below. Or that he had been the one his friends selected to be at the center of the flying wedge they formed to clear the way to the ship's stern. That it was he who they knew, amidships or thereabouts, would be on his own to fight his way alone to the flag, signaling the refusal of the longshoremen to offload the *Bremen*'s cargo in the harbor to protest the new Third Reich's persecution of Jews.

We all want to meet a giant, don't we? We all want to shake hands with a hero. We mark part of our lives by the day we met someone known to be brave, human, foolish, principled, and enduring. Especially enduring. We want those people to endure for us, to be here, to never leave our side. To endure for us. To not leave us to despair in our own small lives, our own lack of what it is to be fully human. The great heroes are compassionate. Above everything, they are compassionate.

I got back from Florida. I whispered, "Coffee and the paper," to Carmen. I crossed another rainy street, bought a paper. Found a chair, drank my coffee and the older gentleman crossed the coffee shop floor to my table, bowed slowly from the waist, placed Bill's obituary before me, turned and walked away.

suit of lights

The bull's stride explodes, spewing chunks off the arena floor. The sand shakes beneath your feet in rhythmic power. He squints you into focus beneath ten-inch horns.

You only have five seconds — three to find the position, two to plant the feet. The beast blasts past, leaving salt, piss, snot and blood over your face. Your rivals hope for the worst.

She waits at home, to give you what you need to stay alive.

ACKNOWLEDGMENTS

There isn't enough paper to name everyone I should acknowledge. Elaine Katzenberger, my editor and publisher at City Lights, for playing a hunch on a book and guiding its writer. Stacey Lewis, also at City Lights, for her invaluable advice. Elizabeth Bell for her sharp eye and easy ways, Yolanda Montijo for her beautiful book cover. And everyone else at City Lights who helped make this book happen.

Henry Rollins —Thanks. Dawn Holliday, Queenie Taylor and Bill Graham, the first to permit me space to work. The classes I taught and read to: "Find a good spot. . . ." Michael Green, James Gammon, Sandy Ignon, Steve Whittaker, Robert Englund, Christopher Buchinsky and Fox Harris for starting me on this path. Jane Handel for more than words can describe. Val Hendrickson and Lorraine Olsen for inspiration. Lydia Lunch for insisting I write. Jim Carroll, Hubert Selby, Jr., Bob Fitzgerald for great company on the road. Dan Fawks for being who he is and always was. The whole Fawks family, god bless them. The Bad Girl from Texas. All those incredible writers and performers I've read and seen who generated that voice inside that said, "I'll never be the same." And Carmen Garcia — the premonition in "Navajo" and my inspiration ever since.